Lieutenant Baker
Longtime Homicide dick—the only Seattle cop
Rossiter fully trusts

Harry Hashimoto
Interned during World War II, he's Miss Jenkins's
first client, and an active member of the Japanese
American Citizen's League

Frank Hashimoto
Harry's brother, a bitter, decorated veteran of the All
Nisei 442nd Regimental Combat Team

Bubbles LaFlamme
Buxom Seattle stripper who might have a heart of
fool's gold

Bunny Sunday
Bubbles's bosom buddy

Marty Haggerty
Rossiter's lawyer whose hobby is hunting big game

Manny Velcker
Pool shark, wolf, and part-time operative of the
Rossiter Agency

Sayonaraville

Curt Colbert

UglyTown
Los Angeles

First Edition

Text copyright © 2003 by Curt Colbert. All Rights Reserved.

 UGLYTOWN AND THE UGLYTOWN COIN LOGO SERVICEMARK REG. U.S. PAT. OFF.

Library of Congress Cataloging-in-Publication Data

Colbert, Curt, 1947–
    Sayonaraville / by Curt Colbert.—1st ed.
        p. cm.— (A Jake Rossiter & Miss Jenkins mystery)
    ISBN 0-9724412-1-2
    1. Private investigators—Washington (State)—Seattle—Fiction. 2. World War, 1939–1945—Veterans—Fiction. 3. Japanese Americans—Fiction. 4. Seattle (Wash.)—Fiction.
    I. Title.
    PS3603.O53 S29 2003
    813'.6—dc21   2002155084
                                                   CIP

Find out more of the mystery: UglyTown.com/Sayonaraville

Printed in the United States of America

10 9 8 7 6 5 4 3 2 1

This book is dedicated to the 442nd Regimental Combat Team

Sayonaraville

Chapter

1

I'D JUST PUT CREAM IN MY COFFEE, WHEN Miss Jenkins ran into the office screaming that our insurance agent down the hall just had his head chopped off with a Samurai sword. Needless to say, I let my java get cold.

My girl Friday beat me back to the body and stared at it like she'd never seen a stiff minus his head. I thought I was going to have to calm her down, but that wasn't the case. Far from it. Always full of surprises, Miss Jenkins seemed to be utterly fascinated by Henry Jamison's beheaded corpse. She knelt down beside the late proprietor of Seattle Life & Property and examined him more closely.

Henry's bald head lay about two feet away from the body. His Coke-bottle, wire-rimmed glasses were askew, hanging down from one ear at a crazy angle just above his pencil-thin moustache.

"Didn't your mother teach you that it's not polite to stare?" I asked Miss Jenkins.

"Look at the expression on his face," she told me. "Except for his glasses, he looks utterly at peace; like he's just having himself a nice nap. I always thought your eyes would be wide with terror and your mouth would be open big as a barn door from screaming or something."

"Poor bastard. Hope he wrote a policy on himself," I said.

My flippant comment aside, I was actually pretty sure that he *was* carrying life insurance on himself. You never knew when the Grim Reaper might pay you a visit. Old Henry never failed to mention that fact to a prospective client. That's how he sold me my first policy, always harping about how unexpectedly you might meet your demise: you could get run over by a bus, have your elevator fall from the thirtieth floor of the Smith Tower, maybe be in the wrong place when the Commies dropped the Atomic Bomb that some folks feared they were developing. According to Henry, the actuarial tables proved that it was getting more dangerous every year and 1948 was no exception. Especially for Henry, who probably hadn't factored in the odds of decapitation by Samurai sword.

But there was something wrong with the sword that had been used on Henry. It was rusty. This told me right away that it hadn't been wielded by a Jap. Not by a Jap of any real breeding, at least. All those Tojo joes had passionate love affairs with their swords. Had some type of spiritual connection to them, too. Even gave the damned things grandiose names like *Singing Chrysanthemum* and other hotsy-totsy boloney of the same ilk.

While true Samurai warriors had long been nixed in Japan, there was still some kind of class thing about owning one of those swords. Only Japs I ever saw carrying them during the war were officers. It was like some sort of badge for them. Way I heard it, the Jap brass thought Samurai swords were more important than women: you could always replace a woman, but you could never replace the sword that had been handed down in your family, maybe for centuries. Those joes would commit Hari-Kari before they'd ever allow a single speck of rust to tarnish their prized pig-stickers.

As if to further prove my point, the three-foot, bloody sword that lay next to Henry had four distinct nicks in the slightly curved single-edged blade. No way in hell would any fancy-schmancy neo-Samurai ever let that stand. They'd as soon toss their own baby out with the bath water.

I fired up a Philip Morris and blew a couple well shaped smoke rings that grew wider and wider as they drifted out over Henry's severed head. "I imagine you think it was a Jap who killed him," I said to Miss Jenkins.

"Not necessarily."

"Yeah? How so?"

She began pacing back and forth in the small office, as was her wont when putting her thoughts together, then started spitting out, almost verbatim, all the thoughts I'd been having about how the Japs felt about their swords. I'd been thinking that I could use this lesson as an educational opportunity for her nascent private dick career, but by the time she was through blabbing, she'd even told me a few things that I didn't know about Samurai swords and their history.

"And there's another thing, too," she told me, stopping her pacing beside Henry's head.

"What's that, pray tell?"

"Check the stubble on Mr. Jamison's face, boss." She bent down and pointed at Henry's middle-aged mug. "It looks like he hasn't shaved for two days or so. He was always clean-shaven and spiffy. Not once in the three years since he moved into our building have I ever seen him less than fresh. Even when I knew he'd worked late and come in early the next morning."

"And just what do you deduce from that?"

"Nothing specific yet," she said. "But it could be important."

I didn't respond, just gave a "harumph-harumph" and nodded knowingly, even though I knew full well that my apprentice partner had noted the *how-could-you-miss-it?* two-day growth of beard on Henry's face way before I did. Miss Jenkins suddenly turned and strode toward the front door, her curly strawberry-blonde locks bouncing as she went.

"Where are you going?"

"To get our camera and take our own pictures of the crime scene while you call Lieutenant Baker," she answered, pausing momentarily at the door. "That's what you were just going to tell me to do, wasn't it?"

"Uh, sure . . . of course," I told her. "Well, don't dally. Move your caboose, doll."

She flashed me one of her extraordinarily pretty but knowing grins, then exited the insurance office. As I listened to her heels click quickly up the hall, I spun the dial for Police Headquarters. I knew I'd have to really stay on my toes around my eager and deceptively bright rookie assistant. Otherwise, Miss Jenkins might just end up owning the joint.

"Hell, Rossiter," said Sergeant Steve Burnett, newly arrived at the crime scene. He took a seat across from me at the late Henry Jamison's desk, where I was finishing my breakfast.

"It stinks in here. How can you eat in the same room with this stiff?"

"I'm hungry, what d'ya think?" I told him, very much liking Jamison's spacious and tidy desk. Far cry from the normal junk pile on my desk. The only thing on it that was out of place at all was his Thermos of lukewarm coffee and a half-eaten cinnamon roll sitting on the edge of his desk-pad. Not wanting to be stuck answering the phone, I had assigned Miss Jenkins that onerous task and carted my breakfast down to Jamison's office before it got too cold. Here, I had peace and quiet and all the space in the world to spread out my morning repast across his fastidiously neat oak desktop. Even had plenty of room for my pitcher of grapefruit juice and coffee pot. I could do this every day of the week if I just managed to keep my desk as perfectly organized as Jamison did. But that was probably one of the reasons that I had more aptitude for private dick work than selling insurance.

"What a mess," muttered Burnett, surveying the bloody scene on the green linoleum. He lit up a Chesterfield, threw in a couple "tsk-tsk's," then said, "I hope this is going to be simple. I managed to finagle getting the afternoon off so I could roll some practice frames before bowling league tonight."

"Yeah?" I asked, sopping up the last of my egg yolk with a piece of toast. "When was the last time you ran across a joe with his head chopped off by a Samurai sword that turned out to be simple?"

"Shit."

"By the way, where's Lieutenant Baker? He said he was coming out personally on this one."

"Oh, he was having an argument with your good pal, Captain Blevens. I came up alone because they told me to scram until they got finished. Guess they're still down in the car jawing."

"Blevens? Here?"

"In the flesh," Burnett told me, spitting out a wayward piece of tobacco. "Captain got wind of you being involved and said he was coming out personally on this one."

"Shit."

"That about sums it up," he agreed, making a face. "What'd you ever do to old Blevens to make him worship your name the way he does? Oh, yeah . . . had something to do with Fat Floyd, didn't it? Him and Blevens started out as beat cops together way back when. You pinned some dirt on Floyd last year and ended up killing the fat fuck. Rumor had it they were tight as ticks and some of the stink's hung around Blevens ever since. That about right?"

"Something like that."

"Whatever," he said, nodding his head and throwing me a wink. "I ought to be getting busy," he added, pulling a note pad out of his Herringbone sports jacket. "Or at least act busy. No offense, but the last thing I need is to look too chummy with you when Blevens blows through the door."

"No offense taken," I told him. I dug out the last of my egg-white and flicked off the little piece of shell that inevitably came with it. As I popped it in my mouth, I thought about our erstwhile police captain, Harvey Winfeld Blevens. It made my egg taste as rotten as he was, so I spit it out. He'd sat out World War II with a cozy draft deferment because he was a high ranking cop needed on the home front to provide security during the national crisis, or some such malarkey. Fact was, he was only a sergeant when the Japs bombed Pearl Harbor. But the instant we declared war, his crooked mentor, Fat Floyd, used his juice to grease a quick promotion for Blevens so he wouldn't have to serve. Bounced him up the line ahead of a lot of other cops, including Lieutenant Baker, who were far more deserving of promotion. All the while, decent citizens went and fought for their country and never came home. Got shot and blown to hell from Iwo Jima to Normandy, while Fat Floyd and Blevens sold a few War Bonds and played patriotic to cover their rat-asses as business went on as usual collecting enough graft from shake-downs, payoffs, and other illicit rackets to buy themselves spanking new upscale houses during the war years. Not to mention the best clothes, silk stockings for their bimbos, copious amounts of fancy foods—though everything was strictly rationed—even new tires for their personal automobiles, when virtually all the rubber was supposed to be going to the war effort.

This was the state of things, when my right-hand operative, Heine, and I came home after our service in the Marine Corps. While we'd fought to throw the Japs out of the Pacific, the rats had been busy at home, growing even bolder and fatter than usual. In the three years since the end of the war, we'd managed to exterminate quite a few of them, including Fat Floyd. But there were always plenty of other rodents in the nest. Including loads of cops, of course. There was only one flatfoot who I knew for sure wasn't on the take, Lieutenant Baker, who'd helped me trap Fat Floyd last year. But other than him, the vermin ran the gamut from law enforcement to politicians to assorted racketeers and crime bosses. You name it.

I lit a smoke and belched a sour burp. My morning had been spoiled by my life insurance agent's shocking murder. My breakfast had been spoiled by thoughts of Captain Harvey Blevens. And now my whole day was spoiled because the good captain was tagging along with Lieutenant Baker, no doubt eager to throw a few monkey wrenches at me. If he played true to form, he'd look for some angle to tie me into the homicide, if for no other reason than Henry sold me my insurance policies. Failing that, which of course he would, Blevens would do everything in his power to try and tie up my time with it. Jack me around and affect my ability to make an honest living. I didn't get paid by the hour, and he knew it. Anything he could do to put the kibosh on my cash flow, he always did with gusto and relish. Just last month, he'd had me jailed as a material witness to the big Queen Anne Trust & Savings heist downtown. That I'd been standing in line, like any other working stiff, just trying to make a deposit, didn't matter. All that counted was that I was in the wrong place at the wrong time. When Captain Blevens heard that I'd been involved, he sent a few of his minions over and had me thrown into the slammer. For my own protection, said the material witness warrant, signed by Judge Stewart, who just happened to be Blevens's brother-in-law. Being late on a Friday, by the time my lawyer got me sprung, on Monday, I'd lost the new paying client whose case absolutely, positively had to be handled over the weekend that I'd just spent in jail. The very same case and weekend, I should note, that Miss Jenkins had kindly offered to cover for me, but I'd said, "Tush-tush, doll. You've put in too many weekend hours already this month. No, you take your mother on that boat trip up to

Victoria, just like you've been planning. And here's an extra ten-spot, on me, for mad money. I'll handle it. What could possibly go wrong?"

The sound of the office door opening interrupted my reveries. "Well, I'll be damned," said Captain Blevens, his large frame filling the open doorway. A thin smile crossed his ruddy face. He glanced at Jamison's corpse, then back at me, his cold blue eyes narrowing as he continued, a tone of mock surprise in his low whiskey voice. "If it ain't Jake Rossiter himself. Fancy meeting you here."

"Hey, Burnett!" I called to the detective, who stood, note pad in hand, making busy over by the body. "You've got to do a better job watching the door. We've got some riff-raff crashing our party."

Burnett suppressed a smile. "Morning, Captain," he said.

Blevens ignored him and barged right in. He stuck a fat stogie in his beefy mug as he veered around the body, then came straight at me. Lt. Baker brought up the rear, shaking his head and hunching his shoulders in a Sorry-Jake-I-couldn't-help-it-shrug.

"Yes, do come in," I told Blevens, raising my coffee cup toward him. "If I'd only known you were coming, I'd have had my butler set an extra place at the breakfast table. As it is, I'm afraid all I can offer you are a few crumbs and some dregs."

"Arrest him," Blevens told Lieutenant Baker.

"Hell, Captain," Baker protested. "For what?"

"Material witness," said Blevens, with obvious relish.

"Bullshit," I said, standing up. "I haven't seen anymore here than you have, Captain. I only came down here to keep an eye on things after my partner found the body."

"Oh, yeah?" he inquired. "Your partner found the body, huh? That lady private dick . . . where is she, anyway?"

"I'm right here," said Miss Jenkins, appearing at the doorway. "What's going on?"

"Arrest her, too," said Blevens.

"What?" exclaimed Miss Jenkins, her green-blue eyes growing wide as two saucers.

"Put the cuffs on 'em!" bellowed Blevens.

"For what?" asked Miss Jenkins.

"Material witness," I told her, tamping down another Philip Morris and getting it lit.

"But who's going to answer the phones?" she asked, her fingers starting to twitch, like they always did when she got agitated. "We'll be missing business."

"Ain't it tough?" said Blevens, with the biggest smile since Joe E. Brown. "Now get 'em outta here! And don't book 'em until I get back to the station house. Keep 'em on ice awhile. Looks of this mess, I might just be here all day."

"Sure," I said, stating the obvious. "And our lawyer can't do a thing to spring us until we've been officially booked."

"I don't make the law," said Blevens. "I just enforce it."

"This is terrible," said Miss Jenkins, as Sergeant Burnett slowly handcuffed her, being careful, I noted, not to put them on too tight. "Just terrible."

"You can say that again," I told her.

"Tsk-tsk." Captain Blevens looked around the room, then flicked his cigar ash toward the ashtray on the desk, but missed it by a country mile. "I got the feeling this is going to be a real complicated investigation. On second thought, I'll probably have to be here well into the evening."

"Sorry, Jake," Baker told me, as he relieved me of my cigarette and snapped the cold cuffs around my wrists.

"You can say that again."

Chapter
2

SOMETIMES CLOUDS HAVE SILVER LININGS. Rarely. But this seemed to be one of those occasions. On the short drive to the pokey, while Captain Blevens was doing his best to rain on my parade, Lieutenant Baker informed me that there was a ray of sunshine waiting for us at the downtown booking office: none other than my right-hand operative, Heine, who should have our attorney in tow, itching to use his legal legerdemain to spring us the instant we got there.

"I called Heine as soon as Blevens horned in on my case," Baker explained, glancing back at us over the mohair front seat as he wheeled the powerful Ford cruiser south toward downtown. "The captain was just looking for an excuse to roust you, so I dealt you a trump card."

"Thanks," I told him.

"By the way," Baker continued. "There's something else you should know."

"I'm all ears."

"Eddie Valhalla's back in town."

"What?" I yelled, the news making me feel the same way I did when the Japs pulled their sneak attack on Pearl Harbor. "Why the hell didn't you tell me?"

"Just did, Jake. I only found out this morning. I was going to call and let you know when the report came through about your insurance agent getting killed."

"I'll be a sonofabitch . . ."

"This is not good," said Miss Jenkins, with a shake of her head. "Why did you have to tell him?"

"He had to know sometime," Baker told her.

"Where's Eddie staying?" I asked.

"He took the Penthouse Suite over at the Edmond Meany in the University District," said Baker. "Him and ZaZu. Hotel Dick's an ex-cop—he tipped me."

"ZaZu too, huh?" I mused, thinking about Eddie's Hungarian bimbo with the hot gams and heart of ice.

"Listen, Jake," Baker said, taking his eyes off the road and jabbing me in the shoulder—getting away with it because he was one of the few people I'd let jab me that way. "You got every right to know Eddie's blown into town. But you go gunning for him, I'll arrest you myself and throw away the keys."

I wasn't listening to him. I was focused on Eddie. Him and me and Heine went way back. Grew up in the same orphanage, St. Joseph's Home for Boys. Ate meals together, learned to swim together, got our knuckles rapped by the nuns together, had more than one fight together, and ran off from the orphanage about the same time, age fourteen, scrabbling our way through the Depression as best we could. But where Heine and me turned our hands to a little honest rum-running near the end of Prohibition, Eddie turned his to strong-arm stuff and worse. Started liking it and began hiring himself out to the highest bidder. Got away with extortion to murder from Seattle to Chicago and all points in between. Rumor had he even did a little journeyman work for Capone's old Chicago gang after Big Al got himself jammed up with the Feds and sent off to Alcatraz. That's when he supposedly got to be an artist with a tommy-gun.

In any event, Eddie and I used to be pals. But that's when we were young. Back when his name was just plain old Eddie Larson. Back before he took on the sobriquet of "Valhalla" . . . chosen, he explained with his wicked laugh, because that's where he always sent the joes he took contracts to rub out.

ZaZu Pinske was another story entirely. She and I had never been friends. Lovers, briefly, one drunken evening when I was new to the private dick business and didn't have a clue that she and Eddie were a tag-team. All I knew was that I'd managed to pick up this knock-out, platinum blonde, green-eyed sex-pot down at Ben Paris's cocktail lounge. She seemed plenty amenable to a little tussle between the sheets, and I was flush with enough dough to splurge and rent us a ritzy room for the spur-of-the-moment occasion.

We blew down to the Olympic Hotel, finest in town, which dripped with as much class as my hot date. By the time ZaZu and I finished our wrestling match, I'd spilled the beans about an important witness that I'd dug up who was set to finally blow the lid off police corruption in Seattle. She had me so full of Scotch, and so full of myself, that I even bragged about my witness being safely squirreled away a few floors above us, waiting to testify before the Grand Jury.

The next thing I knew, I woke up in an empty bed feeling like a hand grenade had just gone off inside my noggin. ZaZu had slipped me a Mickey, then taken my secret straight to Eddie Valhalla, who, in turn, had used a real hand grenade to eliminate my witness.

Nothing was ever proven, of course. Nothing except what a sucker I'd been. I chalked it up to experience. Bad experience. Eddie and ZaZu had turned my first big case into goulash. So I did what my mom always taught me to do before she died—learn from my mistake and move on. But never forget about it. Like the other run-ins I'd had with Eddie Valhalla over the years. None of them good. And the last one even worse. That particular set-to with Eddie left him with a slight, but permanent limp, and me with some slight, but permanent bridgework.

"Boss, you listen to Lt. Baker," Miss Jenkins told me. "You'll just get into another jam with Eddie. Besides, you promised to help me with the Hashimoto case."

"No, I didn't," I said, as Baker wheeled the squad car off First Avenue at Cherry Street. He ground the gears a bit shifting into low as we started up the steep hill toward the downtown station house. "Don't put words in my mouth," I continued. "You wanted that Jap crap as your first official case, against my better judgment . . . Well, you got it. I don't mix with Japs. Not since the war."

"But—"

"Anyway," I said, lighting up a smoke just to get the taste of the word "Jap" out of my mouth. "You make your own mistakes. That's the only way you'll learn. I will share one small piece of advice with you, however: you'll find in short order, Miss Jenkins, that it does help to take on paying clients in this game. You want to be soft-hearted, that's all well and good, but it doesn't do much to pay the bills and put bread on the table."

"But you helped Roosevelt Tyree last year," she quickly countered. "And he didn't have any money."

"That's different."

"Ah-ha!" she exclaimed, seizing the debating point and stabbing a delicate finger at me. "You can help a broke Negro, but I can't help a broke Japanese? That's not fair."

"Who's Hashimoto?" asked Baker, turning into the underground, police parking garage.

"Just some Jap," I said.

"He and his family were interned during the war. They managed to keep their store and get it going again after the war ended, but then they were burned out," said Miss Jenkins, warming up to her favorite sob story.

"Tough," I said.

"It was their only way of making a living," she went on, glaring at me.

"Double tough," I said, blowing a series of lazy smoke-rings.

"So?" asked Baker, a little distracted as he pulled the car into his designated parking slot in the dimly lit garage. Pretty impressive—I'd never driven into police headquarters with him before. He had his own private parking space, complete with a sign that read RESERVED — LT. BAKER. He was still quite a ways down in the old upper echelon pecking order, however. I noticed that his slot was clear down at the far end from the elevator.

"He wants to get their five & dime going again, but they

don't have any money," said Miss Jenkins, taking a small compact out of her purse and using its mirror to double-check her make-up.

"Neither do a lot of people," I told her.

She snapped the compact closed with an audible click and kept talking to Baker, faster and faster. "Mr. Hashimoto claims that somebody burned his store on purpose. And I tend to believe him. The Japanese had to sell out real quick before they got sent off to the camps. They were lucky if they got ten cents on the dollar for everything they owned. But the Hashimotos had just enough money to keep paying their property taxes and—"

"Well, I don't know anything about that," Baker interrupted, as he turned the engine off.

"And then they had the fire and they lost it anyway," Miss Jenkins rattled on. "And some Chinese people own the store now and they hate Japs and won't even talk to them and—"

"We ought to be going in, Baker," I suggested.

"—they haven't got hardly any money," she continued, repeating herself. "And they've all been living crammed into this crummy little boarding house, because nobody else would rent to them."

"Should've thought twice before they bombed Pearl Harbor," I told her.

"The Hashimotos are Americans," she said, her eyes blazing. "They're not the ones who bombed Pearl Harbor."

"Hey!" said Baker, his voice loud enough to command our immediate attention. "Time out. You two can squabble about the Japs later. Right now we need to get inside and get this little booking charade over with so your lawyer can send you on your merry way. Or would you rather keep arguing and have Blevens show up and squelch the whole deal?"

"'Nuff said," I gladly agreed with Baker. I got out of the squad car quickly, so as to not give my persistent partner another opportunity to open her trap. Which, of course, she did anyway.

"It's not right," Miss Jenkins said, bailing out her side and slamming the door shut. She kept running her mouth, trying to get in the last word. "One of the Hashimotos is even a war hero," she blurted. "He fought with that famous all-Japanese regiment in Italy."

"Good for him," I said, giving Baker a prod. We made quick like bunnies for the nearby glass doors that led to the elevators, Miss Jenkins complaining as she brought up the rear, her heels clicking up quite a racket in the mostly empty parking garage.

"You're not listening to a word I'm saying."

"Oh, I'm listening all right," I called over my shoulder. "I'm just not responding," I added. We went over and caught an elevator. I paused and bowed, gesturing broadly for the scowling Miss Jenkins to go in ahead of us. "After you, doll," I told her, doffing my fedora. Once inside, I said, "Feel free to carry on your little crusade after we get sprung, my dear. Right now, just shhhhh! already. We've got more pressing matters to attend to."

For once, she didn't talk back. Just put a major pout on her pretty face. I winked at Baker. The silence was simply wonderful as we rode upstairs.

It was short-lived, however. We got off the elevator into a hubbub of activity. The first floor of downtown police headquarters was old, cavernous, and unbelievably noisy. Its twelve foot-ceilings, faux marble walls, and brittle white-and-blue tile floor, cracked and chipped from countless years of crime-busting, all combined to magnify and echo with the slightest sound. And it was very busy, even at mid-morning, the boys in blue dragging in the crooks they'd collared and hollering at them, and the crooks hollering back. The detectives at their oak desks at the rear of the room tried to make themselves heard on the phones, and people bustled all over the place, various civilians and cops alike. Those who weren't bustling were either chowing down on donuts or gathered around the water cooler jawing and laughing at some joke or another. Above it all, the desk sergeant, a brawny gray-haired Rat City veteran, sat behind his high counter in the middle of everything and bellowed occasionally as he tried to make some kind of order out of all the rhubarb and commotion.

Our sleepy little burg of Seattle, a.k.a. Rat City, was in the middle of yet another crimewave. All the prosperity after the war had been a real bonanza for the crooks, bringing as many opportunities for them as it did for the average working stiff. Same-same for your typical flatfoot: gave the ones who weren't square like Baker, which was most of them, much fatter pickings.

"Is this place always like this?" asked Miss Jenkins, taking off her light floral print jacket.

"This is only the first of the month, when the checks come out," Baker told her. "You oughta see how this joint starts jumping when there's a full moon."

"Hey! Rossiter!" came a booming voice from across the way, somewhere near the jostling crowd surrounding the desk sergeant. "Shake a leg, Jake! I'm due in court in less than an hour."

It was Marty Haggerty, my lawyer, big as a Sherman tank and just about as tough. He emerged from the throng along with my main operative, Stanley Heinselman, who was equally heavy-set, and hurriedly motioned for us to join them.

I led the way, purposely sauntering slow as I could. "What, you mean you work for some other client besides me, Haggerty?"

"You know it," he said, making a sour face at my leisurely pace. "What you pay me barely keeps me in cigars."

"What he spends on cigars, I could live on for a week," quipped Heine, as we approached. "Hey, Jake. Troubles, huh?"

"Has Carter got pills?" I joked, shaking his hand. I shook with Haggerty too, but was careful to keep it brief. The big lug had a grip like a bear trap.

He, in turn, extended a hand to Baker. "Glad to see you, Lieutenant."

"Glad to see you, too," said Baker, smiling, but keeping his hand to himself. "Cops around here spot me swapping handshakes with a defense attorney, I'll be out of donuts for a week."

"True," said Haggerty, with a big laugh. "But you know as well as I do, that half of them will probably end up needing my services one day." He turned his attentions to Miss Jenkins, his six-plus feet and two-hundred-and-fifty-pound frame, all decked out in a wide double-breasted serge suit, positively dwarfing my diminutive partner. "Ah, my dear Miss Jenkins," he said, his hammy hand causing hers to completely disappear within his grasp. "When are you going to finally come big-game hunting with me? From what I hear, you're a crack shot."

"Yes, I am," she said, gradually retrieving her hand. "It's nice of you to offer, but right now I just want to get out of here."

"As soon as the lieutenant gets you officially booked," he promised. Then he turned to me, suggesting for about the umpteenth time, "You'd give her a few weeks off to go on safari with me, wouldn't you, Jake?"

"I think he's got a crush on you, doll," I told Miss Jenkins.

"He'd crush her, all right," Heine commented to Baker.

"You just *haven't lived* until you've been on safari," said Haggerty, expansively and loud enough that we started drawing more than a few looks from around the room. "Think of it, Miss Jenkins," he continued, really warming up to his favorite subject. "Blazing our way through darkest Africa, spending hot days on the Savannah bringing down charging rhinos and elephants with a single shot, then long nights beneath the stars, just you and me and a little gin and the rustling breeze against our tent, the howl of the big cats under the full moon, the lions, the leopards, the panthers—"

"Not to mention the wolves," she interrupted. "I thought you said you were in a hurry."

"Yeah," I said. "Lay off mashing with my partner and spring us already." I knew Miss Jenkins didn't really mind his rakish nature. And neither did I, as long as it didn't go too far. Haggerty was a good man. A real man's man, unlike most attorneys. Kind of a big overgrown Clark Gable with an extra ration of brains. But playtime was over. I had some serious things to delve into. Not the least of which being my insurance agent's murder and the disturbing return of Eddie Valhalla.

"O.K.," said Baker. "Let's go see the desk sergeant and get it over with."

"How long will this take?" asked Miss Jenkins. "We won't actually have to get locked up, will we?"

"Not while I've got any pull around here," Baker reassured her.

"Oh, good," she said, visibly relieved. "I can't imagine sitting around in some holding tank with the kind of low-lifes who come into this place."

"But you will have to get fingerprinted and have your mug shot taken."

"No!"

"Don't worry, kiddo," I told her. "New police photographer's loads better than the last one. You'll be the prettiest face in all the files."

She took a couple steps back. Looked like she was contemplating a jailbreak. "But I heard that once you have a police file on you, it stays with you for the rest of your life. Whether you've done anything wrong or not."

"No easy way to put it," I told her. "The short answer is yes."

By the look in her eyes, I thought we'd have to drag her over to the desk sergeant kicking and screaming. But, ever amazing, she suddenly composed herself. Her eyes narrowed and her expression went hard as nails. "Let's do it," she said, and marched quickly over to the desk sergeant, the rest of us hurriedly bringing up the rear as she muscled her way through the various cops and their collars who were all stacked up in front of the tall oak counter.

"Move. Get out of my way," she ordered, as the crooks and cops parted before her irresistible force. "I have to get booked."

"Miss," said the desk sergeant, pushing up his wire-rimmed glasses and giving her an odd and exasperated glance. "I don't know who you are, but most folks aren't in such an all-fired hurry to get into jail. Have you ever heard of waiting your turn?"

"No time," she told him. "I'm a desperate criminal. Do what you must."

"Sarge," said Baker, as we squeezed in beside Miss Jenkins. "Let me explain."

"Somebody better, Lieutenant," he replied, while half the joes around us began to snicker and chuckle. "Brother, and I thought I'd seen it all."

Baker laid it out for him fast and neat. Quietly reminded the sergeant that he owed him a favor, then told him to play dumb and get us booked, whether Blevens wanted it that way or not. "Captain didn't want 'em booked, you said. He's gonna chew me a new asshole over this," said the sergeant, slowly shaking his head. "What the hell. Old Blevens would find something to yell about today, anyway, I suppose." He jotted down the info about us being material witnesses to a murder, then directed his assistant, a gawky young cop with a hayseed cowlick, to take us back and get us fingerprinted. "But this squares us, right?" he told Baker, as the young flatfoot motioned us to follow him.

"Even-Steven," said Baker, with a tip of his hat, before tagging along with Miss Jenkins and me.

"All right!" I heard the sergeant yell behind us. "What are all you dumb jamokes just standing around for? Step up to the plate! We gotta get your collars booked and you back out on your beats, toot-sweet. There's a crimewave going on out there or ain't you heard?"

While we got fingerprinted, Haggerty skipped out to see the judge he'd lined up to O.K. our release. He wasn't gone more than ten minutes or so, when he came back all smiles, happily waving the bail documents that sprung us on our personal recognizance. Good thing he was quick, because Miss Jenkins's new found resolve had just about reached its breaking point after the rookie cop got fingerprinting ink all over her new white blouse.

"Who's going to pay for this blouse?" she fumed, dabbing furiously at the ink spot, which only made the spot get bigger.

"I'm sorry, ma'am," said the young cop.

"The Department will pay for the cleaning," Baker told her. "Don't worry."

"Don't worry? This is real silk. From Frederick's, too. It'll never come out. Never!"

"I've got to get to court," said Haggerty, handing the bail papers over to Baker.

"I'll walk out with you," said Heine, knowing it was best to stay well clear of Miss Jenkins on the rare occasions that she blew a gasket.

"It's ruined . . . ruined!"

"Here's a ten-spot, my dear," said Haggerty, peeling a bill out of his fat money clip and handing it to her. "That should more than cover it."

"Well . . ." said Miss Jenkins, not thinking twice before taking it. "Thank you. At least there's one gentleman around here."

"Gentleman?" I scoffed, while Haggerty looked like the cat who just ate the canary. "All he's going to do is add that ten-spot to my tab."

"And the Department will pay you back, Jake," said Baker. "Don't worry."

"We need to get out of here," said Heine.

"But I haven't done the mug shots, yet," stammered the young cop.

"Oh, no. You're not coming anywhere near me again!" Miss Jenkins barked, flames in her eyes.

"You better get out of here, kid," Baker warned.

"But the mug shots—"

"I'll handle it. Scoot back to the desk sergeant while you've still got your hide."

"Yessir," said the cop. He headed for the door, giving Miss Jenkins a wide berth as he passed her. "I'm really sorry, ma'am," he said one last time, then quickly popped through the doorway as Miss Jenkins threw him more of her patented flame thrower glares.

"Forget the mug shots," Baker told Miss Jenkins. "You've had enough for one morning."

"Thank you, Lieutenant," she said. Then she stared holes through me, saying, "That makes two gentlemen around here, anyway."

"Well," I said, "now that this fiasco's over, I've got places to be. You mind giving Miss Jenkins a ride back to the office, Baker? I'm going to hitch a lift with Heine. We've got some things to go over."

"Such as?" asked Baker, sounding suspicious.

"Such as some *private* private detective stuff," I told him. "Since when do I have to tell you everything?"

"Since Eddie Valhalla blew into town," he shot back.

"Go get the car, I'll meet you out front," I told Heine.

"You got it," he said. "Catch you 'round the campus," he told everybody, then went right out to get his wheels. Heine was a good man, no B.S., went straight ahead when you put him on to something. That something could be as simple as sticking to a tail like contact cement, or getting in the way of a bullet if need be. Something he'd done for me more than once in the past.

"Don't go after Eddie," Miss Jenkins told me.

"Don't you have to meet with this Hashimoto character?" I asked, changing the subject.

"Not 'til around lunch," she said, her pretty green-blue eyes as distrustful as Baker's. "We haven't set up an exact time for him to come by the office yet."

"Well, all I'm doing is absenting myself for a while. I got other cases, you know? Besides, I don't want to share my office with a Jap, anyway."

Baker stepped up and poked me in the shoulder. I didn't like it, and he knew I didn't like it. "Jake, my men are sitting on Eddie as we speak. You show yourself anywhere in the general vicinity, I'll put you in the slammer so fast your head'll swim."

"He's just trying to protect you from yourself, boss," Miss Jenkins said.

"You hear what I'm telling you, Jake?" said Baker, his finger poking me again. I slapped his hand away, spun around and headed for the door. "Thanks for all your help, Baker," I said, over my shoulder.

"Jake!"

I paused and looked back at him. "Listen. I've no more

intention of going after Eddie Valhalla than I do of jumping off the Aurora Bridge," I said, with a straighter face than Bud Abbot. "Satisfied?"

"No," said Baker.

"No," said Miss Jenkins.

"Ho-hum," I told them, with a dramatic sigh. "You can please some of the people some of the time, but you can't please all of the people all the time."

Haggerty, who'd been uncharacteristically silent for a while, added his two cents. "Rossiter," he said, sucking on his huge cigar. "If you take my advice, which you rarely do, you'll think twice about going to where you're claiming not to be going."

"Well," I said, throwing him a wink. "That's a mouthful of high-priced gobbletygook, even for you, Haggerty. Just send me your bill. I'll see if I can pay it." I tipped my hat to one and all, then high-stepped away from their protestations, out to the street where Heine had his brand new '48 Ford idling, its powerful L-head V-8 all revved up and raring to go.

"Drive," I said, as I slipped into the Mohair seat beside him.

"Meany Hotel?" he asked, peeling away from the curb.

"How'd you guess?" I fired up a Philip Morris and thought it tasted just about as good as bashing Eddie around would. "Let me borrow your blackjack, Heine."

"You gonna let me have a piece of him?" he asked, handing over the heavy cudgel he always carried in his vest pocket.

"No." I squirreled the blackjack away into the bottom right pocket of my houndstooth sports jacket.

"Selfish," he chuckled, turning onto Westlake Avenue and gunning the Ford north toward the U. District, about four miles distant.

We rode in silence until we hit the University Bridge. As the tires squealed across the heavy metal grating in the center of the bridge, Heine said, "Too bad about your insurance agent. You think a Jap killed him?"

"Wasn't any Jap did it." I filled him in about the Samurai sword, its low quality, and its poor condition. Heine had been all through the Pacific with me during the war. He knew just what I meant.

"So, somebody did him and wanted it to look like a Jap, huh?"

"Could be," I said.

"Any ideas why he got bumped off?"

"Nary a one. Don't really know that much about the man. Jamison was pretty quiet. Hard-working, nose-to-the-grindstone type. Married. No kids. Smoked cheap cigars. I think he sat out the war, 4-F. Had a ruptured eardrum. That's about it."

"He sure must've pissed somebody off," Heine said, swerving to avoid an old jalopy that was doing the speed limit, which we certainly weren't, not with Heine's lead foot. "We gonna help find out who did it?"

"Think so."

"Any money in it?"

"Better be," I told him. "Hell, I'd bust the case open just to throw it into Blevens's ugly mug, but I've got people to pay, you included. I'll work the widow for some dough. At least our usual, plus expenses. Miss Jenkins will be lucky if she even gets a bottle of saké out of those Nips. Can't pay the bills with rice wine."

Heine chuckled, and we ate up the distance to the Edmond Meany in no time. We took a right on the main drag, North 45th Street, then rolled the last few blocks up to the hotel. About twenty stories high, it had a tall neon sign on top of it that alternately flashed EDMOND in green, then MEANY in red. Situated on the northwest corner of 45th and Brooklyn Avenue, it was by far the tallest building in the whole University District, visible for miles around, dwarfing even the highest spires on the nearby University of Washington campus. Opened in 1929, just as the Depression hit, it had survived hard times, mostly because it was the only fine hotel between downtown and the city limits out on North 85th Street. I'd stayed there a few times, myself. Wasn't cheap, though. Its big airy rooms were a fair value, but the penthouse was way out of my price range. Took a high-roller like Eddie to afford digs that ritzy. Naturally made me curious as to the source of his moola these days. He only traveled all expenses paid from what I heard.

I'd told Heine to be on the lookout for Baker's men, and we spotted them right off the bat. Figured they might be out on the street keeping an eye on the front of the hotel. Sure enough, that's exactly where they were. Slowing to a crawl as we hit the intersection of 45th & Brooklyn, we made their unmarked police cruiser. Big indigo blue Chevy pulled over at the curb not a quarter block off to our left, parked smack across from the Meany's main entrance, saw the two plainclothes joes sitting in it plain as day through its oval rear window. Even though it was like a million other post-war Chevys on the road, it stood out like a bad toupee because of the big chrome spotlight mounted beside the driver's side-view mirror.

Heine knew not to drive right by them, since they might spot us. Instead, he juiced the Ford through the intersection, and we breezed past the Neptune Theatre and up another block, where we turned right on University Way, then circled around to the alley that ran in back of the hotel. The alley was empty, except for a red *&* white Carnation Dairy truck backed up to the hotel's loading dock.

Our tires *ca-chunk-ca-chunking* against the alley's old and uneven brick pavement, Heine said, "Not much going on back here. This a good spot to drop you off?"

"Roger," I told him. "I'll take the freight elevator up to visit Eddie."

We stopped parallel to the nose of the milk truck, and I got out. It was a nice quiet morning, no sounds to disturb my concentration on just how bad a hurt I would put on Eddie, other than those of the milkman clanking his bottles as he unloaded them, and a few seagulls screeching overhead.

Before I closed the car door, I asked, "Where you going to be?"

"I'll park it up the side street, over on 43rd," Heine answered, his right hand resting on the ball-tipped gearshift lever. "While you're stompin' at the Savoy with Eddie, I'll be incognito down in the main lobby keeping tabs on things. You just ring the front desk and have 'em page 'jarhead' if you need me. Otherwise, I see any trouble coming, I'll find you before it does."

"Good enough."

"Give old Eddie a few extra rabbit punches for me, huh?" He grinned as I closed the door. Then he motored up the alley.

I sauntered over to the loading dock like I owned the joint, feeling more and more on top of the world the closer I got to Eddie and ZaZu. I took the short stairs up onto the dock two at a time. Striding past the back of the dairy truck, I gave the young milkman a friendly nod. He was in the process of stacking bottles of un-homogenized milk, the kind with the cream floating at the top, just the way I liked it—same way my mom used to get it.

The milkman smiled and tipped his striped cap at me. "Morning, sir. Hope I'm not in your way."

"Not at all, my good man," I told him, full of high spirits. "As a matter of fact, what the world needs are more good honest dairymen like yourself, and a few less hoodlums. I'm just on my way to correct that inbalance."

"Uh, sure, pal . . ." He gave me an odd look. "Whatever you say." Then he got quickly out of my way, even though I had plenty of room to go around him.

"Carry on," I told him, then went inside, whistling a happy tune. I found the freight elevator in short order, passing only one other joe, the janitor, as I strolled over to it. I doffed my hat and wished him a fine and pleasant day. He didn't say anything. Just leaned on his push-broom and stared quizzically at me as I boarded the wide wooden-floored elevator and pulled its expandable metal-mesh inner door shut. The elevator was so old, it didn't have any push-buttons for the floors. Instead, it still operated with a large brass lever that you pushed up for "up," and pulled down for "down." I pushed the lever, and the creaky elevator took off for the top floor like a shot. During the short ride, I double-checked my arsenal: black stiletto in my pants pocket, trusty .45 automatic firmly in place in my shoulder-holster, little .25 auto squirreled away in my left vent pocket for emergencies, and Heine's heavy blackjack resting comfortably in my right pocket for Eddie's thick skull.

Ready for most anything, I slowed down as I neared the twentieth floor. Not really used to the old manual operating lever, I figured that I'd come closer to lining the elevator up with the floor level if I went slow. I didn't gauge it too bad—was only off a couple inches when I stopped and opened the door. I didn't bother trying to adjust it. Just stepped up and off the elevator, and found that the service hallway I was in was pretty dark. The glass ceiling-globe directly above me threw out a little light, but none of the other fixtures seemed to be working all up and down the long hallway to my left and right. No bother, I thought. Knowing that the penthouse suite faced south, I turned right and made my way into the increasing darkness.

I'd only gone about forty feet, when the lights really went out. Of course, there was a sudden burst of light and a bunch of bright swirling stars when I first got koshed. I remember thinking that they were very pretty. But I didn't have much time to enjoy them. A crashing pain replaced them as the floor rushed up to meet me and everything went darker than black.

I came to just long enough to see ZaZu Pinske's gorgeous face floating right above me. Her striking good looks would have been even finer if I hadn't caught sight of Eddie Valhalla's handsome but sinister mug drifting into view just

44

behind her. He smiled that tight-lipped smile of his, and ZaZu pressed something deliciously cool to my forehead, and said, soft and soothing, "Don't worry, Jake. You're in good hands."

Cold comfort, I thought, then passed out again.

Chapter

3

I saw stars again when I finally woke up. Thousands of them, glinting and sparkling above me. Took me squinting three or four times to realize that what I was looking at wasn't stars, but a large crystal chandelier. I was flat on my back, surrounded by pleasing cream-colored walls and a bunch of nice paintings.

Hell . . . I was in the penthouse. *With Eddie and ZaZu . . .*

I sat up so fast I thought I was going to pass out again.

"Take it easy," said Eddie, lounging against the mahogany-paneled front door, about thirty feet across the large room. "You'll strain your brain."

I shook off the cobwebs and reached for my .45. Found the holster empty.

"We took your toys away," Eddie told me, withdrawing a gold cigarette case from the deep maroon, satin smoking jacket he wore. "Didn't want you to hurt yourself," he added, calmly taking out a fag and tamping it down against the case.

"You had a lot of toys," came a smooth voice from behind me. I jerked around, which hurt my head, and saw ZaZu, her shapely legs gracefully crossed, sitting in a cordovan leather armchair near a wide picture window with a panoramic view of Capitol Hill and the Lake Washington ship canal. The way her figure curved under the black, clinging, Chinese-style silk dress she wore, she could've knocked me out all over again.

"Yeah, lots of toys," Eddie said, sauntering over from the door and taking a seat in the brocade lounger opposite me.

I swung my feet off the blue sofa I was on and turned to face him, running my hand over the huge knot on the back of my noggin. "Why didn't you finish the job?"

"We didn't kosh you," said Eddie.

"We rescued you," ZaZu said.

"In a pig's eye." I reached into my rumpled jacket and fumbled for my smokes.

"Try one of mine," said Eddie, flipping open his cigarette case and offering it to me. "Hundred-percent imported Turkish. Even stronger than you, big guy."

I passed. Found my pack of Philip Morrises, pretty crumpled from the fall I'd taken, and managed to pull out a fag that wasn't broken.

"He's ungrateful as ever, isn't he, Eddie?"

"Sure is." He cut loose with one of his wicked little laughs.

I studied him for a minute. Eddie hadn't changed much. Almost my height but slighter of build. Probably went no more than a hundred and sixty pounds soaking wet. Longish blonde hair, pushed up slightly at the front with a little extra hair grease—same as he wore it way back at St. Joseph's. High cheekbones, square chin with a cleft in it. It struck me that he looked exactly like that new actor, Richard Widmark, who'd been playing all the heavies of late. Miss Jenkins had dragged me to see his first big movie

47

last year. What was the name of it? *Kiss of Death*, that's it, with Victor Mature playing the hero. Clear case of art imitating life. Evil and deadly as Widmark was in his flicks, he couldn't hold a candle to Eddie in real life. Except, maybe, for being unpredictable. "Always good to see ya, Jake," said Eddie, his narrow smile still in place.

"Maybe our guest would like a drink," said ZaZu.

"Looks like he could use a drink. I'll get it for him," he added, quickly getting to his feet. "You stay put over by all his nasty little toys, ZaZu. Wouldn't want Jake to make a grab for 'em while you were busy being hospitable."

"That would be rude. You wouldn't do something like that, would you, Jake?" she asked, nonchalantly picking up my .25 and running a crimson-polished, long-nailed forefinger down its short barrel.

"Furthest thing from my mind," I said, tapping the ash from my smoke into the big brass ashtray sitting on the table in front of me.

Eddie walked over to the cherry wood liquor cabinet that stood next to the high archway that led into the suite's dining area. He opened the cabinet's double doors and twin hidden shelves swung out, loaded with about every type of booze imaginable. "I'm sure Jake still likes his Scotch," he commented, picking up a bottle of Cutty Sark and setting it on top of the cabinet. "But how about you, baby?"

"You know what I like," said ZaZu.

He nodded and took out a bottle of Smirnoff's vodka. "And for me," he said. "I'll just go with a little—"

"Tequila," I said.

"You remembered," he told me, with an overblown tone of appreciation and a big smile to match.

"How could I forget?"

"Yeah, I do love my cactus juice." He picked up a bottle of the Mexican rotgut, held it up, and looked at the bottom of it. "This is the good stuff, too. Got that little, dead, green worm floatin' down there and everything. This hotel's class, what'd I tell ya?" he said to ZaZu, who rolled her eyes like maybe she'd rather be staying downtown where most every other big hotel in Seattle was located.

Eddie ignored her and got us our drinks, both straight, no ice. He brought them over and served ZaZu first, me second. Then he went back for his tequila. I nursed my Scotch while he poured the fiery hooch into a tall highball glass, growing more and more tense as he filled the big glass almost to the brim, then topped it off with enough extra that some spilled over the edge. I was plenty tense to begin with, but put Eddie and his damned tequila together, anything could happen. He always claimed that he liked the stuff because it made him a little loco. Fact was, he always was a little loco to begin with. Drinking tequila just made him even more loco. A few stiff belts would get him down and dirty. A few more would get him absolutely ugly. Any more than that, you took your life in your hands just trying to share the same side of town with him.

I figured I ought to ask a few questions before the tequila worked its old black magic on him.

"What brings you to town, Eddie?"

He took a big gulp of his tequila before returning to his seat opposite me and answering my question. "The cherry trees," he said, slugging down more of his drink. "I wanted to see the Japanese cherry trees in bloom over at the University of Washington."

49

"That so?"

"Sure, they're just lovely. They got the most delicate pink blossoms," he said. "Some law against it?" He tipped back half the tall glass at one draught.

"Not that I know of."

"Cops seem to think so. They leaned on me almost as soon as we checked in."

"Your reputation precedes you. They're just trying to do their job, Eddie."

"Yeah?" he said, throwing back more tequila like it was so much water. "Since when did you get palsy-walsy with the coppers?"

"Flatfeet and me aren't exactly buddy-buddy," I told him. "I've realized that they're not all bad, that's all."

"Yeah?" His eyes narrowed like his smile. "Talk like that makes me worry about you."

"He always was a goody-two-shoes," said ZaZu, one perfectly plucked eyebrow arching as she pushed back a stray lock of her long, platinum blonde hair.

"Dicks who grilled me were still parked out front last time I looked. Those coppers with you, Jake?"

"Hardly."

He tossed off the last of his drink and stood up. "As if I couldn't give 'em the slip anytime I wanted," he laughed. "Say, Jake, you've hardly touched your whiskey. Don't tell me you've become a damned teetotaler, too. Drink up. I'll get you another."

I held onto my glass. "I'll tell you when I'm ready for more."

Eddie's smile vanished for a second, then came right back. "Well, I'm always ready for more. Say, how about we have some music, too?" He headed over to the big floor model radio that stood near the liquor cabinet. "They still got that station here that I like?" he asked, turning on the radio and spinning the dial as it warmed up. "One with all that good swing music. Here it is," he said, finding his radio station, but not getting much more than a bunch of loud static.

"If you didn't kosh me, who did?" I asked.

"How should I know?" he answered, distracted by his inability to get his music to come in. "Hey, that's Benny Goodman!" he yelled, trying to adjust the dial, but only catching bits and pieces of Benny's sweet clarinet over the increasing static. "I love old Benny. What the hell's wrong with this thing?" He gave the radio cabinet a violent shake. Just got more static for his troubles.

"Eddie, you'll break it," said ZaZu.

"I want my tunes!"

He was getting worked up, never a good sign. "How long you staying in town?" I asked him, trying to change the subject.

"Just change the station," ZaZu told him.

"I'll change the station!" he yelled. Then he kicked his right foot completely through the big cloth-covered speaker at the bottom of the radio, all the glass tubes inside breaking and crashing. "Friggin' thing! How's that?" he said, a low hum now the only sound coming out of the broken radio.

"That's one way of doing it," I said.

ZaZu started to say something, but Eddie cut her off. "Keep your trap shut!" he told her, then turned back to me. "You think that's funny?"

"Yeah, actually, I do."

He glared at me, his gray-blue eyes going glacial. Then he laughed abruptly and grabbed the bottle of tequila from the liquor cabinet, swilling some straight from its long neck. "That's what I always liked about you," he told me, wiping off his mouth with the back of his hand. "You got balls, Jake. Always did. Sense of humor to match." He took a couple more healthy slugs, then brought the bottle with him and sat down.

"We used to be good together, you and me. We was real pals, Jake. Damned shame we went different ways."

I didn't respond.

"Now everybody's scared of me," he continued, guzzling more tequila. "Even ZaZu, sometimes," he laughed. "But not you. Huh, big guy? Well, here's to ya." He offered the tequila bottle as a toast.

I picked up my glass and clinked it off his bottle, and we both drank.

"So," I repeated my earlier question, "how long are you staying in town?"

His eyes went mean. "Maybe you oughta be," he hissed, leaning in at me. "Scared of me, I mean. Maybe you oughta be."

"Not on your life," I told him, staring right back into his eyes and noting that they'd gone all bloodshot from the booze.

"You oughta be!" he snapped, suddenly slapping the glass out of my hand. I jumped to my feet. So did ZaZu. She trained the .25 on me as Eddie stood up, his eyes as wild as his crazy grin. "I'm disappointed in you, Jake. You come to see me armed to the teeth, then get yourself blindsided and blame me when we give you a hand. You damned ingrate!

By God, I say it's time to see who's the better man!" he screamed, throwing his tequila bottle across the room, where it shattered against the wall.

"You know the answer to that," I told him. "I'm ready anytime you are."

"Don't fight in here, Eddie," said ZaZu, quickly stepping in while keeping the drop on me. "You two mix it up, the hotel dick will be knocking at our door in a second. We don't need that. Take the fight somewhere else."

"Out back," said Eddie, his loony grin glued firmly in place. "We'll take it out in the alley."

"Anywhere you want, you crazy bastard."

Every muscle in his body tensed when I called him crazy. He didn't like being called crazy. Especially since it was true. I thought he was going to go for me right then. But he didn't. Which was fine by me. I didn't really want the hotel dick to show up and bust things up while I was busy busting Eddie up. I didn't want Baker's detectives or even Heine to spoil the show, either. I was finally getting the chance to do what I'd come to do.

"Let's go," Eddie said, peeling off his fancy smoking-jacket and rolling up the sleeves of his crisp white shirt. "Don't worry," he told me, as we headed for the front door, ZaZu following me, my own little .25 automatic pointed at my back through the bottom pocket of her silk dress. "It'll be a fair fight."

"Sure," I said sarcastically, going out the door after him. "Just you and me and ZaZu and her pistol."

"She won't use the gun." Eddie smirked, glancing over his shoulder. "Will you, baby?"

"Of course not," she said, smiling prettily as we went

down the back hallway and boarded the service elevator. Eddie laughed his wicked laugh and shut the door. ZaZu slammed down the brass operating lever.

The alley was deserted when we got out back. The milk truck was gone, the loading dock empty, and not a soul in sight. The only spectators were the few gulls still circling and screeching overhead. The truck zone in front of the loading dock was the widest space around, so we settled on it as the best spot to hold our little shindig.

I folded my sports coat and laid it on the steel lip of the dock, keeping one eye fixed on Eddie, watching to see if he took any hidden weapons out of his pockets. He just leered at me from about twenty feet away, his dukes hanging loose at his side, patiently waiting. Not wanting him to wait too long, I closed right in. We circled each other, about six feet apart, each trying to figure out if the other's fighting style had changed since the last time we'd mixed it up.

"You never could take me," Eddie grinned, bobbing and weaving as he moved to my right.

"Vice versa," I told him, remembering that during our last bout, he'd suddenly rushed in under my guard and tried to knee me in the balls. So, I lowered my stance and crouched slightly, ready to put my own knee in his groin if he tried it again.

He read my mind and cackled that crazy staccato chuckle of his. "I never make the same move twice," he said, then quickly feigned a punch with his right fist. I didn't fall for it. Knew he'd wing a left hook upside my head if I took the bait. Instead, I put two stiff left jabs straight into his nose. He countered with a left of his own, then landed a hard right cross into the bridge of my beak in return.

We circled some more, both our noses bleeding.

"Tit-for-tat," said Eddie, wiping at the blood from his schnoz with the knuckles of his right hand.

"Get him, Eddie!" hollered ZaZu.

"Who are you working for?" I asked him.

"I'm on vacation," he said, jabbing a left at me, which caught me flush in the nose again. The blood now gushed out like a Texas oil well. "This trip's personal," he added, catching me with another left. "Just rest and relaxation."

Bleeding so badly that I had to start breathing through my mouth, I purposely threw a slow, weak jab at him. He thought I was getting winded, fell for it, and tried to hit me with a leading right—just what I expected. I slipped it and countered with a loaded left hook. It whistled in over his lowered guard and caught him square in the temple. It rocked him, but he didn't go down. I tried to follow up with a right cross, but he nailed me with an uppercut that felt like it shook all my fillings loose. I wouldn't go down either. We came in close, went toe-to-toe and gave it everything we had. Kept hitting each other so hard, it would've K.O.'d the average elephant. Then up came his frigging knee into my groin, and I rammed my elbow into his solar plexus in return. Gasping, the wind knocked out of both of us, we went into a clinch. That should've given me the advantage, but Eddie was a lot stronger than he looked. We grappled, each trying to gain some leverage. Bam, he gave me a head butt. Bam, I gave him one right back. Then, like a damned dirty dog, he bit into the flesh under my right cheekbone and wouldn't let go. His teeth sinking deeper and deeper, I found his left eye with my thumb and gouged at it for all I was worth.

Then I saw stars again.

More stars than in all the heavens.

They twinkled brightly for a moment, then went out one by one, faster and faster, until all I could see was the big, black, empty sky.

For just a second, the sky lightened again. ZaZu entered the picture above me. She was smiling and tapping Heine's blackjack into the palm of her hand. Eddie's bruised and battered face replaced hers, his tight-lipped grin showing through all the blood spattered across his mug.

"ZaZu shouldn't have koshed you. I apologize," he told me, his voice sounding like it was somewhere clear across the universe. "You and me will have a chance to finish up proper some other time."

I didn't say anything. Just thought about what great pals he and I used to be. How nice it was to have somebody you could count on. Things were easier back in those days. Seemed so simple and clear cut. Now I only trusted a few people in the whole world. And Eddie used to be one of them.

"I just want you to know something," he was telling me, seeming further and further away with every word. "ZaZu clobbered you now, yeah. But we didn't have anything to do with bashing you earlier. I just found you in the hall when I stepped out to get the morning paper. You better watch your back, Jake."

Then Eddie's face faded away. So did everything else. Faded out like in the movies, when the screen starts slowly going dark before the next scene. I thought it ironic that I'd come into this scene with a bash to the back of my noggin and was going out of it with yet another bash to the back of my noggin. I really wanted to see what the next scene was going to bring. But the screen stayed dark and the curtains began to close . . .

Chapter

4

I CAME TO IN LESS THAN A GOOD MOOD. I couldn't see straight. My right cheekbone hurt, and some big palooka was pressing something against it that made it hurt worse. I didn't like that much and tried to give him a good sock in the kisser.

"Hey, Jake, take it easy," came Heine's voice. He grabbed hold of my arms and gave me a hard shake. "For crying out loud, it's me, Heine. You been out for the count."

My right-hand man's beefy face slowly came into focus. So did everything else. I was still out in the alley, smack on my butt over by the loading dock. I struggled to my feet, dizzy and pissed.

As I brushed the dirt off myself, he said, "You're pretty wobbly, jarhead. Maybe you oughta—"

"I'm fine," I told him, even though the world was spinning like I'd drunk too much bad hooch. "Just gimme my coat."

"O.K. Don't listen to me. Do whatever you want. You always do, anyway." He got my coat and gave it to me, followed by his handkerchief. "At least keep this up against your cheek, huh? What the hell happened? Looks like somebody tried to take a bite out of you."

"He did."

"Eddie?"

"Yeah."

"Didn't know he bit."

"Ha-ha. Where's my hat?"

"It's right here. I think somebody stepped on it."

"Swell." I smoothed out my fedora. The crown was crushed, but it popped back into place well enough. "How'd you know I was out here?" I asked, gingerly putting my hat on my aching head.

"That broad, ZaZu, found me down in the lobby. What a knockout. She ain't changed much. Told me you were out here and needed a little tending to."

"That was sweet of her." I dug out a Philip Morris and got it lit. Had to smoke it out of the left side of my mouth, however, because the right side was puffed up about the size of the Goodyear Blimp.

"I would've leaned on her but she skipped out as soon as she mentioned your whereabouts," Heine continued. "By the way," he said, reaching into the front pockets of his brown Eisenhower jacket and withdrawing two pistols. My pistols. "Here's your .45 and that worthless little backup piece you carry. Courtesy of ZaZu." He handed them over. "Of course, there ain't any ammo left in 'em. She ditched the clips before she gave 'em to me. Probably a good idea considering you ain't exactly the most forgiving sort."

"I've still got a bullet left for each of them," I said, checking my guns over. "They may have taken out the ammo-clips, but they forgot one important thing: I always keep an extra round in the chambers."

"You're not going to do anything stupid are you?"

"Nah," I said, putting my pistols back in their proper places. "I've already been stupid enough for one morning."

Heine smiled. "At least you're smart enough to admit it. Say, ZaZu forked over my blackjack, too," he told me. "Mighty decent of her. Course, there's some dried blood on it that needs to be washed off. Yours?"

"I need a drink."

"What you need is a doctor."

"I can get both back at the office. Scotch and a little attention from 'Nurse' Jenkins. She's got more practice patching me up than most sawbones. Let's go." I turned and walked up the alley toward 43rd, where the car was supposed to be parked.

"Miss Jenkins ain't gonna like what she sees," he said, catching up to me.

"I don't either," I told him, trying to walk in a straight line but doing a piss-poor job of it.

"Good Lord," said Miss Jenkins, dabbing at the copious scab on the back of my noggin with a big cotton-ball. "Good Lord!" she exclaimed for the umpteenth time.

"Will you stop saying 'good Lord' and just get on with it?" I told her, not wanting to let on how much it hurt, because she'd just say "good Lord" again. I thought I'd feel better once I got back to the office and sat down at my own desk. But the only thing better about it was the bottle of Cutty Sark that I'd been nursing while Miss Jenkins nursed me.

"Hold still."

"It's a mite hard to hold still when you keep murdering

me with that hydrogen peroxide. It's just a bit sensitive back there, you know?"

"Good Lord, look at your cheek," she said, coming around my high-backed desk chair and staring all wide-eyed at me like I was Bela Lugosi. "Those bite marks go almost all the way through."

"Tell me something I don't know."

"You may need stitches," she commented. I grimaced through the searing pain. "You really ought to see a doctor."

"Don't need a quack," I said, wishing she'd get done with my cheek so I could suck down some more booze. "Not when I've got you, Florence Nightingale."

"Don't count on me for much longer," she told me, tossing the crimson colored cotton ball into the waste basket. "Mr. Hashimoto's due any minute."

"What, you'd throw me over for some Jap?"

"Good Lord, I can't imagine what Hashimoto would have thought if you'd barged in on us in your condition."

"Poor Mr. Hashimoto." I grabbed for my Scotch as she grabbed for the iodine bottle. Luckily I beat her in time to get one good gulp of hooch before she got the cap off of it.

"This is going to hurt," she told me, wetting a new cotton ball with the iodine.

"You're a mistress of understatement, my dear." When she hit me with the iodine, I felt like one of the Japs I'd seen nailed by our flame throwers on Okinawa. I didn't say anything, though. Don't think I could have if I'd wanted to in that raging burning moment. At least nothing that would have been appropriate in mixed company.

Heine stuck his head in from the outer office. "That Jap's

here to see you, Miss Jenkins. Mr. Moto, I think he said his name was."

"That's *Hashimoto* and you know it," she corrected him. "Shhhhh! He'll hear you."

"Fine by me," he said loudly, then stepped all the way into my office, leaving the door wide open behind him.

Heine and me had been in too many jungles with too many Japs to worry much about their feelings.

"Shhhhhh!" Flushing mightily, Miss Jenkins made like a bunny for the open door. "I'm sorry, Mr. Hashimoto," she apologized through the doorway. "I'll be right with you." She slammed the door shut and turned back to us. "You should be ashamed of yourselves!"

"Yeah, I'm a dirty rat," said Heine, taking a seat in the chair opposite my desk and pouring himself a couple fingers of Scotch.

"Me, too. We feel just awful about it," I said, as sorrowfully as I could. "You run along and take care of Mr. Moto, doll. We'll be busy committing Hari-Kari with the Scotch."

I thought she was going to yell at me. Instead, she simply took a deep breath and quietly said, "This is my first real case. You stay in here and nurse your wounds. Don't you dare embarrass me." Without another word, she went into the outer office and closed the door.

"You think we were too hard on her?" asked Heine.

"Nah. She can take it." I popped four aspirin into my mouth, chewed them so they'd work faster, then washed down the bitter mess with a big swallow of 86 proof.

"Well, she did a damned good job patching you up," he said, pouring more Cutty for both of us. "You just look all beat up now, instead of half-beaten to death."

"Thanks," I told him. "Drink up. I need you back out on the street."

"Figures."

"You sit on Eddie and ZaZu until I tell you otherwise."

He tossed off the last of his booze and stood up. "You think they were telling the truth about not blind-siding you the first time around?"

"When have they ever told the truth about anything?"

"Yeah, ain't that the truth?" He took his fedora off my desk and put it on, then adjusted it to the jaunty angle that he favored. "Well, just in case they were playing it straight, you got any ideas who might have done it?"

"Dunno. There's probably a hundred joes who wouldn't mind giving me a bash or two. Take your pick."

"True enough." He turned to leave but stumbled over the hooked rug in front of my desk. "Hell's bells," he said, catching himself. "When you gonna get this rug fixed? I trip over it every time I come up here."

"It's a good conversation piece. I shot Big Ed on that very rug last year. It came back from the cleaners all curled up. I tell a new client about how Ed met his maker, it gives them faith in me right off the bat."

"Yeah, that's definitely a story worth repeating." He chuckled and headed for the door. "By the way," he asked, before he went out. "What are you going to be up to while I'm gone?"

"I'm going to give Henry Jamison's office another look-see. Really go over it with a fine-tooth comb. Just in case I missed something the first time around."

"Watch your back. I'll go out real quiet-like so as to not disturb Miss Jenkins."

"Disturb her all you want," I said. "Likewise that Jap. Maybe he'll get his bowels in an uproar and leave."

Heine laughed. "*Sayonara*," he told me, then vacated the premises.

I leaned over and turned on the new Philco portable radio that I kept on the bookshelf beside my desk. I was hoping to catch a few tunes and take five while the aspirin and Scotch went to work on my infirmities. But all I got was the news report. The announcer was blabbing about the Commies again. How they were everywhere these days and might have even wormed their way into the University of Washington faculty. He added that there were rumors that the House Un-American Activities Committee might be holding hearings in the near future about these professors who were suspected of being Red sympathizers. If they were Commies, we could all be assured that they'd be rooted out.

I turned the radio off, didn't even bother changing the station. Commies on the campus . . . Judas. What next? Whole lot of good joes had just laid down their lives during the war trying to straighten things out, and it had already come to this in barely three short years. Crooks had had a field day while we were gone, and now there were Commies on the campus and Tojo sitting in my outer office crying the blues to Miss Jenkins about how unfairly his race had been treated. Those cozy internment camps they'd been in were a damned sight safer and more comfortable than the fox-holes Heine and I had shared, that was for damned sure. Nobody could ever give *us* back what we'd lost during the war . . .

Only answer to this convoluted crapola was another few

fingers of Scotch. Which I had. Then a few more. Didn't fix anything, but it dulled the throbbing in my noggin and steered my brain back to the situation at hand. Namely, who bumped off Henry Jamison and why? Not to mention who had clubbed me on my way up to see Eddie Valhalla and why? Plus, what the devil were Eddie and ZaZu doing back in town, anyway? Hell, those were plenty enough conundrums for now. Albert Einstein couldn't tackle them all together. Best way to play it was to just try and unravel them one by one.

Deciding it was high time to take my gander around Jamison's office, I picked up my aching bones and strolled out past my partner and her Tojo. He was tall for a Jap, in his mid-twenties, and wore a sharp blue suit and red tie. Miss Jenkins introduced me like she was happy to see me.

"Mr. Hashimoto, this is my boss, Jake Rossiter."

He jumped to his feet and offered me his hand. "Glad to meet you, Mr. Rossiter. I can't tell you what it means to my family you agreeing to help us and all."

"Yeah," I muttered, giving his hand more of a quick brush-off than a shake. "I'm blowing down the hall for a bit, Miss Jenkins."

"No problem at all, boss," she told me, motioning behind Hashimoto's back for me to get the hell out. "I'll hold down the fort as usual."

Hashimoto's eyes wandered over the bandaged and bruised terrain of my face. "Mr. Rossiter, if you don't mind me asking . . . Were you in some sort of accident? Are you O.K.?"

"They're just old war wounds I got in the Pacific," I told him. "Never healed."

His gaze went downcast for a moment. The room was quiet as a church. I could tell that he was hurt by my remark. Almost made me sorry I'd said it. But only for a second. "See you," I told Miss Jenkins, then mobigated out the door.

Down the hall, I paused and listened outside Jamison's office. Weren't any noises coming from inside the place, no light showing through the textured glass door panel bearing the gold-stenciled SEATTLE LIFE & PROPERTY, either. Satisfied that Captain Blevens wasn't still lurking about, I picked the lock and stole into the scene of the crime.

The joint was dark, but not too dark. Had kind of a twilight quality to it from what sunlight filtered through the tall outside window's partially opened venetian blinds. Plenty enough to see that not too much had changed since my earlier visit. Except that the body was gone. Likewise Henry's head and the Samurai sword. My coffee mug and breakfast dish still sat where I'd left them on his desk. Only additions to the room were the white chalk marks outlining the bloodstained former positions of Henry's head and body, plus six or seven spent flashbulbs littering the floor in the same area. No respect. You'd think the damned police photographer could pick up after himself. Aside from that, I couldn't miss the fact that every drawer in the joint had been pulled open and left that way. All the desk drawers, the four drawers in the oak credenza back by the window, and even the wide drawer under the glass-fronted bookcase. Last but not least, all nine drawers in Jamison's three, high, battleship gray filing cabinets had been pulled out and left open, a few of their manila folders fallen to the floor, and a few more files resting at odd angles on top of the obviously ransacked drawers.

What had old Blevens been after, anyway? You usually didn't tear hell out of a place just on a preliminary murder inquiry. I had filched a couple files for myself, earlier, mainly to spite the rotten bastard; but also on the off-chance they might contain some clues. Way this joint looked, maybe I should've kyped a whole lot more.

I got busy playing second banana and went through all the opened drawers. I normally wouldn't have ever followed in Blevens's wake: too polluted and stank too much. But this was different. Little bird told me that something was more than rotten in Denmark.

I fished for quite a while without any bites. My initial go around turned up nothing more than a desk full of paperclips and staples and assorted rubber stamps, followed by a credenza full of extra business forms and such, and finally, endless file cabinet drawers full of banal life insurance and property policy records, most of them current, some closed, but not a whole lot stamped as "paid out," which fit the bill for most insurance carriers: they just loved to take your dough, but did everything they could to Scrooge you if pay-up time ever rolled around.

Hell . . . Nothing to do but go over everything again. I was nothing if not a bulldog. Then, "Voila!" as Miss Jenkins would have put it, I found something taped to the bottom of the desk's pencil drawer. Turned out to be some photos of Henry with a bunch of different dames, including one dog-eared photograph of Henry Jamison and some fair-haired bimbo, both in their skivvies, sharing a bottle of bubbly while they snuggled on the rug in front of a scraggly little Christmas tree.

Why Henry, you sly dog, who'd a thunk it? None of these dames was his wife. I'd met her once when I was giving Henry the first payment on the new liability policy he'd written for my up-and-coming detective agency. Mrs. Jamison had brought Henry his egg-salad sandwich because he'd forgotten his lunch at home. Fairly plain, but not un-attractive, pleasant and pushing the fat side of chunky, she said that her hubby simply couldn't get along without his favorite egg-salad. Also mentioned that she was glad to meet me and was real pleased that I'd given her husband more of my business. Then she left. But not before she'd planted a big slobbery kiss smack on top of Henry's shiny bald pate. The instant she went out the door, Henry dumped the sandwich in the wastebasket.

My second discovery of the morning was a bit more enigmatic. As I thumbed through the file cabinets, I realized that about half a dozen file sections looked a little empty.

The two manila folders I'd snatched for myself had been in the *A* section. Strangely enough, there were now only a couple folders left in that same *A* area. There'd been more than a dozen in there, I was sure, when I had my sticky fingers. Continuing my search, I found that one alphabetical heading, *D*, was completely empty, contained no folders whatsoever. Four other headings, *H*, *M*, *P*, and *T* had only one or two folders each, while all the other headings were crammed fat with folders. Somebody had followed my little burglary with some light fingers of their own. At least in the *A* file. That was for certain. But who and why?

Captain Blevens came immediately to mind. What he'd want with them, I didn't have a clue. But any number of other folks might have been in here in the hours that I'd been gone, as well. Maybe even poor Henry's widow, Mrs. Jamison. I didn't know if she'd been notified of his death yet, but I assumed that she probably had. Be easy enough to find out. If she hadn't, I really didn't want to be the bearer of bad tidings, but she was high on my list for a few questions anyway. Especially with the snapshot I'd found of her hard-working hubby's extramarital hijinx.

There was no point in taking any additional files. Whoever had rifled the cabinets had obviously gotten what they came for. But I took some file from each of the ransacked sections anyway. Just in case they might shed some light on the original files that I'd swiped earlier in the day. Could be that the files I already had in my possession might be important to somebody. Could even have been a motive for murder. So I beat feet back to my office eager to take a hard look at them.

Miss Jenkins was alone at her desk, staring bullets at me, when I came in. Her Jap client had evidently gone, and that was fine by me. I ignored her scowl and blew past her to my inner sanctum, where I began to pore over Henry Jamison's files.

I'd barely started when Miss Jenkins filled the doorway, everything about her stern as a nun, including her crossed arms and rapidly tapping right foot. "How could you?" she said. There was no question in her tone whatsoever. Just accusation.

"How could I what?"

"You know *exactly* what."

"Look, doll," I said. "I don't have time to play 'Twenty Questions.' Can't you see I'm busy?"

She strode forward, all five feet-two inches of her towering over me. "How could you insult Mr. Hashimoto like that?"

"Oh, that," I said, glancing up at her. "I wouldn't lose any sleep over it. Japs don't really get insulted. They're stoic, don't you know?"

"You should be ashamed of yourself!"

I ignored her.

She stalked away, saying, "I officially took his case. So there!"

"It's all yours. More power to you."

She paused at the door and said, "I wouldn't ask for your help if you were the last man on Earth!"

"Well, since there are about a billion of us men still around, I guess I'm safe for a while."

She stormed out, slamming the door so hard that it rattled the pictures on my walls. A couple of them were left hanging at crazy angles by the time the place fell silent again. I couldn't have cared less. The few pictures I had never seemed to hang straight anyway. But I did take the time to readjust the one that hung directly above my desk. My favorite picture in all the world: the big black & white glossy that showed Heine being presented his Silver Star for saving our platoon on Guadalcanal when he single-handedly wiped out the two Jap machine-gun nests that had been cutting us to pieces. Ever humble, he looked more uncomfortable getting that medal pinned on him than he ever had in combat. What a tough nut. Wasn't much I wouldn't do for that joe.

Heine's photo hanging straight again, I went back to my look-see of Henry's files. But just as before, Miss Jenkins was bound and determined to interrupt me.

The door suddenly opened and she took two small steps into my office, then stopped dead in her tracks. She didn't say a word. Didn't have to. The look on her face told me something was wrong.

"What's up?" I asked.

Her expression grew more worried looking, which concerned me. Then she blurted, "I don't really know where to begin."

I rose to my feet. I'd never seen her quite so nervous. "Fill me in, doll, whatever it is. And I'll try to take care of it," I told her. "Is there a problem with Captain Blevens or Jamison's murder or what?"

"Not that." She fell silent again. Finally, she spit it out. "I don't really know where to begin with the Hashimoto case."

I had to laugh. If for no other reason than to relieve the tension. She didn't like it.

"Well, I've never really worked on a case all by myself before," she said.

"Maybe you're not ready for it."

"Am so!"

"Fine. You asked for it, you got it," I told her, sitting back down at my desk. "Say, I've got a good idea. Maybe you could begin by calling Hashimoto and telling him you're not going to take his case after all."

"Very funny. Thanks for nothing," she said, then flew the coop again. Her last words before slamming the door were, "You'll see!"

I lit a fresh smoke and went back to work on the files. If I'd been too hard on her, maybe she'd ditch the frigging Jap case, and things would get back to normal around here. Normal being that I could put her to work helping me go over all these damned dry files. While I was fairly certain there might be something important in them, they were about as tedious as being dragged out to a Seattle Symphony performance at the Orpheum Theatre. There seemed to be nothing whatsoever in the files but the endless names of folks who had policies with Henry's insurance company. Life insurance, property insurance, liability insurance, and so on. Most of them were still in force, but some were stamped as PAID OUT—POLICY HOLDER DECEASED. Others showed some pay-outs for various types of losses . . . fire damage, water damage, theft, et cetera, often noting an increase in premium after good old Seattle Life & Property had to cough up the dough.

I kept at it, though. I went through every single file, then stacked them back in order. I was just getting ready to go over them a second time, when Miss Jenkins buzzed me on the intercom.

"Yeah, what is it?" I said, stabbing the talk-button with the blunt end of my fountain pen. "You finally come to your senses and want to help me with some serious work?"

"Ha ha," came her voice over the static. "I just thought I'd let you know where I've decided to begin."

"And where would that be, pray tell?"

"I'm taking a drive down to Little Tokyo."

"There's no Little Tokyo anymore," I said. "Hasn't been since they threw all the Japs into the camps. It's all Chinatown these days."

"I know that," she told me. "But that's where I'm going, nevertheless. Where Little Tokyo used to be."

"Why? Where exactly?"

"Oh, I've got some questions for a few people. There's a couple gambling dens down there that I need to check out."

"What?"

"And one opium den, too."

"What?"

"I'll be gone for the rest of the day. Probably half the night. I'll bring my pistol, so don't worry. Goodbye."

"Now, hold on just a darned minute—" The intercom went dead. "Miss Jenkins? Miss Jenkins!" I yelled. No response. I jumped up so fast that I bashed my knee into the desk and barreled into the outer office, where I found her putting on her coat. "What are you playing at?" I asked.

"I'm not playing at anything," she said, nonchalantly, then withdrew her big .44 Ruger, gave its cylinder a spin, and slapped it back into her purse. "This is a dangerous business."

"It damned well can be. And that can be a rough area. Who are you planning to talk to?"

"Among others, the people who are running the Hashimotos' old store," she said, grabbing her coat. "Their name's Wong. Then I'm going to poke around in those opium dens and Mah Jong parlors. If that doesn't work, I've got a line on a few houses of ill repute and some ladies of the night who might know something." She put on her floral print scarf and headed for the door, saying, "It may be dangerous, but that's what I get paid for."

"Oh, I get it," I said, as she turned the brass door handle. "You're just trying to get my goat, aren't you?"

She turned and smiled. "Goodness gracious. How could you think such a thing? I'm only going into harm's way because I've got to begin somewhere."

"Sure. And the next thing you'll be doing is trying to sell me the Brooklyn Bridge. Well, I'm not buying it, doll. Opium dens and gambling joints . . . What a bunch of baloney. You're just trying to get me worried so I offer to help you out."

"I've got to go," she said, stepping out into hall.

"So, blow already," I told her. "I'm going back to the Jamison files. Five'll get you ten that you're going to be sulking over a soda somewhere, mad as a wet hen that you couldn't get me to fall for this."

She didn't say a thing. Just let the door swing closed and was gone. I listened for a minute as her footsteps receded down the hallway, then went back to my office and poured myself a stiff snort. I lifted it high and toasted myself for not being a sucker. Then I tossed it off and poured myself another.

I was just sipping at it, when Miss Jenkins suddenly threw the door to my office open so hard that I jumped.

"Back so soon?" I asked.

She looked scared half to death. "Boss . . ." she gasped, trying to catch her breath. "Somebody's slashed all the tires on my new car!"

Chapter

5

MISS JENKINS'S '48 PLYMOUTH COUPE SAT at the curb, resting low and squat on its rims. Her tires were slashed all right. Whoever did it had put half a dozen long, deep cuts into the sidewalls of all four tires, which were splayed out flat as could be, a couple of the inner tubes even poking through the space where the rubber had separated from the steel rims.

"That's my first brand new car ever," said Miss Jenkins, standing forlornly on the sidewalk, her scarf pulled tight against the light drizzle, while I walked around her gray Plymouth inspecting the damage. "Gee, it'll probably take a whole week's pay just to replace those tires," she added.

"Don't worry about that right now," I said, noticing that she'd left the car unlocked, as usual.

"Who would do such a thing?"

"I don't know. Kids maybe," I told her. "Anyway, these days, you're better off keeping your car locked up."

"Well, that wouldn't have helped my tires any."

I opened the driver's door. "No, it wouldn't," I said, leaning inside to see if there was any other damage. "But sometimes they'll slash up your upholstery, too."

"They didn't!" she yelped, still behind me.

"No, it's O.K.," I told her. Then I spotted a note addressed to Miss Jenkins laying on the front seat. A very unkind note. I grabbed it up, and stuffed it in my pocket so she wouldn't see it.

"Let's head back upstairs, doll. I want you to call and report this to the cops, while I put in a jingle over to Ray's Garage."

We hopped the elevator and got busy with our respective duties. While Miss Jenkins reported the vandalism to the flatfeet, I went into my office and closed the door. Then I sat down and opened up the crumpled note. The message was short and not so sweet:

> Lay off the Hashimoto case if you know what's good for you. You don't, your pretty face is going to get sliced up worse than your tires. This is your only warning.

"Boss," came Miss Jenkins's voice over the intercom. "I just got off phone with the police. They're sending a squad car over to take a report."

"That's nice," I said, thinking about her pretty face. "Come in here, I want to talk to you about the Hashimoto case."

She came right in, and took a seat in the green leather chair opposite my desk.

"What is it?" she asked.

"You talk to anybody else besides me about this Jap's problems?"

"No," she said, sitting straight up in her chair. "Just you and Heine. Why?"

"You sure about that?"

"Well, Lieutenant Baker knows about it, of course," she said. "And Haggerty, your lawyer, he asked me something about it."

"He did, did he?"

"Yes. You were standing right there, don't you remember? We argued about it in the Police Station before Haggerty got us released. What's going on, anyway?"

"Nothing," I told her. "Except I'm taking over the case."

"Sure," she laughed. "Next, you'll be trying to sell me the Brooklyn Bridge."

"I'm serious, doll. You're off the job."

"What?"

"You heard me."

"But . . . Why?" she sputtered.

"I've got more important things for you to do."

She leaned toward me, her green eyes on fire. "I don't think so."

I crossed my arms, said, "Think what you like." Then I gathered all the files I'd swiped from Jamison's office and pushed them across the desk at her. "Here. These are from the insurance office. I've run into some snags trying to make sense out of them. I need you to go over these with a fine-tooth comb. Particularly the *A* file. Little bird tells me that one or more of the names in there has something to do with Henry Jamison getting bumped off."

"Why me?"

"You're better at it than I am."

"That's not the real reason," she said. "Does this have anything to do with my tires being slashed? Is that it?"

"Of course not. Why should it?"

She studied me for a moment. I stuck on my best poker face. Then she got up and tried a different tack. "You never wanted me to work with Mr. Hashimoto to begin with," she said, pacing the room. "Oh, I get it!" She whirled around and stabbed a finger at me. "You're pulling me off the case because you're going to ditch it. You couldn't talk me out of taking it and now you're just going to let it go, aren't you?"

"Hardly, Miss Jenkins. Truth be told, I'm doing it for your sake, as much as my own. I'll be working on it like there's no tomorrow."

"My sake? I don't believe you."

"Believe what you like. Spend all afternoon fuming for all I care." I picked up the insurance files and walked around my desk and handed them to her. "Just so long as you go over these files. Now scoot, I've got work to do."

"It's not fair," she said, juggling the files a bit before getting a firm grip on them.

"Like they say," I told her, sitting back down at my desk. "Fair's for horseshoes."

She was temporarily at a loss for words. Then she found the phrase she was looking for. "Oh, go soak your head!"

Files in hand, she tromped into the outer office and slammed the door behind her for the third time in less than an hour.

I got her on the intercom. "Bring me the Hashimoto file."

"Get it yourself!"

Not feeling like arguing, I did just that: went out and got the file for myself, leaving her sulking at her desk, and returned to my office. I poured myself two fingers of Cutty Sark, then looked over the Hashimoto file.

Miss Jenkins was anything if not thorough—she'd listed a short history of the Hashimoto family since they arrived in America, complete with bios on each family member, and a rundown on the business they'd operated before the war.

The father, Subaru Hashimoto, and his brother, Hideki, had emigrated to Seattle from Nagasaki in 1910. They got work as field hands for one of the larger Japanese-owned farms on Bainbridge Island, then heard of the money-making opportunities available in the Alaskan fish canneries. They promptly headed north to make their fortunes. After three years in the canneries, saving most every dime they made, they had squirreled away enough dough to afford to get married and start their own business. Returning to Seattle, they both found brides, then bought a small variety store on South Jackson Street. The two couples shared living quarters above the place while they made it into a going concern. In 1917, the year America entered World War I, each couple had their first kid. Then Suburu and Hideki joined the Army. But Suburu had a heart murmur and sat out the war 4-F, while his brother shipped out to France and came back a hero. Wounded in action, Hideki returned with a Purple Heart and both a Bronze and Silver Star for valor. Unfortunately, his wife and kid, as well as his brother's first born, all died in the Influenza Epidemic that followed the war. Hideki never remarried, but Suburu and his wife had three more kids over the years.

Harry Hashimoto, who'd hired Miss Jenkins, was the oldest. He had graduated from Cleveland High School, on Seattle's Beacon Hill, a year before Pearl Harbor. While in the internment camp during the war, he was very active in the J.A.C.L.—the Japanese American Citizen's League. Though he never served himself, Harry was instrumental in getting many of his fellow internees to sign up for duty with the Armed Forces in order to demonstrate their loyalty and patriotism.

Frank Hashimoto, the next oldest son, finished his senior year in the internment camp, then went on to join the Army in early '43, when the Japanese Americans were first allowed to do so. He served with the 442nd Regimental Combat Team in Italy and Germany, and was highly decorated, as was his entire unit.

The youngest, Bobby Hashimoto, got through with school in '43, the same year Frank joined the Army. He, however, didn't share Harry and Frank's idea of proving his love of America by enlisting in the service. He and at least half of the other Japanese Americans in the camps felt that they were already American citizens, and, thus, didn't have to prove their loyalty in any way at all. When he got his draft notice in '44, he refused to be called up, and got sent to prison as a draft dodger. He died in a federal penitentiary of tuberculosis in 1946.

More sad news followed about the father, Subaru Hashimoto. All the file said was that he'd been shot and killed by a guard during some fracas at the Minidoka Camp in early '44—didn't explain any more than that.

I set the file down. I'd read enough. What the hell was it about these Japs that somebody was threatening Miss Jenkins over? I didn't have a clue, but it was time for some digging.

I got her on the intercom and asked, "Miss Jenkins,

refresh my memory: what's the name of those Chinamen running that five & dime, again?"

"It's all in my file."

"Meaning I should look it up for myself?" I asked.

Her answer came by way of clicking off the intercom without another word. She was pretty hacked off. Tough. It was for her own good. But I'd buy her a dozen long-stemmed roses, anyway, after I'd made sure she was safe, in order to make amends. I dug the name Wong out of the file, grabbed my hat and coat, and prepared to pay these Chinamen a little visit.

"Where are you going?" asked Miss Jenkins, as I blew by her on my way out the door.

"It's all in the file," I told her, then hit the hallway and didn't look back.

The midday cacophony of Chinatown was going full blast when I stepped out of the Roadmaster and plugged a nickel into the parking meter. Chinamen milling everywhere, the air reverberated with their sing-song language, the sounds of busy traffic, and the ever-present keening of gulls from nearby Elliott Bay. The air also offered quite a range of smells, some pleasant, some not so pleasant. A Chinese BBQ joint butted up against the Wong's five & dime, its big windows filled with row upon row of glistening, brownish-bronze cooked ducks and other fowl. The door to the place was partially open, and it smelled damned good. A few doors down, though, stood a large fish market. It had a couple tables set out in front of it on the sidewalk, holding big basins full of ice, which displayed every type of fish and seafood you could imagine, including sea urchins and sea cucumbers and some other types of sea life that looked like you wouldn't touch them with a ten-foot pole. It smelled salty and just a bit off. Topping everything, however, a low, one-story brick building sat directly across the street from where I'd parked. I couldn't read the Chinese characters on the sign above its double doors, but I didn't have to in order to figure out what kind of business it was. In the time it took me to stub my smoke out on the curb and lock the car, I saw half a dozen folks come out of the joint holding large, squirming paper bags, a white chicken head poking out from the top of each brown bag, clucking and squawking like mad as they were carted off to end up on somebody's dinner table. Just the sight of them took me back to the smell of chicken shit from all the stinking chicken coops Heine and I had cleaned out while trying to get by during the Depression. Whether I could really smell chicken shit coming from the live poultry market or not, I thought I could, and that was enough to send me in to question the Wongs post-haste.

The old hardwood floor creaked and groaned as I walked up to the long oak sales counter that stood near the front of the five ∂ dime. Bigger than I thought it would be, the place seemed to have been recently expanded. The main room of the store was about forty by sixty feet, and held row after row of everything from costume jewelry to buttons and notions to cheap kitchenware and a bunch of stuff in small boxes labeled with indecipherable Chinese lettering. Part of the side wall had been knocked out, forming a still unfinished archway that led into an adjoining space of about equal size. I glanced inside as I moseyed up to the old

Chinese lady who stood, eyeing me with some suspicion, near the sales counter's big, ornate brass cash register. The new room, which must have been the next door business at one time, was pretty much of a mess, the floor all dusty, some carpenter tools laying here and there around it, and a bunch of new display shelves partially draped by a tarp and stacked against the far wall. Business must be good, I thought, even though there was presently nobody else in the store except me and the old Chinawoman.

"Mrs. Wong?" I asked, stepping up to the counter.

"No English," she said, shaking her head. The woman was dressed like a coolie, in this black, pajama-like outfit.

"Ah," I commented, noting that she had an open book laying face down on the counter beside her wrinkled right hand: *Huckleberry Finn* by Mark Twain—and it sure wasn't printed in Chinese. "No speakee-the-English, huh?"

She shook her head again.

I picked up the book, fanned the pages, then said, "Sure is a lot of English in here."

"Can I help you?" came a male voice from right behind me. I spun around to find a tall Chinaman, about thirty or so, wearing dusty tan overalls and holding a big claw hammer in his left hand. He smiled and said, "Grandmother doesn't trust foreigners, please excuse her."

I took a step back from him and his hammer. "She's excused."

He casually slipped the hammer into one of the loops at the waist of his overalls. "My name's Charlie Wong," he said, offering me his hand. "We don't get many Occidentals in here. What's your name?"

I shook with him, noticed he had a grip like someone

who worked with his hands a lot. "Jake Rossiter," I told him.

"Should I be glad to meet you?" he asked.

"That's up to you, Mr. Wong."

"You a cop?"

"I'm private."

The old lady said something to him in Chinese.

"This about the Hashimotos, again?" he asked, his friendly expression turning a bit sour.

"What do you mean, again?"

"You'll have to leave," he said.

"You asking me, or telling me?"

He pointedly rested the palm of his right hand on the head of the claw hammer.

I thought about decking him right there and then. But, since he looked like the type who probably wouldn't stay down, I changed my tone and said, "Look, Mr. Wong, I don't want to cause any trouble. I just want to ask you a few questions."

The old lady said something else in Chinese. I gave her a quick glance, saw that she'd picked up the receiver to the big black phone that sat beside the cash register. "What'd she say?" I asked Wong.

"Grandmother wants to know if she should call the cops."

I smiled. "You really think they'll bother with you folks down here in Chinatown?"

He smiled. "Yes. They take pretty good care of us, actually." He spit some Chinese at his grandmother. She began to spin the dial.

"Why so antsy?" I asked. "Makes me think you've got something to hide."

"We have nothing to hide," said Wong. "We've got a business to run. If the previous owners had troubles, well, that's too bad. Life goes on."

"Hello, police?" asked the old lady, in perfect English.

"Whoa!" I said, holding up my hands and waving them for emphasis. "O.K. I'm going, already."

Wong gave his grandmother a sharp nod. But instead of hanging up the phone, she said, "Hold on a moment," then covered the mouthpiece with her right hand and stared icicles at me.

I tipped my hat to them. "Thanks for the hospitality," I said, heading for the front door. I got it open, then turned around for a final comment. "Maybe we'll be able to chat some other time."

"Goodbye, Mr. Rossiter," said Wong, with barely a trace of emotion.

As I stepped out onto the sidewalk, I wondered about a lot of things, but, in particular, about what Wong had said regarding the cops. My experience with Orientals was that they never trusted cops. And my experience with cops was that they didn't give a rat's ass about Orientals, unless they had the opportunity to shake them down. Could well be the case with the Wongs, I was thinking, when I spotted a familiar figure not fifty feet up the street: my very own Miss Jenkins! She turned away the instant our eyes met, but I would've recognized her petite and shapely form even if I hadn't seen her pretty face and strawberry blonde locks curling out from under her trademark floral-print scarf.

"Hey!" I yelled.

She scooted up the street like greased lightning and disappeared into the alley between the fish market and an overhanging neon sign that advertised some joint called the Shanghai Chop Suey Parlor. I sprinted after her—had almost reached the mouth of the alley—when a shot rang out. Another shot followed almost immediately, also from down the alley—but this one was much louder, had a real booming report. I filled my hand with my .45, and crept up to the alley. "Miss Jenkins!" I hollered. No reply. I crouched, then ducked around the corner.

Chapter

6

SILENCE. JUST THE SOUND OF MY RACING heart and my Oxfords edging up the block-long alley. I couldn't see Miss Jenkins anywhere, only the shaded, brick-paved corridor that stretched ahead of me between the old buildings, the whole thing lined with galvanized garbage cans and strewn with wet newspapers and other assorted litter. I wanted to call out her name again, but that would give away my position if somebody had more shooting on their mind, so I made my way up the alley, trigger-finger at the ready, taking cover where I could find it—behind a garbage can or in some of the many back doorways that lined the alley.

If she'd gone and gotten herself killed, by God, I'd never let her hear the end of it. What a crazy thought . . . But I should've expected something like this—should've known that Miss Jenkins wouldn't give up her first case so easily, and might follow me down here to the Wong's five & dime. Dammit, where was she?

I heard a low groaning up ahead, off to my right, and instantly drew a bead in its direction. I followed the barrel of my .45 to its source, went right up to these three, big, overflowing garbage cans before I got a look at the person making all the noise: Miss Jenkins, smack on her butt just on the other side of the cans. Her floral-print scarf hung loosely around her neck, and she lay very still, her big .44 Ruger clutched in her outstretched right hand, as blood ran down her forehead.

I rushed over and knelt down beside her—got her .44 instantly pointed at my nose.

"Don't move!" she yelled, her glassy eyes locked onto mine, her gun hand shaking enough that I thought she might just drop the hammer.

"Hold it," I told her, not liking the view down the Ruger's wide bore. "I'm glad you're alive, but I'm one of the good guys, remember?"

She stared at me for a minute like she *didn't* remember.

"Oh . . . It's you, boss . . ." The pistol slipped from her grasp, hit the pavement hard, and went off, the .44 caliber dum-dum ricocheting down the alley. Miss Jenkins jumped at the report, yelled, "He's shooting at me again!"

I scooped up her pistol, and held her tight. "Don't worry, doll, nobody's shooting at you anymore."

"Oh . . . good . . ." she said, burrowing into my arms. "I feel a little dizzy . . ." I dabbed at the blood on her head with my handkerchief, was glad to see that the bullet had just creased the top of her head, leaving only a nasty little two-inch furrow across her scalp.

She suddenly popped up bright-eyed and alert, just like her normal eager-beaver self, and smiled up into my face, announcing, with a great deal of pride, "I think I got him, you know?"

"Sure, kid," I said, not trusting her seeming recovery— I'd seen too many joes wounded during the war who seemed fine one moment, then turned into basket cases the next. "You just take it easy, I'll get you—"

"No, I'm serious," she protested, pulling back from me. "I remember clearly now: one minute I was running away from you, then all of a sudden there was this pain in my head, and I fell down right here in this very spot, and I looked up and I saw this man in the shadows down the alley pointing a gun at me, and, well, he must have thought he'd killed me, but boy did he get a surprise when I pulled my revolver out and shot him—*yes, I did*—and it smacked him up against that wall down there and then he ran away and you showed up, and that's exactly how it happened."

"You sure about that?" I asked.

"Of course I'm sure," she told me, struggling to her feet. "Sure as I'm sure that I'm fine now . . ." She wobbled a bit, then leaned against the wall, and slowly sagged back down to the pavement. "Well," she said, her voice quavering, "maybe I'm still a little woozy, at that . . . But I'm sure I shot him . . . positive."

"I'll take your word for it." I glanced up the alley, saw no movement whatsoever. "You get a good look at this joe?" I asked. "Would you recognize him if you saw him again?"

"No. It all happened so fast . . ."

I handed her my handkerchief. "Stick that on your noggin, doll, while I go check things out where you say that shooter was. Let's hope you gave as good as you got."

"Better," she said, gritting her teeth, and pressing the handkerchief against the top of her head. "I want my gun back."

"You in any shape to use it if you have to?"

"Of course I am," she said, sticking out a hand. I gave her

the Ruger. She put it in her lap, then went back to dabbing at her head. "Ouch."

"Just don't go pointing it in my face again," I told her.

"Very funny."

"You sure you're going to be all right?"

"I'm fine," she said. "Just go find the bum who shot me."

Always tough and scrappy. That was my Miss Jenkins. I gave her a kiss on the cheek, and added another for good measure, then set out to hunt down the worthless son-ofabitch who'd tried to kill her.

As I cautiously made my way up the alley, I half expected to hear sirens, the police roaring in to respond to the report of gunshots. But I heard nary a one. Way people kept to themselves down here, it probably hadn't even been reported. And even if it had, the cops usually left the Orientals to their own devices. Which was fair enough, the way I felt at the moment: if I got my hands on whoever had tried to bump off Miss Jenkins, I didn't want any flatfeet interfering with my revenge.

The alley came to a dead end about half a block away from where I'd left my junior partner. Empty. Wasn't a single spot for anybody to hide. Where the hell had the shooter gone? I checked the couple fire escapes that lined either side of the alley, but none of the iron ladders were pulled down, each still firmly in place in each of the grated landings that stood about a story above the pavement. But I noticed a little blood on the bricks—just a trace of it, in the general vicinity where Miss Jenkins had placed her attacker—a few drops here, a few drops there. Anybody shot by that Ruger should have been bleeding like a stuck pig. She could've just nicked him, or he might be bleeding internally, either of which could account for so little blood on the ground.

The crimson drops did form somewhat of a trail, however. They led to a peeling green door near the far end of the alley. I tried the door handle—locked—got something sticky on my hand. Closer inspection showed it to be a pea-sized lump of coagulated blood—more of it, barely visible, smeared across the badly tarnished, brass lock plate under the door handle. This is where our boy made his getaway, all right. I shoved against the door, gave it all I had. It wouldn't budge. There was no sign on the old door, but it led somewhere into the same building that the Wong's five & dime occupied.

I went back to Miss Jenkins, afraid for a moment that I really shouldn't have left her, no matter what she said. I breathed a sigh of relief when I found her exactly as she'd been a few minutes ago: sitting on the pavement, looking no worse for wear, still dabbing at her pretty head with my handkerchief. She didn't say anything when I came over to her, just looked up at me, her eyes asking whether or not I'd found the shooter. I shook my head, *no*.

She nodded, then said, "Hold me for a minute, will you, Jake?"

I knelt down and took her in my arms. She nestled her head into my shoulder, and sighed. She was soft and sweet, felt just right there, wasn't like other women at all. She was different. Other dames, well, you wined and dined them, hoping to get further than dessert. You whispered sweet nothings in their ears, when that's what you really meant: nothing. You promised them the world, but saddled up and galloped out of Dodge at first light. But Miss Jenkins, well, she made you think about coming home and having someone to hold in the night.

I was almost ready to tell her that, when I realized that she'd passed out colder than a fish. Damn! She was hurt way worse than she'd let on. She needed some medical attention but quick!

I picked her up and kind of panicked as I carried her out to the Roadmaster—stumbled and nearly dropped her in the process. Damn my hide, I should have never let her get involved in all this.

As I laid Miss Jenkins across the back seat, more than a few Chinamen stared at us, but only briefly, before going back to minding their own business.

Good damned thing nobody'd been shot around here or anything, I thought, as I gunned the Roadmaster and burned rubber all the way to Seattle General Hospital.

Chapter

7

"SHE GOING TO BE O.K.?" ASKED BAKER, hurrying toward me down the emergency room corridor. Following in his wake were two of the biggest uniformed cops I'd ever seen. If they'd been gorillas, they'd have given King Kong a run for his money. Their faces were as grim as Baker's, and I was glad they seemed to be on our side.

"Yeah," I told him, standing up from the hard bench I'd been occupying for the last twenty minutes. "They just wheeled her out. Nasty concussion and a dozen stitches. Got her sedated, wouldn't let me go up to her room yet."

"Sonofabitch," said Baker, pushing his brown fedora up a bit. "What'd you let her go down there for?"

"I didn't *let* her go anywhere," I said. "I told her to stay put at the office, but she followed me, anyway. You know what a mind of her own Miss Jenkins has."

"Sonofabitch," he repeated. "What's this about a note you found threatening her life?"

I dug it out of my pocket and handed it to him.

He read it over, then shook his head. "You should've called me."

"Well, I didn't. We just going to stand around here debating, or are we going to go down to Chinatown?"

Baker turned to his men. "Let's go bust some heads, boys." The two huge cops smiled like they'd just been given free, all-day passes to the carnival rides at Playland.

The sledge hammer hitting the door made a sound like a 90mm mortar round exploding. Green splinters flew everywhere as the old door caved in. We could've just gone into the building through the main entrance, of course, but given our present dispositions, and the fact that the shooter had absconded through this particular exit, we needed to burn off some physical energy. Gun drawn, I went in first, Baker and one cop hot on my heels, the other cop having been sent around to guard the front door. "This is a roust!" Baker yelled, at the top of his lungs. But we didn't get anybody's attention; found ourselves all alone staring down a dark and narrow hallway. Didn't seem to be a light switch anywhere. Baker's cop pulled out a flashlight and handed it to him. He cast its wide beam down the hallway, which seemed to go on forever. "Careful with any gunplay in here, boys," Baker told us. "We're packed in pretty tight. I don't want to be filling out any reports on how we shot the shit out of each other."

"Shine that flash over here, Baker," I said. "Yeah. See it? Blood trail from our boy."

"I see it," he said, slowly moving the light up the old, bare plywood floor. "Time to see where it leads."

We made our way forward, barely room for two men shoulder-to-shoulder in the tight confines. The drops that formed the blood trail got closer and closer together as we progressed. The shooter had evidently bled more and more as he made his escape. As much blood as we kept finding, I started worrying that we might come across this joe some-where with his ticket punched. I wanted him alive.

The corridor took a couple turns, then came to a dead-end up against a brick wall after we'd gone a hundred feet or so.

"What the hell?" said Baker, shining his light all around, but there wasn't any other way out except back the way we'd come.

"This is like a damned carney funhouse," said the beefy cop behind me. In the flickering light, he looked like some zombie in a Boris Karloff movie. "I don't like it."

"Blood goes right up to that brick wall," I told Baker. "You thinking what I'm thinking?"

"Yeah," he said. "You want to do the honors?"

"What are you talking about, Lieutenant?" asked the beefy cop.

"You never worked this neck of the woods, before, did you?" Baker asked him.

"What's that got to do with anything?"

"Watch Rossiter and learn," he told him.

I switched my .45 to my left hand, then pushed against the wall with my right. It seemed solid at the center and on both sides. But when I gave it some extra muscle on the left, it suddenly swung in about a foot, while the other side swung out, just like a revolving door, which is exactly what it was, covered with fake brick less than an inch thick. I shoved it open a little more, grabbed Baker's flashlight, and poked my head in and took a peek on the other side: the same narrow hallway continued on perhaps another thirty feet, then branched off into what looked like two separate corridors. "It's clear up ahead," I told Baker.

"Damn," said the beefy cop. "A false wall. I thought they only had these things in the flicks."

"Got 'em all over Chinatown," Baker told him. "False walls, secret passageways, you name it."

As I pushed the fake wall open wide enough for us to get through it, the cop asked Baker, "From Prohibition, huh?"

"Further back than that," I told him. "They've always run gambling, prostitution, opium, and such down here." I switched my Colt back to my right hand. "I'll give you a history lesson later. Let's go find our man."

We went through the opening, and up the new hallway. It smelled musty, dank, had a slight dampness to it that reminded me of the troop ships I'd ridden in during the war. It also contained another odor that reminded me of fighting the Japs—metallic and faintly salty.

"What's that smell?" asked Baker.

"Blood," I told him. "Our boy was bleeding bad by the time he got this far."

"Yeah," he said, shining his flash directly on the floor. "There's damned puddles of it everywhere."

"I don't like this," mumbled the beefy cop, stepping on my heel.

"Buck up, man," Baker told him. "What, are you afraid of the dark?"

"No, Lieutenant," he said. "I just never liked spook-houses, you know?"

We paused when we came to the spot where the hallway branched off, couldn't see what might lay around either of the corners, left or right. Baker signaled that he'd take the right, so I took the left. We raised our pistols, then, on the whispered count of three, popped around our respective corners, ready for anything.

"It's clear on my side," said Baker.

"Same-same, I think," I said, peering into the darkness on my side, seeing and hearing nothing, but wishing I had my own flashlight. "Shine that flash up here, just to be sure."

Baker's beam showed an empty hallway that went about forty feet before turning off to the right.

"Same as the hall on my side," said Baker. "It goes on a ways, too, before taking a turn."

"No blood trail up here," I said. "Shooter must have gone your direction."

"Hell," he said. "I thought he went your way."

"What do you mean?"

"There's no blood up the other hall, either."

"Got to be." I took the flashlight and double-checked—wasn't any blood in the hallway to the right whatsoever. "I'll be damned. Must be another secret passageway around here somewhere."

"Oh, jeez . . ." said the big cop.

The blood trail stopped right at the wall between the two corridors, actually formed a pool about as big as a king-sized flapjack, like our quarry had spent some time standing in one spot. The wall here was of plaster and lathe construction, had some big chunks of the plaster fallen out of it, exposing the narrow lengths of lathe underneath. We couldn't see anything obvious, so Baker and I felt all along it, trying our best to see if we could find any hidden seams. Nothing. Then I spotted it.

"Trap door," I said.

"Where?" asked Baker's flatfoot.

"You're standing on it."

He jumped back like he thought he'd fall through it or something. I had to laugh.

"It's not funny," the cop said, his teeth clamped together so tightly that I thought he might break them.

"No, it's not," I told him, kneeling down and pointing out what had tipped me on the trap door. "See that little piece of splintered plywood sticking up? There's a seam showing there where it came up. Clever," I continued, getting a fingernail under the edge of it. A hinged square of plywood, about 4"× 4", lifted back from the flooring. "This little piece of wood's a hidden handle," I said.

"Look at that seam," commented Baker, going down one knee beside me. "You can barely see it."

I pulled on the handle, and up came the trap-door, a $2^{1}/_{2}$ × $2^{1}/_{2}$ foot square, its edges beveled at a 45-degree angle, which accounted for the tightness of the seam. Baker's flashlight showed a metal ladder leading below, about as steep as you'd find on a ship. Looked like it went down a full story into the basement, which was blacker than the Ace of Spades where the light didn't reach.

"I ain't going down there," said the big cop, his upper lip twitching like he had a tickle.

"What's with you?" asked Baker. "I've seen you go up against some of the toughest hoods in town. Can't let a little thing like that scare you."

His man shook his head.

"Fine, then, you can bring up the rear," Baker told him.

"Uh-uh," mumbled the big lug, taking a step back.

"I haven't got time for this," I said, preparing to climb down the ladder.

Baker walked up to his cop, and poked him in the chest. "You go down with us, or you're going to be left up here all alone in the dark. Long way back outside without a flashlight."

"Shit," he said. "O.K., Lieutenant. Sorry."

"Don't worry," I told him, taking my first steps down the ladder. "Nothing down here but a few monsters."

"Shut up, Jake," said Baker. He came over and showed his light into the trap door so I could make out where I was going. I clung to my .45 as I climbed down the steep ladder. I didn't want to say so, but I myself had a few gallons of adrenaline flowing over what might lay below.

Baker's cop had good reason to be nervous once we all got into the basement. Instead of a nice, big open area, we found ourselves in yet another corridor, this one somewhat wider than the others, but all made of cold, clammy brick, with a rough and uneven concrete floor.

"Shit," I heard him stammering behind me in the dark, as I moved ahead on point with Baker, cobwebs brushing against my cheeks every now and again. "Shit-shit . . ."

We went on like that for sixty feet or so, before coming to another metal ladder. This one stood dead center in the middle of the brick corridor, which continued into the darkness ahead, as well as snaking off to the left and right, forming two new brick roads into God-knew-where. The choice was pretty easy, though, since the bunches of blood we'd been following ran out at the base of the ladder.

"Listen!" said Baker, in a loud whisper. "You hear footsteps?"

"Yeah," said his cop, looking up toward the ceiling.

I heard them, too—muffled, at first—then more clearly,

like heels on a hardwood floor somewhere above us, but a ways off on either side of the ladder.

"I'm going up first!" shouted the big flatfoot. He didn't wait for anybody's agreement, just scampered straight up the rungs like his life depended on it.

"Hold on . . . damn," muttered Baker.

I went up fast after the panicked cop, afraid that he'd blow the game in his haste, Baker hard after me. Without a single nod to caution, his cop threw open the trap door at the top, and clambered through it, breathing heavy and making enough noise to wake Rip Van Winkle. The sudden light hurt my eyes when I quickly popped up after him like a jack-in-the-box. I found myself in a large, old storeroom of some kind, lined with dusty, empty wooden shelves, and lit by a large, bare bulb hanging down from the tall ceiling by a chain. The big cop was leaning against a bank of shelves near the trap door, gasping for breath. I grabbed one of his meaty biceps, shook him, and told him to be quiet and get a grip, as Baker came up through the floor behind me.

I'd just noticed that the blood trail led to a wide, metal-covered door at the other end of the big room, when the door got thrown open, and none other than Charlie Wong stepped through it, his claw hammer held high in his right hand like he was ready to bash some brains. But my .45 and two .38 Police Specials convinced him otherwise real quick.

"Mr. Wong," I said. "Fancy meeting you here."

"Drop the hammer," ordered Baker.

It thunked to the floor, Wong asking, "What's going on?"

"You tell us," I said.

"I heard noises." He stared at the open trap door, then at the puddles of blood that trailed right up to his work-booted feet. "I came back, saw blood in the rear hallway, heard you in here," he continued. "Didn't know what to think—thought somebody was breaking into my store."

"Likely story," scoffed Baker, making a beeline to him. "Face the wall, lean up and spread your legs." He frisked Wong, then pulled him back to a standing position, and cuffed his hands behind his back. "Where'd he go?" asked Baker, spitting out the words hard and fast.

"Who?" said Wong, shaking his head. "Why are you doing this?"

I grabbed him by the front of his work shirt's collar, and squeezed until he made a choking sound. "Spill it!" I told him. "My partner's in the hospital, you want to join her?"

"I don't know what . . . you're talking about," he wheezed, his eyes starting to bulge.

Baker pulled my hand away from Wong's throat, said, "Let's go find a phone."

We pushed the tall Chinaman out of the storeroom, and down the rear hallway he'd mentioned, the trail of blood ahead of us, clear as the Yellow Brick Road. It stopped where we stopped with Wong, at the door that he said led into the back of his five & dime. A large window was set into the outer wall facing the door. The door was closed tight—the window, however, was wide open, pulled all the way up in its brown-stained, wooden frame. I poked my head through it—wasn't any fire escape outside, just a straight drop of about seven feet into the alley. I couldn't see any blood down below, but it could've been camouflaged easily against the alley's shaded, red paving bricks.

"Be good to get somebody down there to dope it out," I told Baker, who hadn't loosened his grip on Wong one iota.

"I'll go," the big cop volunteered, quick as a bunny. "I need some fresh air."

"Do it," said Baker.

His flatfoot didn't waste time trying to find a doorway to the outside—just piled through the window and dropped to the pavement with a thud.

"Let's go, you," Baker told Wong, shoving him through the door as I got it open.

We came in at the back of the store, near a section full of greeting cards and stationery. Halfway up the aisle leading to the cash register, we ran into two young and attractive Oriental dames doing their shopping. They beat feet out of the store as soon as they saw us coming. Wong's grandmother, minding the check-out counter, didn't follow suit, though—she screamed something at her grandson in Chinese, and grabbed the phone. In the short time it took us to get up front, she was blabbing mile-a-minute English into it.

"You send somebody quick!" I heard her say. "And you get me Lieutenant Giles, you understand?"

"Giles . . ." I said to Baker, while Wong spit some Chinese at his grandmother. "Isn't that—"

"Yeah," said Baker, with a frown. "Captain Blevens's lap-dog down at the South Precinct."

Chapter

—

8

WHILE WE WAITED FOR BAKER'S SPECIAL squad to blow in from downtown Homicide, I had my first blow up with Baker in quite some time. He'd helped save my life last year, when I got the goods on Fat Floyd and Captain Phillips, the last corrupt commanders at the South Precinct, and it had put a new perspective on my longstanding distrust of cops. But it was a very narrow new perspective, only wide enough to include Baker, and the big, mean, squarehead Swede, patrolman Ole Olafson, who'd also come to my rescue.

"Dammit, Jake," Baker told me, while the two flatfeet who'd come with us pulled down the five & dime's blinds and turned the OPEN sign in the front window around to CLOSED. "Look," Baker continued. "If you can trust me, you can trust my boys. Don't be such a hard case. My detectives will be here any minute. Work with them. They're hand-picked men, I trust each and everyone of them with my life."

"You want to bet your life on them, fine," I said. "I've had too many bad experiences with too many crooked cops. I'm not willing to wager my life, or share my info, with any other flatfeet than you."

"We had nothing to do with this," protested Wong, for about the zillionth time, warming a chair beside his grandmother behind the check-out counter. "You can't keep us here like this."

"You'll stay put until we've had a chance to search these premises!" barked Baker. "Including all your damned secret passageways!"

"We didn't know anything about them," said Wong, squirming a bit in his seat, his hands still handcuffed behind his back. "We just—"

His grandmother cut him off with a short burst of Chinese. Wong shut his yap and smiled.

I drew Baker off to the side. "I think the less said in front of these Chinese, the better," I told him. "In fact, the less said all around might be in order. I'm not too happy with Lt. Giles's name coming into the picture. Especially with his connection to Captain Blevens. I'll be damned if I'm going to set myself up to get blindsided again this today."

"Got yourself blindsided, huh?" asked Baker. "Was that before or after you had your battle royale with Eddie Valhalla?"

"How'd you know about that?"

"I had you followed."

"What?"

Baker lit up an Old Gold, said, "Don't act so surprised. Why do you suppose I didn't say anything about the condition your face is in? I knew you'd go after Eddie no matter what I told you."

"I'll be a sonofabitch."

"The tail was just to keep you from killing that rotten

little hoodlum, or vice versa," he continued. "Had a nice report that you gave as good as you got. Something I wouldn't mind doing to Eddie myself. I'd love to have an excuse to give him the 3rd degree, but I operate under a few more restraints than you do."

"Had me tailed," I muttered, so damned mad I could taste it.

"It was for your own good."

"That tears it." I cinched up my overcoat. "I'm blowing out of here."

I headed for the front door. But before I could turn the handle, in came Lt. Herb Giles, squat, ruddy-faced, with bushy eyebrows, and big superorbital ridges like the Neanderthal he was. He glared at me like he'd just lost the winning ticket to the Irish Sweepstakes.

"Out of my way, Rossiter," he ordered.

I didn't budge. "You got here quick," I told him. "What, old Blevens keep you on a leash right up the street?"

"Move!" he yelled, giving me the stiff-arm, and bulling forward. I moved back as he shoved me, but wasn't in the mood to get muscled; decided if he wanted into the joint so badly, the least I could do was give him a little assist: as he shoved into me, I stepped aside all of a sudden, and Giles's momentum carried him forward so fast that he stumbled and fell flat on his butt.

He lay in a stunned heap for a moment, then scrambled to his feet, favoring the small of his back. "You're under arrest!" he yelled.

"What for?" I asked. "For yielding the right of way like you wanted me to?"

"For assaulting an officer of the law!"

"That's not the way I saw it," said Baker, shaking his head. "Looked like Lt. Giles just slipped," he said, pointedly, to his two uniformed cops, whose jaws were still hanging down to their chests. "Didn't it, boys?"

Baker's flatfeet slowly closed their mouths, then grinned, as they nodded to the affirmative. "Yeah," said the biggest cop.

"Yeah," echoed the other one. "That's sure the way I saw it, too."

Baker turned back to the fuming Lt. Giles, who knew he'd been had—couldn't do much more than dust off the seat of his trousers. "You ought to be more careful, Giles," Baker told him. "Damned slippery floor in this place." Baker threw me a wink, and nodded toward his two cops who'd helped back me up. "See what I mean about trusting your friends, Jake?"

I tipped my hat to him, then went out the door, letting it slam behind me as I hit the sidewalk. I certainly knew the value of having loyal pals, but I also knew that most cops were like snakes: it was just in their nature to bite you, whether they coiled up first or not. The two big flatfeet who'd just sided with me over Giles's slip were a good example—they'd followed Baker's lead and supported me— but who knew what they'd do if given contrary orders by Captain Blevens.

I spotted a phone booth up the street by the fish market. I moseyed over, got inside it, and put in a call to Seattle General to check on Miss Jenkins. They kept me holding while they tried to locate her nurse. I wished they'd make it snappy, because the booth reeked of fish. I wasn't too happy having to juggle the Hashimoto case while trying to crack the murder of Henry Jamison, especially when the Jamison case was the only one I'd probably be able to squeeze any money out of. I was just thinking about how I'd divide my time, when I saw a black *&* white police cruiser pull up in front of the five *&* dime down the street. Three plainclothes types got out and went inside the store. Baker's boys, I guessed. The nurse finally came on the line, and curtly told me that Miss Jenkins was resting comfortably, would be kept overnight for observation, and, no, I could only see her during normal visiting hours, which would be from 3:00 to 5:00 this afternoon and 9:00 to 10:00 in the morning. She also offered an unsolicited opinion that women shouldn't be doing private detective work. When I thanked her for her advice and told her that nurses should really just stick to emptying bedpans, she hung up without another word.

I pulled out the phone book, and thumbed the *J*s looking for Henry Jamison's home phone in order to give his widow a call to see if I could come pay my condolences and ask her a few questions, but got interrupted by the screech of brakes. I looked toward the sound, saw another police cruiser pulling to a hard stop in front of the five *&* dime. I forgot all about Jamison's widow when I saw who piled out of the squad car and barreled into the store: Captain Harvey Blevens, a half-smoked stogie clamped tight in his teeth, and a look on his face like a bull charging the matador.

What the hell was going on? I didn't have a clue, except to guess that Lt. Giles had friends, too. Much as I wanted to go be a fly on the wall, I didn't want to chance Giles or Blevens getting a make on me, so I hung tight in the phone booth, figuring all hell was about to break loose in the five *&* dime, and I'd have just as good a view of the outcome from my present perch as I would trying to sneak a peek through the store's front window.

I didn't have to wait long. Baker and his three detectives exited the joint less than a minute after Blevens barged in. I noted that neither the good captain, nor Lt. Giles, nor the Wongs followed them out onto the pavement. Baker's plainclothes dicks wore hang-dog expressions on their faces, looked like they'd just been deep-sixed from some honky-tonk for making trouble. Baker looked pretty grim, as well. He threw his fedora down on the sidewalk, then picked it back up and dusted it off. No question about it— Blevens must have taken over at the Wong's five *&* dime, just like he'd taken over the crime scene at Henry Jamison's office.

After a brief and animated confab with his men, Baker's detectives drove off in their cruiser, and Baker strode over to his ride, the unmarked Ford, and leadfooted it up the street.

I lit up a Philip Morris and waited. Halfway through my fag, the Wongs and South Precinct brass still inside minding the store, I decided that it was well worth being that fly on the wall, after all—and the most unobtrusive way to that end, was the same secret passageway we'd used to get inside the place the first time around.

I made it back to the alley faster than the best thoroughbred out at Longacres, entered the ink-black maze of corridors, and used my Zippo to light the way as I retraced my steps to the ladder that led to the trap-door in the Wong's old storage room. There, I heard a few footsteps above me, just as before, but only the barest traces of a muffled conversation somewhere off in the distance. So, I crept up the ladder, and quietly cracked open the trap-door about half an inch.

"You keep playing along," came Blevens's voice, now more audible, "and everything will be copacetic. Understand?"

"Yes, Captain," answered a male voice that I recognized as Mr. Wong's. "But, this Rossiter—"

"Damn Rossiter!" shouted Blevens. "You just run your business. We got ways of taking care of him."

"Sure do," said Lt. Giles.

"Shut yer yap," ordered Blevens. "You ain't exactly been holding up your end of late."

"Sorry, Captain, I only—"

"You start giving the Wongs and the rest of 'em their money's worth, or my fingers will snap fast as they do down at the jazz club," he interrupted. "See how I aim to please, Mr. Wong? Just remember, though: it cuts both ways. Plenty of Chinamen would kill to have a set up like this. You keep playing ball, or you'll have an empty rice bowl."

"We didn't tell them anything," said Wong.

"Make sure it stays that way," ordered Blevens. He turned to his lieutenant. "Let's go, Giles. I got an appointment with the Weasel, and he don't like to be kept waiting."

I heard their footsteps fade off into the distance—had a quick decision to make: stay and squeeze the Wongs, or try to tail the fat cat who had it in for me, who, the way it had sounded, was off to meet up with some joe with enough juice to pull *his* strings. Easy choice. I could come back to the Wongs anytime.

I hurried back through the passageways and poked my head around the corner of the alley just in time to see Blevens slap Giles silly out at the curb. One-two-three across the kisser like a Three Stooges routine, except these slaps were real, cracked like whips, and must have stung to beat the band. But Giles just stood there and took it like a cowed dog. When Blevens was through, he meekly opened the door to the captain's cruiser for him. Then he rabbited over to his own cruiser and squealed off like his life depended on it.

I wondered where Giles was going in such an all-fired hurry. I made a mental note to lean on him if I ever got the chance. The lieutenant seemed like the type who'd crack given the right pressure, I thought, as I watched as his captain pulled away from the curb. Blevens made a U-turn in the middle of the street, then drove west, toward the nearby waterfront. In short order, I landed on his tail, keeping a discreet follow several cars back.

We ended up next to the Black Ball ferry terminal at the Colman Dock. Blevens parked his car on the water side of Elliott Avenue and took a stroll out onto the adjacent pier. Since it was abandoned, as were many of the old downtown piers in the years after the war, I couldn't follow him. There was just no place to take cover on the bare and decrepit pier. So, I grabbed the small binoculars I kept in my glove box and loitered near the concrete balustrade at the edge of the waterfront sidewalk. There, I mingled incognito with the crowds of pedestrians who usually frequented the area, as I watched him head down the long dock.

The big white ferry boat was all loaded up and ready to go. As it blasted its horn, and pulled out of the ferry terminal next to me, Blevens picked up his pace, and raced to the end of the pier, moving surprisingly fast for a man who was pushing obesity. About twenty feet from the tip of the pier, he descended a gangplank, steeply angled to the low tide, where he met up with a small wooden cabin cruiser moored at the little floating dock. Blevens cast off the mooring lines at the bow and stern of the boat, and jumped aboard as the boat's inboard engine turned over, sending up a cloud of blue smoke. I couldn't see who was in the covered pilot house, but whoever it was gunned the engine, and the cabin cruiser quickly pulled away from the dock, rocking in the wake of the ferry as it roared out into Elliott Bay.

I kept the boat in my sights, desperately wanting a glimpse of the pilot, figuring he must be this joe, Weasel, that Blevens had mentioned. But all I saw was Blevens angrily wave his arms, evidently unhappy with whomever was running the boat, before he joined the person in the pilot house and disappeared from sight. Damn—missed my opportunity. Then I got what looked like another chance, when the boat changed course about half a mile out and motored parallel to the shoreline. It sailed toward the south end of the bay, where Harbor Island lay at the mouth of the Duwammish River, with its many hardworking docks and transfer facilities. If the cabin cruiser held to that course, I could follow it around the water in the Roadmaster, maybe still get a chance to spot the Weasel and I.D. him—maybe even dope out what he and Blevens were up to.

I spun away from the balustrade, ran smack-dab into a little, freckled boy, about four or so, wearing a striped sweater and a brown beanie—had to grab him by the shoulder to keep him from falling down.

"Watch it, kid," I said. "You O.K.?"

"I wanted to use the binoculars to see the boats," explained the boy, as his mother rushed up and took him by the hand. "Could I?"

"Johnny, you have to be more careful," scolded the young woman, her red hair done in a bob.

"Some other time, kid, I'm in a rush." I started to walk away.

"Why did the man put a big, old, rolled-up rug on that boat?" the boy asked. I turned around but quick.

"I don't know," his mother told him. "It doesn't matter. Why don't we get you a nice ice cream sandwich?"

I came over, and knelt down eye-to-eye with the little boy. "What's this about a rug?" I asked, taking a fast glance out at the bay, Blevens's boat still in sight, cruising south. "What boat? That boat out there?" I pointed at the cabin cruiser.

"I can't see it," said the kid, squinting through the balustrade's rails.

"Try these," I told him, handing him the binoculars. He smiled wide as I helped him get the cabin cruiser in his sights.

"What's going on?" his mother asked, hovering over us.

"Is that the boat you saw?" I asked Johnny. "The one with the white trim?"

"Uh-huh, I think so," he replied, jiggling the binoculars so much I thought he might drop them through the rails into the drink. "It has lots of shiny wood. Gee, these make everything come real close—"

I grabbed the binoculars out of his hand, said, "Thanks, kid."

He scrunched up his eyes like he was going to start crying.

I gave him a quarter. "Here, treat your mom to an Eskimo sandwich."

I tipped my hat, piled into the Roadmaster, and lead-footed it around the waterfront. I didn't let red lights or traffic get in my way as I sped to catch up to the cabin cruiser. It kept sailing south at a leisurely rate, like Blevens and its skipper didn't have a care in the world. I managed to close the gap and motor up parallel to them within a few miles. The problem started once I reached that point, because that's where they headed out toward Harbor Island.

I gunned the Roadmaster, then pulled a fast U-turn, getting a blast of a big tanker rig's air horn for my efforts, and sped back up Marginal Way where I connected with the Spokane Street viaduct that led across the flats to Harbor Island.

I hit the island flat-out, passing transfer trucks and other vehicles like they were standing still. The place covered a large area, maybe two square miles, with a million different docks and loading facilities, but something told me that I'd find Blevens somewhere in the vicinity of the late Nick Napolitano's old dock shack on the West Waterway. Napolitano had checked out with Fat Floyd last year when we had our little showdown, but since Blevens and Floyd had been pals, I figured the dock shack was a likely spot for birds of a feather to come home to roost.

I was behind the eight ball with that conjecture. After parking as near as I could get to the dock shack, and hustling through the throngs of longshoremen busily loading and unloading their ships, I found Napolitano's dock shack boarded up and abandoned. Wasn't anything or anybody in sight, except an old rust bucket of a freighter that looked like it hadn't sailed since VJ Day. The whole area around the dock shack was littered with old newspapers, various food wrappers, and a host of empty bottles—beer, booze, and soda pop. Nobody had used this joint in a long time.

I kicked the shack's door in, anyway, just to be sure. The place was bare; just the sawdust floor and circle of bare dirt in the middle where somebody had removed the old potbellied stove that used to heat the shack.

I blew out of there and ran up and down the docks asking every joe who'd answer if they'd seen a white-trimmed cabin cruiser come through of late. I spied a crowd of working stiffs at the near end of the dock adjoining the Byerly Tugboat Pier where I'd parked. By the time I moseyed over to see what was up, a black & white squad car roared onto the scene via the narrow gravel road marked "Transfer Trucks Only."

I sprinted the last twenty feet to the dock, got there just as two uniformed cops bailed out of their car. My initial reaction was less than pleasant, considering they had to have been dispatched out of Blevens's damned crooked South Precinct. But when I recognized the huge moose who'd been driving, I had to smile—something rare as hen's teeth when I bumped into flatfeet.

"Olafson!" I threw him a small salute.

"Rossiter," he responded, adjusting his hat on his big, square head, a trace of a smile on his own lips, even though he looked like he'd still like a piece of me, as usual. "Fancy meeting you here, Mr. Private Dick."

"I could say the same," I told him, as the longshoremen on the dock hollered and gestured for the cops to hurry over to them. "What's the ruckus?"

"Found a floater in the waterway," said Olafson's string-bean partner, Heavey. "Happens all the time around here—no big deal. Detectives should be along in a minute and take it over. May as well do our bit and check it out first, huh, Ole?"

"Mind if I tag along?" I asked Olafson.

He didn't answer, just turned and headed for the dock with Heavey, gesturing for me to follow with a swipe of his hammy mitt.

"By the way," Olafson said, as I fell into step with his close-to-three-hundred-pound bulk. "You owe me a repeat boxing match."

"Should I let you win this time around?"

"*Har-dee-har-har*," he snorted. "That was just a lucky punch and you know it."

"If I remember correctly, it was more like several combinations of *lucky punches*."

He stopped. "We boxing again or not, smart ass?"

"Anytime you want," I told him.

Olafson smiled, then we started for the dock again. "All right!" he bellowed, as the knot of longshoremen parted like the Red Sea before him. "What'cha got for us, boys?"

They pointed at the dirty water lapping against the barnacle-encrusted pilings about fifteen feet below the planks of the dock. There, floating face down and dressed in a suit even browner than the water, was a man's corpse, gently washing back and forth into the pilings, an enormous bullet hole clearly visible in the middle of his left shoulder-blade.

Just then, the homicide detectives rolled up in an unmarked police car and piled out of it. I didn't know either of them—which was just as well, considering the way they brushed me aside getting to Olafson.

While the shorter of the two stared over the dock into the water, his partner commented to Olafson, "Hey, Ole. Another floater, huh?"

"Yup. Third this month. What d'ya want me and Heavey to do?"

"Have him secure the area while you help us fish this joe out," said the detective. "Then you two can be on your way."

"Good," said Olafson. "I got bowling league tonight."

The dock boss showed up, grumbling about lost time, while the homicide dicks borrowed a rope and got a little wet as they and Olafson worked at dragging the stiff out of the soup. I took the opportunity to ask the cluster of longshoremen if they'd seen a white-trimmed cabin cruiser in the area earlier.

"Cabin cruiser?" sneered a wiry longshoreman, about my age, but rougher than I ever looked after my worst bender. "Around here?"

"Yeah, I seen one," a muscular joe chimed in.

"When?" I quickly asked him.

He smiled wide as his face, glanced at his buddies, then back at me. "Last time I was in Monte Carlo," he bellowed. All the longshoremen thought he was a regular laugh riot. "Or was it last summer at the French Riviera?" he added. "Yeah, at the Riviera, when I was making kissy-face with Ava Gardner."

"Rossiter, take a look," yelled Olafson, above the hoots and howls.

I turned, saw that he and the detectives were just pulling

the sopping corpse up and over the edge of the dock like a fat trout on the line. The body thunked against the creosote-covered planks, and ended up face down, just like it had been in the water. While the plainclothes dicks brushed themselves off, Olafson knelt, grabbed a hunk of the guy's long black hair, and lifted his head back so we could see his face better. "You ever see this joe before?" he asked me.

I went over and examined the body more closely—late twenties/early thirties, big nose, swarthy, olive complexion—definitely a wop. He had a four-inch scar across his right cheek, and, lo and behold, a small caliber bullet hole, barely visible, at the base of his skull, which was only about a third as big as the half dollar-sized hole in his shoulder.

"Can't say as I have," I told Olafson. "But five'll get you ten that the coroner finds a .44 caliber dum-dum in him."

"How would you know that?" asked Olafson.

"Oh, just call it a hunch."

Chapter

9

I DIDN'T STICK AROUND WAITING FOR THE meat wagon to show up. It was obvious that somebody had executed the shooter who'd tried to murder Miss Jenkins. Blevens had something to do with it, and I wasn't taking any chances. I high-tailed it straight to Seattle General.

"Oh, hi, boss." Miss Jenkins greeted me brightly, sitting up in her bed and sipping at a glass of orange juice like she was having brunch at the Legend Room rather than being stuck in the hospital with a huge bandage on her pretty head. "I'm sorry about disobeying orders. Before you start yelling at me, I—"

"Am I yelling?" I crossed over and put a gentle hand on her shoulder. "I'm just glad you're O.K., doll."

She smiled up at me. "Thanks. I'm fine, I—"

"*Now, I'm going to yell at you!*"

She looked away, muttered, "I thought so . . ."

I put both hands on my hips. "Just what in the Sam Hill did you think you were doing?! Didn't I tell you to stick in the office?!"

"Yes, but—"

"What the hell were you thinking?!"

"Well, I—"

"You could've gotten killed!"

"Yes, but—"

"No two ways about it!"

She rolled her eyes back and sighed, like she always did if I got too angry with her. Then she calmly set her glass of orange juice on the white metal nightstand by her bed. "Are you through yelling at me for a minute?"

"For a minute." I took a seat in the little, gray chair beside her bed, then fished out a Philip Morris, and pulled the glass ashtray on the nightstand over where I could reach it.

At length, Miss Jenkins said, "You're quite right, of course. I could've gotten myself killed."

I nodded and lit my smoke, glad she'd finally gotten the message.

"However," she added. "I've been doing a lot of thinking about that."

"About what?"

She grinned—grinned that small, smug grin that she always plastered to her puss when she was about to upset my applecart. "It's a good thing I *was* there, actually."

I raised my eyebrows. "How's that?"

She fluffed out the pillow behind her, and sat up much straighter. "Because if I hadn't been there, that thug would've probably tried to kill you instead."

"Gee, I hadn't thought of that."

"Really?"

"Not in a million years." While she puffed all up and looked even more smug with herself, I flicked the ash off my cigarette. "Brilliant as your deduction is, however, there's only one small error with your reasoning, doll."

She quickly leaned toward me. "What's that?"

I leaned toward her, right up to the point that my beak was almost touching her petite and perky nose. "Just this: that hood was undoubtedly following you, Miss Jenkins, not me."

"What?"

"You heard me."

"Oh . . ."

"Get it?"

"Gosh . . ." She leaned back against the headboard again, putting a safer distance between us. "You must mean he didn't know that you'd taken over the Hashimoto case, right?"

"Bingo! He thought you were still on it and tailed you down to the Japs' store because you were the target from the get-go."

"Yeah . . ." she mumbled, mulling it over. "Given the facts, it certainly seems that way, doesn't it?"

"Seems?" I asked. "Seems?" I added, building up another good head of steam. "It's a damned cinch! Whoever's toes we've stepped on, first they slash your tires, then they leave you that note, then—"

"Note? What note?"

"Never mind. You need to—"

"You never told me about any note."

"—start listening to me! When I tell you not to do something, you better—"

"What note?" She leaned over at me, getting all fired up. I shrunk away, sorry I'd mentioned that damned note.

"Look," I said. "Forget the note. The main point is—"

"The note's the main point and you know it! Why didn't you show it to me? What's it say?"

I knew when I was beat and reached in my pocket and dug the note out. I knew I couldn't finish chewing her out until she'd read the blasted thing. "Here, read it for yourself."

She snatched it out of my hand and got it unfolded. As she looked it over, her eyes grew wide as the full moon. "Goodness," she said. "My goodness . . ."

"Nasty little sentiment, huh? Now can you see why—"

"Shame on you!" Her burning, green-blue eyes locked onto mine. "You should've told me!"

I had to laugh.

"What are you laughing at?"

Nobody could twist things around like my Miss Jenkins. Nine times out of ten, I went to give her the rhubarb, but somehow she always turned things around and I was the one who ended up on the short end of the stick. At length, I simply said, "Would it really have made any difference?"

"Well—"

"No. The answer is no, and you know it. Note or no note, you would've followed me down there and gotten yourself shot anyway."

"Well—"

"So screw this damned note!"

She was quiet a moment, then adjusted her bedclothes and sulked. Finally, she said, barely audible, "Sorry, boss, I guess I was just mad about you swiping my case."

Her apology brought me up short. I got precious few of them from Miss Jenkins, and didn't quite know what to say. "Well . . . See that it doesn't happen again."

"*Absolutely*." She looked totally earnest.

"Fine."

"And *you* won't hold out on me anymore, will you, boss?"

"*Absolutely*." I looked totally earnest.

We smiled and nodded pleasantly at each other (me, with my fingers crossed behind my back).

"So," I said. "Now that that's settled, there's something I need you to do for me."

She looked at me suspiciously, like she didn't quite trust me.

"What's that?" Miss Jenkins asked.

"Little bird tells me you never went through Jamison's files like I asked you to."

"Well . . ."

"You were too busy tailing me down to the Hashimotos' old store."

"Well . . ."

"That being the case, I want you on those files as soon as you get out of here."

"But—"

"After I get somebody in place to guard you, that is."

"What?!" She sat bolt upright in bed. "Guard me?! I don't need anybody to guard me."

"*Au contraire*, my dear. Aside from protecting you with all these threats, it'd be worth forking out the dough for somebody just to make sure you stay put in the office this time around."

She was quiet for a moment. Made me uneasy. It wasn't like Miss Jenkins to stay silent for long, especially when she got her dander up.

At length, she asked, "Who would you get to watch me, anyway? Heine's busy keeping an eye on Eddie and ZaZu."

"Ah," I said. "Think you've got me, there, huh? Easy: Manny Velcker."

"Heine's pal? Ha!" she exclaimed. "I don't think so. Manny's still out of town."

"Not so!" I countered. "He blew back in over the weekend. Finished that little job in Frisco early. Brought in some nice cash for us."

She sipped at her orange juice, and I could see her wheels turning.

Finally, she nodded her head and said, "O.K."

"O.K.?" I asked. "Am I hearing things, or did you just agree with me?"

"Sure. Whatever you say, boss."

I didn't like it when she agreed with me—at least, not so easily.

"What've you got up your sleeve, doll?"

"Why, nothing at all." She showed me her arms, both quite bare in the sleeveless blue hospital gown she wore. "See? I don't have sleeves."

I ignored her attempt at levity, got up, and said, "You stick here—I'll be right back."

"Where are you going?"

"Down the hall to use the pay phone. I'm going to ring over to Ben Paris and tear Velcker away from whichever pigeon he's pool-sharking at the moment; get him up here and on the job."

As I went out the door, a heavy-set, middle-aged nurse was just on her way in carrying a thermometer and a large hypodermic syringe, both evidently intended for my contentious junior partner.

"Give her a real good solid jab with that thing," I told the nurse. "She needs it."

I stepped into the narrow booth across from the elevators, plugged a nickel into the slot, and spun the dial for Ben Paris. Velcker must have been playing a table right near the phone, because I only had to listen to the clickety-clack of pool balls caroming off of each other for a few seconds before the manager got him on the line.

"Hey, Rossiter," said Velcker. "Calling me over here, I'm guessing you got another gig for me, already. Better be a good one, 'cause I got a serious mark at my table all set up for the big bet."

"Ditch the pigeon, Manny," I said. "I need you up to Seattle General on the double to ride shotgun on Miss Jenkins. Room 210. I'll explain when you get here. Whatever big bet you're passing up, I'll match it and throw in a bonus."

"Copacetic, Jake." He rang off.

Velcker was a good egg. My kind of man. You asked, you got—any questions or reservations, Manny saved until he'd done the task at hand. With him on Miss Jenkins, I could rest easy.

I was whistling a happy tune when I strolled back into Miss Jenkins's room—*and found it empty* . . .

Damn. She couldn't possibly have flown the coop . . . They must've taken her off for some tests or something . . . I checked her little closet-like commode—empty. Checked the closet itself—empty . . . Hell's bells!

I tore out into the hall. She wasn't anywhere in sight. I located her nurse taking some old codger's blood pressure two doors up.

"Shhhhhh!" the nurse told me, when I barged in. "If you're looking for your secretary, she just checked herself out. Against my better advice, too. When you find her, if I were you, I'd have a word with that girl for her own good."

"And how!" I agreed.

I hit the hall at a fast walk—exited the hospital on the run—ran smack into Manny Velcker on his way up the main steps.

"You lose something?" he asked.

I glanced up and down the street, then shook my head. "Miss Jenkins."

"Figures." Velcker pushed his brown Fedora back on his head, stuck his hands in his pants pockets, and waited for me to make the next move.

I pushed my tan fedora back on my head, stuck my hands into my pants pockets, and tried to figure out what that should be.

Chapter

10

IT STARTED RAINING ON MY WAY OVER TO Mrs. Jamison's. I watched it tick against the Roadmaster's window and tried to take my mind off Miss Jenkins's unknown whereabouts. I'd called the office on the wild hope that she'd gone back there to look over the files like I'd told her to, but only got our answering service, which informed me that Heine had left a message only minutes before: Eddie and ZaZu had given him the slip, but he had some info and wanted me to meet him over at Leo's Grill on Broadway Avenue within the next hour.

So, I detoured to the restaurant. It was only a couple miles away from Mrs. Jamison's place by Volunteer Park. I'd sent Velcker back to the office to try and snag Miss Jenkins, if she ever showed up there, and felt that I had all my bases covered.

The rain and wind really picked up as I parked in front of Leo's. I had to hold onto my hat so it wouldn't fly away in the storm as I ducked inside. Shaking the water off my fedora, I spotted Heine buying a fresh pack of Lucky Strikes at the front counter. He was glum. Didn't say hello. Just motioned me back to his booth. I followed him to the rear of the restaurant, wondering what cat had his tongue, where we settled into the red leather booth. A pretty waitress poured me a steaming cup of java before I'd even had a chance to pull a Philip Morris out of my pack.

"Why so quiet?" I asked Heine.

"I got ditched, Jake."

"Yeah, well, it's not the end of the world."

"We'll see . . ." he grumbled. "Man, Eddie and ZaZu put the slip to me slick as if I'd been some damned amateur."

"Happens to the best of us," I said. I tamped my smoke against my Zippo. "I got ditched, myself. Miss Jenkins pulled a vanishing act out of her hospital room right under my nose."

"Hospital room?!" Heine exclaimed. His coffee mug banged against the Formica table as he set it down. "What the hell happened?"

I filled him in on the history, short and sweet—Miss Jenkins getting winged down at the Wong's store, the bit about the shooter getting shot himself, Blevens's involvement, and my taking over the Hashimoto case.

Heine shook his head. "Shit, and I thought I had a tough day."

"I put your pal, Manny Velcker, on the payroll." I signaled the waitress for more java. "He's over at the office, now, waiting to nab Miss Jenkins if she shows her face. Got orders to handcuff her to her desk if he has to."

"Velcker'll take care of business." Heine eyed the waitress, cute blonde with a run in her nylons, as she finished refilling coffee mugs at the table next to us. "When do you get off, honey?" he asked.

"You're fresh," she said, a twinkle in her eye and a lilt in her voice.

"That I am." Heine smiled, his pearly whites gleaming, his bright blue eyes locked onto her equally blue eyes.

She didn't look away. Took a step closer to us, as a matter of fact. "I get off at five."

"I'll be back."

The waitress smiled, then took her coffee pot around to the other tables. Heine, still grinning, turned back to me, and said, "Direct approach. I always liked it."

I had to smile, myself. "Just one question, Mr. Wolf," I asked him. "How're you planning to pick this chicken up at five when you're still on the clock for me?"

"Vic Croce."

"Vic Croce?"

"Yeah," Heine said, sipping at his java. "I ain't working 'round the clock on this. Not yet, anyway. I brought Vic on for my relief. Tried to get hold of Manny, but he was out. You must've hired him before I could."

"So, now I got both Manny *and* Vic on my tab, huh?"

He threw me a wink. "Anyway, Jake, what you been telling me, and what I got to tell you, you'll be needing them both. Maybe even a third op, too."

"Oh, yeah? Well tell me, already, before I go broke."

Heine laughed and lit up a Lucky. "I'm sitting in my car, running the battery down and listening to some tunes on the radio, when this big, black Lincoln limo pulls up in front of the Meany Hotel's main door. That's some ritzy wheels, I'm thinking, complete with a chauffeur wearing them chauffeur duds—you know, with the hat and gloves—when out comes Eddie and ZaZu. They're arm in arm, all gussied up like they're going out to dinner, even though it's only the middle of the day, and the chauffeur opens up the back of the limo for 'em, and off they go. They lose those dumb cops supposed to be watching them as easy as you please, but I stay on 'em, and finally we go up 45th and into the University of Washington campus. I shadow 'em over to where they park, close to Denny Hall. Chauffeur stays with his ride while they get out and take a leisurely stroll across campus where they planted all those Jap cherry trees.

"I'm thinking, well they got to be meeting up with somebody. But, no, they just spend about fifteen minutes moseying up and down the walkway between all them cherry trees, pointing at them and smiling. And get this—a couple times Eddie stops and recites like, poetry or something, you know? Looks up into those trees and says all this syrupy shit like, well, like that old English joe who wrote all them plays you can hardly understand. You know the cat I mean."

"Shakespeare?" I asked.

"Yeah, that guy," said Heine. "Hell, I know Eddie's a little loony, but that's just nuts, huh? Well, anyway, them trees are all real pretty and everything, all blooming like they are, but what the hell's going on? I keep on their tail, but they don't meet up with anybody. Eddie just keeps on spouting that poetry crap every so often, and they just act like a couple tourists who ain't never seen a bunch of cherry trees before. Then they pop back to the limo, and off we go again."

"That's all they did, huh?" I asked.

"Yeah."

I stubbed out my butt in the ashtray. "Well, Eddie did say that he wanted to see the cherry trees while he was in town."

"Yeah, well, he saw 'em all right," Heine said. "But so what?"

"Where'd they go from there?"

"This is where it gets interesting, Jake, especially with what you told me about Miss Jenkins." Heine loosened his tie—he hated ties, but always wore one with his sports jacket. "They motored south, straight down into Chinatown."

I leaned across the table fast enough that I almost spilled my coffee. "Eddie and ZaZu were in Chinatown today?"

"Hey, watch your java; I don't want it all over me," warned Heine, steadying my coffee mug. "Yeah, Chinatown, that's what I said. We came up South Jackson from Third Avenue, and they turned right to South King Street, then parked for a minute across from the Wang Choi Benevolent Society, one of them Chinese Tong headquarters."

"They meet up with anybody there?"

"No," Heine continued. "That's the funny thing. I thought they would, too. But all of a sudden, the limo peeled away from the curb and burned rubber down the block. They made me, I think. I was half a block back, but I'm sure that's why they pulled over, just to see if I pulled over too, you know? Anyway, I floored it after 'em, but got the surprise of my life when that big limo kept pulling away from me. Hell, I got a V-8 in that new Ford of mine—how the devil could that big tub of a Lincoln be beating me? But it did. I last saw 'em when they turned down this alley over near old Japantown. When I finally got there, I gunned down the alley after 'em, but they were history. I did a block by block search for almost a half an hour, but it was like they'd fallen off the face of the earth. Hacked me off—you know me, I hardly ever lose a tail. Shit."

"Over by Japantown, huh?" I drained the last of my java. "What time was that?"

"About eleven-thirty."

"Damn . . . That's when Miss Jenkins and I were down there."

Heine frowned. "You think Eddie had something to do with the shooting?"

"Not with Miss Jenkins," I didn't think, I said. "But he could have put the hit on the joe who shot her."

"Maybe." Heine thought a moment. "This is all getting real screwy. Who the hell is he working for?"

"Your guess is as good as mine, gyrene. But we'll know in short order if Eddie pulled the hit."

"How so?"

"He'll blow town. You know he never sticks around after he does a job."

"Damn. I better drive over to the Meany," said Heine, "see if they've checked out yet. If they haven't, I'll stick around 'til they come back, then pick up my surveillance again."

"You do that, *compadre*. And call me at the office in about an hour; let me know about Eddie."

"Roger."

We stood up, and prepared to leave.

Heine dug six bits out of his pocket for the coffee. As he laid the coins on the table, I said, "Six bits, huh? That's leaving a big tip for twenty cents worth of coffee."

"Yeah," he said, grinning wide. "I bet that pretty waitress thinks so, too."

We passed the blonde object of his affections as we made for the door.

"See you at five," Heine told her.

The waitress smiled, and went back to clean off our table. Heine whistled a snappy tune as we went outside—seemed to be in a little better mood than when I'd first met up with him.

I found Mrs. Jamisons's house in short order. A big, two-story brick Colonial, it stood on a double lot on East Aloha, just up the twisting road that led past the south end of Volunteer Park. I pulled over in front of it, but didn't get out right away. Instead, I lit a Philip Morris, and tried to get Eddie and ZaZu out of my mind before going in to question Henry Jamison's widow. It wasn't easy.

Damn them anyway. It'd be just like Eddie and ZaZu to have flown the coop already. With them being in old Japantown when the shooting went down, they might well have had something to do with killing the hood who'd gone after Miss Jenkins. And they'd probably be long gone by the time Heine checked back at the Edmond Meany, leaving me with a repeat round of egg on my face. Even if I couldn't pin anything on them, I wanted another piece of Eddie Valhalla—a much larger and more painful piece than I took out of him during our fight. Failing that, Eddie would be laughing all the way back home, just like he'd given me the rhubarb all the other times in the past—just like he'd done to Heine and me the last few years at the orphanage when he started going bad.

Piss on him! There was nothing I could do until Heine got the scoop at the hotel. Better to go straightaway and talk to Jamison's widow than stew another minute over Eddie and ZaZu. Mrs. Jamison's doorbell was one of those fancy gizmos that chimed in three tones. Fast as anybody got the door, it could've chimed Beethoven's whole Fifth Symphony. I rang it twice more, before the door finally opened. I got more than I expected—more, in this case, in the form of Mrs. Alberta Jamison, who carried a good two hundred pounds on her large, roughly five-foot, ten-inch frame. She also had more to say than any grieving widow I ever met on the day of her husband's death.

"Mr. Rossiter!" she beamed, recognizing me right off the bat, even though I'd only met her once. I'm not sure I would have recognized her. She had gained a lot of weight. But she still had a certain appeal. She had a fair complexion, rosy cheeks, and like a lot of chubby-faced people, looked younger than her age. In fact, I thought she might actually be kind of pretty underneath the extra weight she carried. Had all her curves in the right places, too—they were just extra-large curves. "Do come in out of the cold," she continued, quickly. "I've got leftover chicken in the oven, a fire in the fireplace, and so much to tell you."

I followed her inside—actually, got dragged inside by the hand I'd extended while trying to say hello. She kept rattling on as she sat me down on her sofa, and tried to fill my mouth with big, sticky cinnamon rolls.

"Fresh baked," she said, shoving a heaping tray of cinnamon rolls at me like there was no tomorrow. "I always bake when I'm upset. Which I am. As a matter of fact, I like to bake most any time at all. Have one. You're a big man, there's plenty."

"No, thanks," I said, but the tray kept coming at me anyway. I stopped its forward progress, and took the obligatory roll. "O.K., just one." I took a fast bite out of the pastry, proclaimed it "delicious," and got in a quick sentence before she could start blabbing at me again.

"Mrs. Jamison, you almost seem to have been expecting me."

"I've been thinking about you ever since the police called me about Henry this morning," she said, sitting in the wingback chair opposite me on the blue sofa. She put two cinnamon rolls, for herself, on a dessert plate that barely had room for one on it. "I want to hire you."

I smiled, pleased she'd brought up the word *hire* already—it was only a short step from there to exactly how much dough she was going to pay me.

"Henry cheated on me for years, you know," she continued. "I think one of his bimbos did him in."

I stopped smiling, took a napkin off the coffee table, and set my roll down on it. "That's a pretty loaded statement you just made, lady. Henry was playing around on you, and you knew about it?"

She nodded in agreement; took a bite out of her first roll, then quickly took another, larger bite.

"He never seemed the type," I said. "To be a ladies' man, I mean."

"Henry was oversexed." She filled her face with more pastry.

"I see," I said, as if her explanation was sufficient. I thought, for a moment, about how she seemed to be taking all this in stride. "You said bimbos, Mrs. Jamison. As in the plural. Henry had more than one dame on the side?"

"Oh, my goodness, yes." She chewed hard, and washed another big bite down with a slurp of her java. "Way too many to count."

"How long had this been going on?"

"Well," she said. "We were married in '23, so I'd say about twenty-five years. I'm sorry, would you like some coffee?"

I passed on the coffee. "What makes you think that one of his chippies killed your husband?"

"They were no good," she said, with a toss of her shoulder-length brown hair. "None of them."

I leaned toward her. "Is that just conjecture, or have you met any of these broads?"

"You don't have to meet somebody to know they're evil, Mr. Rossiter." She finished off the last of her pastry, then tackled the next one, shoving it in faster and faster as she spoke. "Running around with married men . . . That's no good. Poor Henry, I don't think he could help himself."

"Why do you say that?" I asked. "Because he was over-sexed, as you put it?"

"There is that, of course," she said, taking an enormous bite. "But if a pretty girl so much as smiled at him, he was off to the races. Henry wasn't much of a looker, you know. At best, he was on the shy side of average. I think women were like drugs to him. Made him feel like more than he was. Poor Henry, he just couldn't keep his hands off of them."

"You're being very understanding."

"Henry was a good man. Other than that, anyway."

I kept quiet for a moment. Just watched her eat. I had to wonder if there was more than met the eye with Mrs. Jamison. Way she put it, everything was just dandy about her marriage, except her husband going to bed with every broad under the sun. I wasn't buying it. I'd seen hinkier things, sure, but I really didn't think that cinnamon rolls, even copious amounts of them, could ever be an acceptable replacement for marital fidelity.

"Where were you this morning, Mrs. Jamison?"

"Well, right here," she said, blithely, not seeming to catch the inherent accusation of such a question. "I got up early to do some baking."

I leaned forward, and locked eyes with her. "You didn't, by chance, take a little break from all your flour and shortening, and go down to the office and relieve your errant hubby of his head, did you?"

She choked on her cinnamon roll. "How can you say such a thing?" She coughed and sputtered, and wiped at her mouth with her napkin. "How can you . . . say such a thing . . ."

"Pretty easily, really. I've been in this game a long time, and I don't think I've ever heard such a load of hogwash."

She gasped and started to tear up—just stared and stared at me—her big, brown eyes filling to overflowing. I thought she was going to break down blubbering. Instead, she popped the last morsel of roll into her mouth, and quickly grabbed a third roll off the tray, stuffing, I swear to God, fully half of it into her mouth all at once.

Her cheeks bulging like a hungry chipmunk, she chewed prodigiously, then said, "I know you have to ask those kinds of questions. But I've only been telling you the truth." She swallowed. "I don't know what I'm going to do. Will you please, please help me, Mr. Rossiter? I have the names of some of his girlfriends. Addresses, too. I'll double your usual fees . . . no, I'll triple them. These women had something to do with Henry's death, I just know it, I just know it."

With that, she stopped eating. Let her question hang in the air like the unfinished half of the cinnamon roll dangling from her right hand. Sat frozen that way, waiting for my answer. After a long moment, I had to figure if it was important enough to stop her from stuffing her face, she might just be on the level, after all.

"You've got some names, huh?"

She nodded her head.

"How, exactly, did you come by these names, Mrs. Jamison?"

"They were in love notes, mostly," she said, quickly. "Henry was always writing them. He fancied himself a poet." She went back to work on her cinnamon roll, but took normal sized bites this time around. "He was a terrible poet, of course," she continued, "but he wrote them anyway. Lots of them. I've found them around over the years, in his pockets, in the trash can beside his desk, places like that. I saved them—always saved them."

I didn't say anything. I'd seen some sad crapola in my time, but this lady took the cake.

Finally, I said, "Well, maybe I could take a gander at them. You got any handy, by chance?"

"Oh, yes!" She smiled brightly and jumped to her feet. "I've got all of them. Every one. I saved them in a big scrapbook upstairs—I'll get it for you." She rushed over to the stairwell. "You enjoy your cinnamon roll," she added, moving at quite a clip for a big woman. "I'll be back in a jiffy."

After she'd gone, I just sat and stared at the large tray of cinnamon rolls. At that moment, it looked about as appetizing as a tray full of bricks.

Snap your fingers, she was back. Plopped herself down on the small loveseat beside the sofa, with a big, fat, leather-bound scrapbook, which she placed in her lap and carefully opened to the first page. She beamed as she gazed at the many pieces of stationery that were glued to the heavy, brownish-cream-colored paper inside. Then she smiled at me, and patted the velvet upholstery beside her, inviting me to slide over to the loveseat and share her treasure.

I got up and sat down beside her. Mrs. Jamison snuggled up against me, hip to hip, and positioned the open scrapbook halfway across each of our laps.

"See?" she said, proudly, pointing at the four notes that filled the first page. "These are all to the same woman, Annie. I'm sure he wrote more to her that I didn't get my hands on, but I'd decided to make this up by order of name. I've alphabetized them, too," she commented. "I thought that was a nice touch."

"Yeah, it's just dandy," I said, slowly pulling the scrapbook away from her. I scooted over, but couldn't get much distance between us, and prepared to go through it. She was shoulder to shoulder with me again though, before I'd managed to turn the first page. She smelled of cinnamon and some type of sweet perfume that didn't really go with that particular spice.

I moved over a hair more. So did she. Soon, I found myself trapped between her and the arm of the small loveseat. Short of being rude and getting up, it looked like I was stuck for the duration, so I tried to ignore Mrs. Jamison's increasingly heavy breathing as I quickly but carefully perused all the pages.

Anne, somebody named Bubbles, Danielle, Estelle,

Myrna, the list went on and on right up until the name Vivian. Same-same for the love notes themselves—mostly written in fountain pen on small pieces of stationery. It was all pretty awful. Lots of mentions of June and moon, mixed in with a bunch of crudity—stuff like "my hands on your big, ripe tits," and "Regina: I swoon by night, in your sighs and warm, wet cooze," and even one where he badly plagiarized the Bard: "Bubbles, shall I compare thee to a summer's day—how about another roll in the hay?"

"Old Henry sure got around, didn't he?" I asked Mrs. Jamison.

She smiled at me. Smiled warmly. Sighed . . . close enough that her breath was a bit hot on my cheek.

I stood. So did she. I started to feel uncomfortable.

"I think it's time for me to blow out of here," I told her. "Maybe I should take this with me. Look it over more closely when I have a chance. That O.K. with you?"

"You can't stay?" she asked, moving as close to me as she'd been on the loveseat.

"Got places to be," I said, stepping back a few paces. She followed.

"You're going to take my case, then?" she asked, her voice turning husky as she closed in on me.

"Yeah," I told her, clutching the scrapbook and turning for the door. "For the time being, anyway."

I hadn't gotten two paces, when she blurted, "Oh, thank you!" grabbed onto my shoulder, spun me around, and planted a kiss smack on my lips. But it wasn't any little thank you kiss. It was a real kiss. A real big, wet kiss. A real big, wet, long kiss that positively reeked of cinnamon and desire.

How the hell I got away from her, I don't remember exactly. All I remember, with absolute clarity, was sitting in my Roadmaster for a minute, a little shook up, holding onto that perverse scrapbook of hers, not being able to get the taste of cinnamon out of my mouth.

Chapter

11

THERE WERE LOVE NOTES TO OVER THIRTY different dames in Mrs. Jamison's scrapbook. Most of them dated—some going back as far as 1925. As I pulled the Roadmaster to the curb outside my office, I decided to start by bird-dogging Henry's most recent chippies: three separate broads that he'd been seeing over the last year. Had to hand it to the mousy little schnook . . . that was two more women than I'd gotten to first base with during the same amount of time. What the hell did he have going for him? Certainly wasn't looks. Money? Yeah, that was always a good bet. I'd have to keep that in mind when I ran these dames down. Money was the motive for more murders than you could shake a stick at. Put love *and* money together, well, that probably covered ninety percent of the homicides that occurred in the city every year. At least all the ones I'd ever investigated.

It had started to rain hard. I bailed out of the car, and beat feet into my building through the increasing downpour. I guess I'd been preoccupied about not getting the scrapbook wet, and hadn't been thinking much about Miss Jenkins, until I opened the door to my office, and saw her sitting at her desk, like it was just any ordinary day, calmly unwrapping a piece of Blackjack gum and sticking it into her mouth.

She glanced up at me, and smiled pleasantly.

I didn't.

"Where the hell have you been?" I asked, storming in and shaking the water off my fedora.

"Why, right here," she said, innocently. "Where have you been?"

"Don't try to change the subject." I marched straight up to her desk, and waited for an explanation. I noticed she had the files I'd kyped from Jamison's office stacked up in front of her. Nary a one of them cracked open, either.

As if reading my mind, Miss Jenkins selected a file from the stack and opened it up, saying, "You told me to stick around the office, so I came back here and went over these files like you wanted me to. I found something pretty interesting—"

"Sure," I said. "And next you'll be telling me that I won the Irish Sweepstakes."

"But—"

The door to my inner office suddenly swung open, and out popped Manny Velcker, a tumbler of my Cutty Sark in each hand. "Hey, Jake," he said, "fancy meeting you here."

"Likewise," I told him, noting that Manny was still natty as ever. He wore a dark brown & beige, two-tone jacket, with a bright white silk shirt, the collar spread wide over the jacket's lapels, and a crisp pair of double-pleated, light wool slacks, finished off with Argyle socks and a pair of spit-shined Cordovan loafers. "Especially considering you've been lifting my Scotch."

"Oh, this . . ." he said, high-stepping our direction,

sloshing a bit of my hooch onto the carpet in the process. "Don't worry, I left you some. Anyway, I figured Miss Jenkins might need a belt before dinner. You know, what with getting shot and everything."

He handed her a tumbler.

She didn't take it.

"I didn't ask for a drink," she said.

"Good for what ails you, kiddo." Manny set the Scotch on the desk in front of her. "It's good if nothing ails you, too," he added, with the brightest smile this side of Errol Flynn.

"Well . . ." said Miss Jenkins, eyeing the liquor. "I don't normally drink at work."

"Go ahead and have one," I told her. "You're going home early today."

"I am?"

"That's an order."

"In that case," she said, "I will have a drink."

"Better have a double, because you're going to stay home tomorrow, as well."

"What?"

"I want you to take Miss Jenkins home," I told Manny. "Right now."

"You're kidding!" Miss Jenkins exclaimed.

"No. I'm not."

I grabbed her coat and handed it to her. "You might not like it, doll, but it's for your own good. I don't want you to get hurt."

Manny shrugged. "You're the boss, Jake."

Miss Jenkins glared at me, then for just a moment, her eyes softened. So did mine. I think she realized that I really meant it when I said I didn't want her to get hurt. I pulled her to her feet, and helped her on with her coat.

"You take her home, Manny, and keep an eye on her."

He looked Miss Jenkins up and down, then smiled. "That won't be hard."

I was just finishing up in the bathroom, when the office phone rang. By the time I got out to get it, whoever it was had hung up. I checked my Bulova, figuring it might have been Heine, since the timing was about right for the call he promised to give me regarding Eddie. So I spun the dial for our answering service in case he'd left a message with them. I got our usual daytime girl, Dotty. Heine had left word for me. Dotty read his message back to me in the slow, Southern drawl that she'd brought with her from Atlanta when she'd come to Seattle to work making planes for Boeing during the war:

"Jake, you better high-tail it over to the house you were just at up on Capitol Hill. Don't know who you were talking to in there, but Eddie Valhalla's got some kind of interest in them. Him and ZaZu came back to the hotel awhile ago, then went their separate ways, so I stuck with Eddie. Tailed him up to this house just in time to see you ringing the doorbell and going inside. Ain't got a clue who the chunky broad was who let you in, but I followed Eddie around the neighborhood a few times until you left. He's back now, and ain't moved for a while. You wouldn't hardly notice him, but he's the one in the baggy gray overcoat and slouch hat, sitting way back across the street feeding the pigeons in the park. Whoops . . . gotta go . . . He's up on his feet and taking himself a little stroll. Don't know if he's moving to another bench, or going over to that house. Whichever it is, that's the direction he's headed. Get up here pronto, gyrene. Out."

I didn't bother thanking Dotty. I was halfway to Mrs. Jamison's place before she even got the dial tone after I'd slammed down the receiver.

The street seemed quiet when I peeled around the corner, then slowed to a crawl as I approached Mrs. Jamison's big brick house. I parked a block away, switched off the engine, and bailed out. The Roadmaster's eight cylinders may have stopped racing, but my mind hadn't: frigging Eddie Valhalla keeping tabs on Henry's widow, and I hadn't spotted him when I'd left earlier. Took a real pro to escape my notice. And Eddie was nothing if not a pro. What the hell was he up to? Did he have something to do with Henry's murder after all? Whatever the case, I didn't know squat. Not even Eddie's whereabouts at the moment . . .

I entered the park from the side street, and slowly walked through the wet, fallen leaves toward a bunch of empty benches that faced the Jamison place. Like Heine had said, the benches were set way back from her house and were partially obscured by a copse of big elm and maple trees. Even so, I should've made Eddie when I'd first left her place. It ate at me that I'd missed him—ate at me almost as much as not spotting him now—neither him nor Heine, anywhere in sight.

I eyeballed the street, hoping to catch sight of Heine's car parked somewhere. Looked long and hard, but didn't see it; not on the side-street or the main avenue running in front of Mrs. Jamison's joint. Then it occurred to me that Eddie had been heading for her house. Since he seldom went anywhere without mayhem on his mind, Heine would have tagged along after him. God only knew what Eddie might have wanted with Mrs. Jamison, but I bet it wasn't one of her cinnamon rolls.

I raced across the street and quickly cased out the house. Listening for any sounds of violence from inside, I reconnoitered its perimeter. Except for the neighbor's dog barking behind the tall back fence, I saw and heard nothing. Just the chill late March wind rustling through what leaves the big birch tree in the back yard still had left on its limbs.

I quietly climbed the stairs to the back porch and filled my hand with my .45 as I stole a peek through the back door's slightly fogged-up window. Got quite a surprise when I saw Mrs. Jamison calmly at work in her kitchen. She had a frilly, embroidered apron tied around her waist, and was just pulling the leftover chicken she'd mentioned out of the oven. She almost dropped it when I rapped at the door.

"Why, Mr. Rossiter!" A rush of warm, roast chicken-scented air billowed out at me as she flung open the back door. "I'm so glad you've come back to see me."

I went in, side-stepping the big embrace she tried to wrap around me.

"Anybody else come to see you while I've been gone?" I asked, striding across the kitchen and pushing open the swinging door to the dining room. I went through it; found both the dining and living rooms empty. We seemed to be alone; just us and the soft classical music that was still playing on the big Philco floor-model radio.

"No, nobody's been here but you," said Mrs. Jamison, coming out after me, wiping her hands on her apron.

"You sure about that?"

"Well, of course."

"Good," I said, turning back and meeting her under the archway between the two rooms.

Her eyes gravitated to the Colt I still had in my right hand. "Why do you have your pistol out?" she asked. "My, but you have a big pistol, don't you?"

I holstered it. "You know an Eddie Valhalla, Mrs. Jamison?"

"What a strange name," she said, moving close enough to me that you'd have had trouble fitting a piece of typing paper between us. "No, I don't know anybody by that name."

"Well, he knows you." I edged back, getting a safer distance from her.

She edged forward. "How?"

I back-pedaled some more. "Don't know, exactly. Maybe through your late husband."

"Forget Henry," she said, getting a little breathless, and closing in on me until my back was up against the carved mahogany post of the archway.

I rolled away from her, out where I had some room to maneuver by the head of the dining room table. "Pack a bag, Mrs. Jamison," I told her. "I'm getting you out of here."

"Really?" she asked, stalking me once again, slow and methodical. "Where?"

This dame had gone ga-ga for me. What had brought it on, I didn't know, but I'd had enough of it. As she tried to glom onto me again, I grabbed her by the elbows and pushed her back. "Cut it, will you?" I said, sharply. "I'm not playing any hanky-panky here. This is serious business."

"Oh—" she muttered, shocked by my manners. She stood still for once, so I let go of her. Her big brown eyes stared into mine, and she stammered, "I—I—I don't know what came over me, I—" Then her voice trailed off, and she began to sob, great big crocodile tears running down her face and dripping into the hollow between her very large, well-shaped breasts. Hell's bells, women . . . I had every reason not to, but she was making me feel like a heel. So, I did the only thing I could . . . I held her . . . held her tight while she got it all cried out . . . was a bit surprised that the extra-buxom bazooms pressed against my chest were really quite firm.

"Look, Mrs. Jamison," I said, at length, the shoulder of my jacket soaking wet. "I don't think it's safe for you here. I'm taking you to a hotel, O.K.?"

She looked up at me, her tears drying as quickly as they'd started. "Oh, yes, Mr. Rossiter, that would be fine; that would be very nice."

"It may be nothing, but it's for your own safety. Understand?"

"Not really," she said, letting loose of me and drying her eyes with the bottom of her apron, which left small bluish-black smudges on it from the little bit of mascara she'd been wearing. She smiled. "But, whatever you say. I'll be safe with you at the hotel. Yes."

I could see this was threatening to go south again, so I quickly said, "Fine. I'm going out to get my car. I'll bring it around. You pack what you need, fast as you can, and meet me out front. I'll try and explain things better to you on the way. Got it?"

"Oh, yes," she beamed. "Could we go to the Olympic?

That's what Henry liked best. The Olympic. We stayed there on our honeymoon."

"Pretty expensive," I said. "Whatever. It's on your tab."

"I don't mind." She smiled even warmer, then made for the stairwell across the living room. She paused on the landing, looked back at me, and said, "No, I don't mind at all." Then she hurried up the stairs.

On the drive to the hotel, I didn't have much time to worry about where Eddie and Heine had gotten off to. Mostly, I worried about trying to operate the Roadmaster's gearshift lever: Mrs. Jamison sat so close to me that I couldn't shift up to second or down to third without my right elbow coming into contact with some part of her body or other. But I didn't shoo her away, again, this time. I had enough trouble driving without another round of tears and hysterics.

Aside from getting us to the Olympic in one piece, I did manage to cover some important bases with her. I explained, as best I could, the danger that Eddie Valhalla presented. It seemed to blow right over her, though. She reiterated that neither she, nor Henry, had ever had any dealings with anyone named Valhalla, let alone with the sort of riff-raff who would hire a professional killer.

I pressed her more about Henry, anyway. Got basically the same response. He'd dealt with insurance, not thugs; had started his business just after the Great Depression began with a small loan she'd made him from her inheritance. No, she wasn't wealthy, far from it. But her father had died during the Influenza epidemic that came at the close of World War I, and had left a fair amount of stock certificates to Mrs. Jamison's mother. Stock in salt, of all things. Her mom, knowing virtually nothing about the stock market, left the money invested right where it was, in salt. She passed away just after her daughter's marriage to Henry in '23, and being the only child, the salt stocks fell to Mrs. Jamison. Knowing little more about the stock market than her mother had, Mrs. Jamison also left the money invested in salt. Turned out to be quite a break. When the market crashed in '29, salt was one of the few stocks that held its own. It had always provided a dismal return on the investment, but it was cheap, plentiful, and something that everybody always needed. In short, the small dividends it consistently provided helped carry them through the Depression along with the proceeds from her husband's burgeoning insurance business.

I knew damned well that I'd never trust the stock market. No matter how well they said it had been doing since the war, they'd never get a red cent out of me. Bunch of new regulations or not, as far as I was concerned it was just legalized gambling run by a bunch of crooks in suits.

It wasn't all roses for the Jamisons, of course. Henry had had occasional money troubles over the years. Oddly enough, they had been larger and more frequent of late, rather than during the leaner times. He had been after her for quite a while to let him invest her money in something more profitable than salt. But she wouldn't budge. Salt had served her parents well, had kept she and Henry out of the soup kitchens, and had been instrumental in starting his insurance business. What more did he want?

"Maybe plenty," I told her, as we pulled up in front of the hotel. "Don't take this wrong, Mrs. Jamison, but I've been wondering if old Henry had money troubles. Money troubles and bimbos often tend to feed off of each other, in my experience."

She ignored my comment, and slipped an arm around me. "Let's not talk about this anymore," her hot breath said in my ear.

I bailed out. Came around to her side just as a doorman in forest green livery opened up the car door for her. I popped the trunk lid, and he grabbed her suitcase, a big, tan leather one with brass fittings. I took it from the doorman, told him I'd cart it inside, then flipped him two bits and went into the hotel with Mrs. Jamison, who hung onto my free arm and smiled like a schoolgirl.

The Olympic was even fancier than I remembered it. With a lobby big enough to hold two average-sized houses, it had more polished woodwork than a carpenter shop, enough crystal chandeliers to light a small town, and enough deep, plush Persian carpeting to cover two football fields.

The joe manning the shiny walnut check-in desk had one of those hairdos that was parted just above the top of his left ear, then combed over and pasted down to cover up a pate about as bald as a cue ball. But his ritzy threads more than made up for his bad hair: a crisp, custom-tailored blue woolen blazer; a put-your-eyes-out white shirt with a high collar starched so hard it looked like it could cut his neck sure as a stiletto; and a wide, silk tie, maroon with a gold squiggly pattern that probably cost more than my entire present wardrobe. He smiled as we approached, his pearly-whites glinting like the gold pince-nez specs he had pinched onto his narrow, equine schnoz.

"Good afternoon. May I be of help?" he asked, his voice low and sonorous.

"Only if you make large, low-interest loans," I quipped.

His eyes widened momentarily, then he chuckled and said, "Ah, sir is making a joke."

"Sir is checking in," I told him. "We need a room."

"The Honeymoon Suite," said Mrs. Jamison, her tone as rosy as her cheeks.

"The what?" I asked.

"Ah, newlyweds," cooed the desk manager. "Have you reservations?"

"More than you know at this point," I told him. "Look, we'll take whatever you've—"

"Tush-tush," he interrupted, quickly flipping through his register. "Not to worry, sir. It's mid-week . . . not a great deal of demand mid-week in the wintertime . . . yes, it just so happens that the Honeymoon Suite is available."

"We'll take it," said Mrs. Jamison, squeezing the devil out of my arm.

"Congratulations to you both," beamed the manager. "Best wishes."

As he pushed the guest register over for me to sign, his left hand snaked out and rang for the bellhop. Mrs. Jamison didn't give me a chance, though. She'd snatched the fountain pen from the register, and signed us in, before I could even reach for it. Then the bellhop popped out of the woodwork. He was the spitting image of the kid they used in the "Call for Philll—lllip Morrr-rrriss!" ads. Bright and eager, he tipped his little pillbox-style cap, and picked up Mrs. Jamison's suitcase, which was almost as big as he was.

"The Honeymoon Suite, Chester," the manager directed, handing him the key, and glancing at our names in the register. "Mr. & Mrs. Jamison are newlyweds."

"Say, that's swell! Congrats!" said the bellhop. "Follow me, folks." He led the way across the lobby to the bank of glimmering brass-doored elevators. The bellhop was a strong little monkey, carried the heavy suitcase easy as you please, took us up to the top floor, and got the door open to our suite, then stepped aside.

I started to go in, but Mrs. Jamison tugged on my arm and asked, "Aren't you going to carry me over the threshold, darling?"

I looked at the bellhop, who was grinning to beat the band: seemed to relish these moments. Hell . . . I'd gone this far, figured I had to play out the charade. So, I managed to get a grip on Mrs. Jamison, and lugged her over the threshold.

"That was nice," said the bellhop as I set her down. "That was really nice."

He started to bring in the suitcase, but I took it from him and handed him a buck. "Thanks, pal, I'll take it from here."

"You don't want me to come in and get the lights and the drapes and such for you?"

"Thanks, but no thanks," I said, slowly swinging the door closed on him.

"Oh, I get it." He grinned, and he threw me a knowing wink. "You got other things on your mind, don't you?"

"You don't know the half of it."

I went inside, where I found Mrs. Jamison strolling around the expansive suite looking like she was on Cloud 9. "We should order some champagne," she said, dreamily.

"Go ahead," I told her, "but just for yourself." I put the suitcase down. "This is as far as I go."

"You're not staying with me?"

"You'll be safe here. For the time being, anyway. I'm assigning a good man to keep an eye on you. His name's Vic Croce. He'll be contacting you soon. In the meantime, you stay put until I get a handle on things."

Her expression turned all coy. "But can't you stay and watch over me? We can order from room service and—"

"Sorry, I've got places to be."

"But—"

"If you need anything, go ahead and call room service. If you need me, I'll be in touch." I turned to leave.

"You're all the same," she said, behind me.

"What?" I asked, over my shoulder.

"You're just like Henry!" she began to wail, her voice breaking. "Always too busy! Always going somewhere else! Just like Henry . . . Just like Henry . . ."

Brother. Dames, I thought, they could turn on a dime. I got going while the going was good, hit the door just as she shrieked her way into a high-volume crying jag. Got out into the hall and got shut the door behind me, as she yelled and cried louder and louder—so loud, in fact, that it was plain as day outside the room.

I retreated down the hall to the nearby elevators, where our bellhop was just catching one. He held the elevator open for me, shook his head, and said, "First argument, huh?"

"You could say that," I told him.

I phoned Vic Croce over at the 214 Club. I knew he'd be there pool-sharking this time of day. I told him there'd been a change in plans; Heine would have to do without his services for a while; I needed him to pull guard detail on Mrs. Jamison ASAP. Vic said he'd get right on it, but Heine wouldn't be too pleased. I told him Heine would understand. He was a tough nut. He'd survived a lot worse than pulling round-the-clock shifts and missing dates with pretty blondes during the war.

That covered, I headed for the Hashimotos' boarding house on Beacon Hill. I felt it was high time to get some dope on their case straight from the horse's mouth. According to Miss Jenkins's file, they were all living crammed into two little rooms. What with the housing shortage after the war, and them being Japs, I figured they were damned lucky to get two little rooms.

I motored through downtown, then picked up Denny Way, and followed it up the steep hill to 12th Avenue East. Heading back south a few blocks, I went over the high, narrow bridge that connected the southern end of Capitol Hill to the northern tip of Beacon Hill. The massive, brick Merchant Marine Hospital loomed over me as I got to the other side. I always thought it a strange location for a hospital, since everything else around it for miles on Beacon Hill was residential, but figured that the land must have been cheap when the Feds built it in the early 30s. In any event, the area, especially the east side of the hill and a lot of the Rainier Valley below, had been home to most of the city's Italian population for years, hence, the name "Garlic Gulch." While the majority of the area was comprised of well-maintained, single-family homes, the half-dozen blocks surrounding the Marine Hospital were getting a bit run down. Why, I didn't know, but this was particularly so where I found the address I was looking for. It was a couple blocks east of the hospital, just over the crest of the hill.

The street was pretty bleak . . . had a couple boarded-up old houses and a couple others with FOR SALE signs hanging in front of them and blowing in the wind, while the rest of the homes on the block sported peeling paint, patched roofs, and overgrown, weedy yards. The Hashimotos' boarding house stood between one of the abandoned homes and another place with half its chimney fallen in. By far the biggest joint on the block, the boarding house was non-descript, except for looking like it needed to be torn down. A huge, ramshackle two-story joint, it had been added onto enough times that you couldn't really tell what the original house had looked like. As I parked, an older woman stepped out onto the house's wide, covered porch. Built like a fire plug, late fifties to early sixties, with white, wispy hair that fluttered in the breeze, she wore a faded print housedress about as old as she was and carried a small, hooked area-rug that she began vigorously shaking out. She caught my eye as I started up the short concrete steps to the narrow and weedy front yard. She scowled, shook the dirty rug even harder.

"If you're from the city, again, mister, just turn back around and get lost! You can take your building codes and stick 'em where the sun don't shine."

I paused at the top of the steps, and tipped my hat before she got it in her head to try and knock it off. "I'm not with the city, ma'am," I said, pleasant as punch. "I'm here to see the Hashimoto family."

"Yeah?" She draped the little rug over a bare forearm as

thick around as Popeye's and eyed me. "What do you want with *them*?"

"Just a friendly visit."

"Says you." She gave me another once over, her eyes sharp as flint, then said, "Well, com'on inside if that's what you want. They're upstairs in the two rooms at back." I took the stairs up to the porch two at a time and opened the rickety screen door for her. She smiled slightly and nodded her head. "You got manners," she said, pausing before she went in. "You know, mister, I'm a pretty fair judge of people. Got to be, in my game. Nice coat and tie on, I'd say you was here on some kind of official business. You a cop, maybe?"

"No."

"Good," she said, finally stepping through the doorway. "I don't need no trouble with the law," she added, as I followed her inside, "especially over a bunch of Japs."

"You don't seem to care much for them," I said, my eyes trying to adjust to the dim foyer, its only light source a bare bulb hanging down from the ceiling. "Why do you rent to them?"

"Don't have to like 'em to take their money, honey."

I had to smile: the same was often true in my business.

"What're you smiling at?" she asked.

"Nothing. Just economics."

She looked at me like I was talking Greek. "Yeah, well . . . I got work to do . . . you can find your own way upstairs."

"Thanks. You've been most gracious."

"Me?" she laughed, and smoothed back her thin, white hair. "I don't think so. But whatever your game is, I do like a man with manners. If you fancy a snort when you're through with those Japs, come see me out in the living room. I've got cleaning to do, but I always keep a bottle of bourbon squirreled away."

"I'm on a pretty tight schedule, ma'am, but I might just do that if I have time," I said, although I felt the same way about bourbon as I did about tough old birds.

"You won't," she said, matter-of-factly, then walked off without another word.

I watched her fade away into the dark and sparsely furnished living area to the left of the staircase. The beat-up sneakers she wore squeaked against the scratched-up, soft-wood floor as she went. Strong old coot or not, I noticed she shuffled a bit as she passed the narrow table by the front window, which had chipped veneer and a couple withered jade plants on it. Like this whole section of Beacon Hill, her joint had definitely seen better times. And so had she. But I still didn't care for bourbon.

There were six rooms lining the long, dim hallway at the top of the stairs, each with big brass numbers on their doors. The place had paper-thin walls. I could clearly hear some of the tenants gabbing as I made my way to the Hashimotos' two rooms down at the end of the hall.

"Look, I'll pay up, I promise," came a man's voice, from Room #6, evidently in deep to some bookie or loan shark. "You gotta give me another week . . . yeah, I'm on the square . . . for God's sake, just carry me another week . . ."

Some dame in #7 was singing along with a record player . . . loud and off-key.

Whoever was in #8, yelled, "Keep it down, will you?!"

From #9, came a woman's voice, "You louse! You heel! You lousy heel!" This was followed by a man's voice, "But, baby—" He was interrupted by the unmistakable sound of getting his face slapped. Hard. Hard as a thunderclap when lightning strikes right above your roof.

Normally, I might've stuck around to see if the joe slapped her back, but all the tenants seemed as low-down as the joint itself, and I wasn't in the mood for any cut-rate entertainment.

The doors to Rooms 10 and 11 faced each other at the end of the hall. According to our file, Room #10 was home to the Hashimotos' mom, while the two sons occupied #11. I heard soft swing music playing in #11 as I prepared to knock on their door. I was interrupted, however, by a heated exchange coming from the mother's digs.

"Mom, I keep telling you," came a man's voice, "we're doing the right thing. We can't take this laying down."

A female voice spit out some rapid-fire Japanese. I couldn't decipher it, but she didn't sound too happy.

"There's nothing to be ashamed of, Mom; this is—"

She said something else in rapid Japanese. Hearing the language spoken gave me a chilly sense of *déjà vu*: reminded me of the war, the jungle, and Japs about to go on the attack.

"Mom, I *am* a dutiful son. We both are. But look where it's gotten us. We're doing this for you."

I knocked on the door. The room went silent. It stayed silent long enough that I was just about to knock again, when the joe who'd been speaking English asked, "Who is it?"

"Jake Rossiter. I've got some questions for you." I didn't get an immediate response, so I added, "You want to open up? I usually don't make a habit of talking to doors."

The door slowly opened, dropping down a bit at the top due to a broken hinge. Harry Hashimoto filled the doorway, even taller than I remembered him, still dressed in his blue suit. He looked surprised to see me.

"Mr. Rossiter . . ." he said. After a moment, he put a small smile on his face, and extended his hand. When I didn't shake, he took his hand and smile back, then asked, "Where's Miss Jenkins?"

"She's busy."

"I don't understand."

"There's a lot I don't understand, either. That's why I'm here. You going to invite me in?"

He hesitated. Behind him, I caught a glimpse of his mom's room. Small; Spartan; wooden floor painted a dull gray; double bed with a peeling, white headboard set beneath a narrow window, its yellowed blind pulled halfway down; small table and two chairs, beside a blue-tiled counter with a two-burner hot plate sitting on it.

His mom appeared behind him. Harry introduced me to her in Japanese. She barely acknowledged me, and bowed a short bow.

"Yeah, nice meeting you, too," I responded, off-handedly. His mom said nothing, just kept staring at me. Didn't even blink. No expression on her face or trace of emotion in her eyes. Only the long stare. Inscrutable, like they always say. "She speak English?" I asked.

"When she wants to," said Harry. "I'm sorry. My mom's real old school, thinks this is unseemly. She isn't very happy with me hiring a private detective."

"Neither am I," I told him. "So, why don't we cut to it, pal? I'll ask my questions, then blow."

"Let's go to my room," said Harry. He stepped out into the hall with me. His mom slowly closed the door behind him.

I followed him into the room. Small, like his mom's room, one side of it held a roughly hewn, knotty-pine bed. An olive drab army cot lay against the wall near the bed. Just past the cot was a peeling Formica-topped counter and two single-burner hot plates. Three folding chairs and a gray, metal card table stood across from the sink. The other side of the room was packed with old steamer trunks, and slat-sided wooden fruit crates, their flimsy tops held on with lengths of jute twine wrapped several times around each one. From what I could see into the crates, they contained everything from books to dishes and various kitchen gadgets to some small, framed pictures, a bathroom plunger, a bunch of towels and washcloths, and a whole scad of other odds and ends.

"Looks like you've got half a house stuffed into this place," I commented.

"Just about," Harry said, gesturing for me to have a seat at the card table, as he turned the portable radio down.

I took off my trench coat, put my fedora on the table, and pulled up a chair.

"You like some coffee, Mr. Rossiter?"

"Sure, if you've got it."

"We've got it," he said, heading over to the sink, where he filled up a quart-sized pot with some water. "Hope you don't mind your java boiled; our old percolator bit the dust."

"The stronger, the better."

I noticed a large shadow box hanging on the wall over the

old army cot. While Harry worked on the coffee, I went over and looked at it more closely. It contained three Purple Hearts, two Bronze Stars, and a Silver Star. It also had an arm patch for the 442nd Regimental Combat Team mounted at the top of the box, as well as two photos of the same Jap in it: one, a standard boot camp graduation photo; the other, a photo of his company at attention, and him being presented with a medal—the award ceremony, the inscription on the picture read, for his Silver Star in Italy. I figured this had to be Harry's brother, Frank Hashimoto. For one joe, he had a whole lot of medals of valor.

I went back to the table and let my eyes wander over the jumble of trunks and crates again. "You manage to save all this stuff before you went into the camp, or what?"

"Some of it," he said, taking a seat across from me while waiting for the water to boil. "The government offered free storage, but we didn't trust it. Good thing, too . . . most people who took Uncle Sam's offer came home to find their belongings ransacked, stolen, or just vandalized and destroyed."

"Yeah, well," I said, lighting a smoke and thinking about a lot of my buddies who didn't make it home from the Pacific. "Whole load of things got destroyed in the war."

"Yes, they did, Mr. Rossiter," he said, evenly, locking eyes with me for a minute. He got up, and threw a couple double-measures of Eight O'Clock Coffee into the boiling pot on the hotplate. "Anyway," he continued, returning to his seat, as the java boiled away, filling the air with its heavy aroma. "The old Nippon Kan Theatre had a sub-basement in it. They kept stuff for a lot of folks there, free of charge.

The building owners were sympathetic to us. We were lucky. It was all still there when we came back from Minidoka."

"Glad to hear it. Now, let's get down to the questions I've got for—"

"Oh, this isn't everything we had," he interrupted. "Not by a long shot. We saved five times this much stuff. Lost all the rest of it in the fire. Took almost all of our savings to keep up the property taxes on our store while they had us locked up. We had just enough left to re-stock the inventory when we came home. But that was O.K. We moved back into our place above the store and figured we were lucky, had it better than most. Business was slow at first, but we were about the only store still operating in Little Tokyo; all the places boarded up around us, it was a real wasteland. But we kept at it, made enough to get by. Then they burned us out."

"You saying it was arson?"

"You bet it was arson." He got up and took the boiling pot off the hot plate. "It was started by gasoline in three different spots down in the store. Had gas poured under our front door upstairs, too. We were lucky to get out alive."

"They catch who did it?" I asked, as he poured our coffee into two thick mugs, using a small strainer to keep the grounds out.

"Of course not." He brought the mugs over, and sat back down. "Hope you don't mind it black, we haven't got any cream or sugar."

"I take it any way I can get it," I told him, sipping at the thick, bitter brew . . . reminded me of the java we got in the

Marines: so heavy, more often than not, that you could just about eat it with a fork.

"In any event," I said, at length, "you must have had insurance. Why didn't you fix up the damage and get it going again?"

"That's what we planned to do." He shook his head, then pulled a pack of Luckys out of his suit coat's inside pocket. Tamping one down against the table, he added, "But no soap."

"Why's that?"

"We filed a claim, of course," he explained, taking a small box of stick matches out of the same pocket and firing up his butt. "Our agent told us that these things take time. So, we waited. Couldn't live in our apartment anymore, it was all scorched. Just about couldn't live anywhere . . . nobody would rent to us. Finally found this dump and squeezed in here."

"What about the insurance?"

He laughed. Kind of a funny, hollow laugh. "Like I said, we waited. And waited some more. Couldn't blame our agent; to begin with, he came over right away, himself, to inspect what was left of the store and fill out the damage report. He explained that it was complicated, especially with an arson investigation still in progress . . . no offense, but they had to rule out that we hadn't torched the place ourselves." He laughed again, soft and sardonic. "Like we'd set fire to our own home and store after everything we went through to keep it."

"So, what was the upshot?"

"You know insurance companies, Mr. Rossiter: they're in business to take your money, not pay it out. We got grilled good by the arson investigator. He didn't like people like us, you could tell. He kept after us for almost a year. He's still after us. Him and some cop who worked with the arson squad. The insurance company wouldn't settle with all that going on. Finally, our agent told us that the best they would do was five hundred dollars. And that's only if we dropped the matter for good and signed off on it. Five hundred bucks on over ten thousand in damages. We were stuck. Broke. But we still wouldn't sign, and he upped it to a thousand dollars, said he said he was doing us a favor to get anything at all. Said we better take it, or the likelihood was that we'd be brought up on charges of arson and insurance fraud."

"Sad story," I said. "I'll look into it for what it's worth. What was the name of your insurance agent?"

"Jamison," he said. "Henry Jamison, Seattle Life & Property."

Chapter

12

"I KNEW HENRY JAMISON. HE WAS MY insurance agent, too," I told him, wondering at the coincidence of Henry being connected to the Hashimotos. "Too bad he's dead, I wouldn't mind asking him about this settlement offer you got."

"Dead?"

"Murdered. Had his head lopped off with a Samurai sword."

The door opened behind me. "You don't say?" asked a man's voice. I turned, saw it was Frank Hashimoto, the war vet, recognized him from the photo above his cot, the one where he was being presented with the Silver Star. Tall like his brother Harry, he had a much more muscular build, wore dungarees with a blue work shirt rolled up at the sleeves. He stood in the doorway with his arms crossed, holding a half-empty pint of cheap Four Roses Whiskey. He stared straight into my eyes. It wasn't a friendly stare.

I didn't bother getting up. Just stayed turned part way around in my chair, and said, "You make a habit of listening at doors?"

"It's my room," he said, quietly, his lips barely moving under his short, black moustache. Cool customer. Didn't mince words. I smiled. "Glad to see we've hit it off so well," I told him, then spun back around in my chair to face Harry Hashimoto, who looked embarrassed by his brother's rudeness. "You might want to close the door," I added, over my shoulder, "there's a draft."

The door slammed shut.

"Frank," Harry said, "I was just telling Mr. Rossiter about the fire we had at the store."

"Swell." Frank came to the table, smelling strongly of the whiskey, pulled out a chair, turned it backwards, and sat down straddling it, his arms resting across its top, holding the pint of hooch by its short neck. "And I suppose you told him about me getting arrested for it, huh?"

"No," I said. "That's news to me."

"My brother had nothing to do with it," Harry said.

"So, why'd you get rousted, then?" I asked Frank.

His lips curled into a faint grin. "Probably because I'm a Jap," he answered, giving added emphasis to the word, even as he slurred it ever so slightly.

"Got to have been more to it than that."

"Plenty enough reason," he responded, his eyes narrowing as they stared holes through me.

"Frank—" Harry began.

"You don't like Japs much, do you, Rossiter?"

"No."

Frank stood up quick, knocking his chair back as he did so. "Yeah, well, I was in the war, too, buddy! How'd you like a good sock in the jaw?"

I came to my feet. So did Harry. He stepped in front of his brother. "Don't, Frank."

Frank shoved him, but Harry held his ground. Harry

kept him back and turned to me saying, "Frank's been drinking . . . Don't get into it with him . . . He shouldn't be fighting, I'm sorry. He's got a steel plate in his head from the war."

"So what!?" yelled Frank. "Get out of here before I throw you out, Rossiter!"

I really wanted to see if he could throw me out. But I couldn't very well hit some joe with a steel plate in his noggin—rude Jap or not—so, I told Harry so long and took my leave.

Not being able to bust Frank Hashimoto in the kisser left me in a foul mood. I dashed through the cold rain and blowing wind, piled into my Roadmaster, and headed downtown to Ben Paris. I was hungry, and could get some good grub at the joint's restaurant. But I could also bust something there. Namely, a rack of 8-ball in their pool hall. Way I felt, I'd break so hard that my cue ball would send the other balls flying clear off the table, breaking customers' glasses and who knew what else? And maybe some joe there would even take offense at it, and I'd get the chance to bust somebody's kisser after all.

I found parking right outside the place, plugged a couple nickels into the meter, then went into the building and descended the wide stairwell that led to the Ben Paris complex in the lower level. My heels clicked across the large marble foyer, as I passed the shoe-shine parlor, gift shop, and restaurant, and made a bee-line straight for the pool hall. Stepping through the entrance, the click of billiard balls in play was drowned out by the click of my fast heels. I pulled off my overcoat and got ready for some action.

Much to my surprise, I spotted Heine, getting some

action of his own, hustling a pigeon at the table nearest the door. Heine was a pool shark par excellence, spent most of his free time down here relieving marks of their dough, but I didn't expect to run into him just then—thought he was still out, trying to catch up to Eddie and ZaZu.

Playing with a young joe of only about eighteen or nineteen, I watched as Heine quickly ran the last three balls off the table, then sunk the 8-ball in the corner pocket, and took his winnings, two sawbucks, from his sad-faced opponent.

"Hey, gyrene," Heine called, spotting me as he pocketed the kid's dough. "Brother," he told the guy, "I'd like to give you another chance to win your moola back, but that's my boss who just blew in. Duty calls, you understand."

"Fine by me, mac," said the fair-haired joe, putting his wallet back in his trousers. "I got half the wife's grocery money left, anyway. That's better than I usually do. See ya around."

I walked up and joined Heine at the table.

"Lifted the poor kid's grocery money, huh?" I said.

"Yeah. I should feel guilty," Heine quipped. "I don't."

I set my fedora on the lip of the pool table. "What's up, *compadre*? I didn't expect to run into you here."

"I didn't expect to be here, either," he said, putting his cue down onto the dark green felt. "Cruel fact is, though, that Eddie and his broad gave me the slip again. And I mean the total slip. Twice in one day. Judas, I may as well have been chasing around trying to find a single leaf in the forest. Figured I'd come down here to my old haunts and cheer myself up. I don't lose a tail too often. You know that. Like almost never."

The thought of Eddie and ZaZu being out on the loose left me at a temporary loss for words . . . something that hardly ever happened to me. I picked up Heine's cue ball and smashed it into the pool table's nearest pocket. It didn't help much, but improved my mood ever so slightly.

"Looks like you need some cheering up, too," Heine said. "Let's amble over to the restaurant and get a little chow and a whole load of whiskey."

Two straight shots of Cutty Sark before our steaks arrived further boosted my mood. But not by a whole lot. Heine's straight shots of Old Gran-dad cheered him up slightly as well, until I told him about squirreling Mrs. Jamison away at the Olympic, and getting his man Vic to guard her, meaning he'd be working around the clock, and miss his date with the pretty blonde waitress after all.

"Shit," he said. "Shit and double-shit." He downed another shot of Old Gran-dad, then added one more, "shit," for good measure.

"Dammit, Heine," I said, as I sliced into my blood-rare rib steak. "This is a big enough can of worms as it is, but I've got to tell you, working with these Japs has got me on edge."

"Sorry to say this," he told me, "but glad it's you and not me."

"Thanks."

He took a bite of Porterhouse big enough to choke a horse, then washed it down with a whole shot of Old Gran-dad. "I never lose a fucking tail," he said, quietly, cutting out an even bigger piece for his next mouthful.

"Happens."

"Not to me."

I waved my empty glass at our waitress, a perky brunette, with an even perkier figure. She lammed right over with more booze. Normally either Heine or I would've tried to make time with her. I think she knew it, too. But she was brainy enough to recognize how down in the dumps we were and just set our drinks on the table and left well enough alone.

We drank and ate in silence for a time.

At length, Heine said, "So, we just going to sit here and get drunk, or make something happen?"

Good old Heine. Wasn't much that could keep the big jarhead down for long.

I smiled and said, "How about getting drunk *and* making something happen?"

He flashed me his pearly whites. "Sounds good." Gesturing to our waitress for another refill, he added, "What've we got to go on?"

We put our heads together and did a recap of everything that had transpired so far. We needed to get the big picture to see if anything added up. Unfortunately, all we had when we were through blabbing was just the same bunch of stray numbers—still no sum.

"Well," said Heine, "sounds like we got ourselves a lot of spaghetti, but no sauce. Crap. I told you all I know so far, which isn't much. You got anything else?"

"Just these snaps," I said, remembering the photos of Henry with different bimbos that I found squirreled away in his office. I pulled them out of my inside pocket and fanned them like a hand of cards in front of Heine.

"That mousy little joe," he said, taking a gander at the dizzy dames wrapping themselves around old Henry.

"Who'd a thunk it?" he continued, echoing my original thoughts when I first saw the photos. Then, bingo! Heine stabbed a finger at the snap showing Henry with the buxom dame in front of the sad little Christmas tree.

"Hey! That's Bubbles LaFlamme, the stripper!"

"Who?"

"Jeez, Jake," said Heine, still going ga-ga over the photo. "I thought you got around. Man, she can make them tassels on her big titties twirl around fast as the props on a Mitchell bomber. You telling me you ain't ever seen Bubbles LaFlamme?"

"I don't think so."

"You wouldn't forget her if you had. Hot'cha!" he whistled. "But what's a hot number like Bubbles doing with that milquetoast? Especially looking like she's on Cloud 9. What's he got that I ain't got?"

"For one thing, he's got his face between her big bazooms."

"Yeah, ain't it the shits?" Heine shook his head. "But it don't figure. It's gotta have to do with money. Dame like that don't go around with Henry's type for anything less."

"A little bird tells me somebody ought to have a little talk with Miss LaFlamme," I said.

"You don't have ask twice, brother," Heine said, perking right up. "She's stripping down at Club Rialto." He checked his watch. "Late afternoon show starts pretty quick, too. I'm on my way."

"Not you, jarhead. I was talking about me."

"Hell . . ."

"You've got to find Eddie and ZaZu."

"It ain't fair."

"Whoever said life was fair, Heine? But don't worry, I promise not to do anything with Bubbles that *you* wouldn't do. Let's blow."

Club Rialto was a bit of a paradox for our normally sleepy little burg. Seattle was the biggest town north of Frisco, yeah, but the nightlife was mostly comprised of movie theatres, jazz clubs, and big dance halls, like the Trianon Ballroom. Most burlesque acts were hidden away in private clubs, or booked into certain roadhouses outside the city limits. The City Fathers had always frowned on the lewd and risqué, unless it was kept safely tucked into the shadows. But, as during Prohibition, a little grease went a long way: pay off the cops and politicos, they'd look the other direction, often join in—maybe even own a piece of the action.

Such was the case with the Rialto. It operated right out in the open. Began as a small downtown vaudeville house, went to showing flicks for a few years, burned down just after the Depression began—some said for the insurance money, though nothing was ever proven—then got rebuilt as a supper club, with a well-known speakeasy in the base-ment. Rumor had it that they showed blue movies down there during the war. I didn't know for sure—I was stuck in the Pacific for the duration. But come about a year ago, they started with the strip acts at the Rialto. Tame at first, but right up-front for all to see. Didn't get raided, let alone closed down. Just got raunchier and more popular. So popular, they had to add afternoon shows later on. Even Miss Jenkins wanted to see what it was all about, inebriated one night after she'd had a few pops with me. I told her, "hell, no," and took her out for a hot roast beef sandwich and a nice chocolate malted instead, which promptly made her sick. Girl never could hold her liquor.

Anyway, all I could figure was that the proprietors of Club Rialto applied more grease to much bigger fish than anyone ever had before. Otherwise, they would've been shut down in a heartbeat, or zoned out by some ordinance, especially as they were located just a block up from the big, downtown Congregationalist Church on Marion Street.

I motored up and parked just across the street from the joint. I hadn't been in for quite a while. Had only frequented the place a couple times, very drunk on both occasions, actually, which was the best way to tolerate their watered-down drinks. It hadn't changed much, except for the addition of a large glass case containing a big picture of their top-billed act, a statuesque stripper named Bunny Sunday, just beside the double-doored entryway. Getting second billing was Bubbles LaFlamme, a small photo of her occupying the bottom right corner of the case.

Just at the north end of the building, was the same narrow, dark stairwell that led down to the sheet metal door where you used to gain entrance to the speakeasy. That brought back some memories for me: it was one of the joints on my normal delivery route back in my rum-running days. You knocked twice, then waited to the count of three, then knocked once. The door would open, and in you'd go. Sometimes there'd be more women than men in the place . . . women who occasionally thought that an eighteen-year-old bootlegger was cute stuff. Quite a thrill.

Today, of course, there were more men than women in Club Rialto. In fact, I didn't spot any dames at all, except the working girls: three cocktail servers, a pretty cigarette girl making the rounds, and the coat check girl, who seemed bored with her job, but managed a weak smile as she took my overcoat and fedora.

The host, ferret-faced with too much pomade in his 'do, came up and offered to get me a table. I told him I didn't want to sit down yet. He eyed me suspiciously, then said to give him the high-sign when I was ready. Weren't any strippers on the stage, so I figured they were between acts. Bubbles LaFlamme must be back in her dressing room . . . I'd probably have to mosey on back there to catch her.

A huge, hulking joe, standing at the bar off to my right, saved me the trouble. I was just about to head backstage, when the big moose stepped aside and revealed none other than Bubbles herself lushing it up at the bar. She looked even better than in her photo: buxom, long, wavy red hair, leggy as Rita Hayworth, and a waist so tiny it looked like I could get one hand around it. She had four empty martini glasses in front of her and one that was half-empty in her hand.

The big guy pleaded with her. "Bubbles, you shouldn't oughta drink so much. You gotta go back on stage in a little bit."

She ignored him, tipped off her drink, and called for another.

I walked directly to the bar but didn't get ten feet from Bubbles before the goon stepped between me and her bar stool, and stuck a bear-size paw in front of my mug.

"Hold it, mac," he growled. "Where d'ya think you're going?"

"Isn't it obvious?"

"Hey," he scowled. "Miss Bubbles don't talk to just anybody between acts."

"I'm somebody."

"Says who?"

"Says this." I handed him one of my business cards.

He glanced at the card, then his eyes, brown and bloodshot, drifted back up and locked onto mine. He was so damned ugly it hurt to look at him.

"Private heat, huh?" His thick lips barely moved. "What d'ya want with—"

"Give her the card," I ordered. "Tell her it's about Henry Jamison."

I saw Bubbles's eyes go dark for a moment at the mention of Henry's name. "Give me the man's card," she told her goon.

He turned and handed it to her. She glanced at it, laughed sardonically, and patted the bar stool next to her, telling her hulking boy to get out of the way so I could join her. About four inches taller than my six feet, and built like the proverbial brick shithouse with a square chin about as broad as my chest, the big monkey grumbled but did as he was told. As I pulled up a stool beside Bubbles, though, he took up a station not six inches from my right shoulder and loomed over me.

"He reminds me of a junkyard dog I once met," I told her. "Doesn't he have something better to do?"

"This is what I do," the goon said. "I watch out for Miss Bubbles."

"Don't mind Tony, Mr. Rossiter," Bubbles told me. She smelled like sweet perfume and gin. "He just watches over me, like he said."

"Tony, huh?"

"Yes," she said. "Tony. He goes by Tuna, but some folks call him Fish. Only, don't ever call him Fish, Mr. Rossiter. He doesn't like that at all. Not one bit."

"Got it," I told her. Then I looked up at the big lug. "Hey, *Fish*," I said. "Don't you have a bone you can go chew on?"

He looked like he was going to pop his thermometer, but Bubbles told him to cool off.

"You're a smart aleck, aren't you, Mr. Rossiter?" she said, sizing me up like I'd just asked her for a dance and she liked the cut of my jib. "I like smart guys." Then she went cold as ice. "But as you may have guessed, Tony here's not too smart. If you're smart, you'd realize sometimes even I can't control him."

"O.K.," I said. "But if he keeps crowding me, I might have to put your statement to the test."

"Go sit down, Tony," she told him.

He pulled up the bar stool next to me and sat down.

I offered Bubbles a smoke. She declined.

"So," she asked, "why's a private detective wanting to see me about Henry?"

"That's what I'd like to know."

She smiled and lit my cigarette for me with the big table lighter from the bar. "Henry gave me things. I gave him things in return."

"I bet you did."

She toyed with the lighter, flicking it on and off.

"How'd you know about Henry and me?"

"I've got pictures."

"So have I." She was quiet for a minute. "But that's all

I've got now," she added, ruefully. She tipped off the last of her martini. "You wanna buy a sad girl another drink?" she asked, her words starting to slur, as if the buckets of booze she'd been drinking were hitting her all at once.

I flagged the bartender, who brought her another belt. I passed on any for myself. She was swilling enough for both of us.

"Why so sad?" I asked, while she sucked on the fresh martini. "Henry?"

"Who else?" she mumbled. "We were going to Tahiti. Now the only place I'm going is back on that frigging stage."

"Tahiti, huh? You mean he was leaving his wife?"

"What do you think?"

"When?"

"This morning," she said, twirling the olive around in her drink. "We were going to catch the Frisco train from King Street Station, then the South Seas boat from there and live the life of Riley. Hell, I quit my job and everything yesterday. But he never showed up at the train station." She quit swizzling the olive around; picked it up by its toothpick and stabbed it into the remaining hooch, knocking the glass over. "Dammit!" she yelled. "Why'd he have to go get himself killed? Now I lost my top spot, and all I got is lousy second billing. I loved him. I really loved that bald-headed little runt." She started to cry. Not very loud—just a series of small sobs—but I did notice that she seemed to be shedding real tears.

"Hey," came Tony's gruff voice from the other side of me. "You got Miss Bubbles all upset."

I handed her my handkerchief. She dabbed briefly at her

eyes, then used it to mop up the spilled booze that was trickling down the bar.

The house lights suddenly dimmed, then came back up. This repeated twice.

"That's my cue," said Bubbles. She got up. So did her guard dog.

"I've got more questions for you."

"Later. I've got a show to do." She turned, wobbling slightly from all the booze, and started to leave.

"Hold on a minute," I said, getting to my feet—well, actually, not quite to my feet. I was almost to my feet when big Tony's hammy mitts came down on my shoulders and jammed me back into my seat so hard it's a wonder the bar stool didn't break.

"She said later, bud!"

"Come backstage after my act," Bubbles called over her shoulder, already halfway to the exit door to the right of the stage. "Tony, come," she ordered.

He lumbered after her.

I thought about following, but my tailbone wasn't quite willing, yet. So, I settled for a double shot of Cutty Sark instead, brought to me by the bartender, who said, "You're lucky, mister: Tuna usually lays 'em out colder than a fish."

My chair was just starting to feel comfortable again, when the three skinny joes who made up Club Rialto's band took up their stations with their instruments at the far left of the stage. There wasn't any warm-up. The drummer sat down behind his kit, the saxophonist picked up his tenor sax, and the bass player took hold of his bass fiddle, and: "Da-da-ta-ta!" they played an introduction, loud and a little off-key.

The blue velvet curtains parted, revealing the ferret-faced joe who had first tried to get me a table, who also evidently doubled as the M.C.

"Welcome to Club Rialto, folks!" he hollered, adjusting his out-of-kilter bow tie. "We're proud to present one of your favorites! So, without further ado, I give you one of the Pacific Northwest's hottest sex kittens, the one and the only, *Miss Bubbles LaFlamme*!!!"

"Hubba-hubba!" yelled a bald-headed joe seated near the stage.

The rest of the crowd cheered as the band struck up the music, then fell silent, except for a lone wolf whistle, as Bubbles made her entrance from stage left. She wore a different outfit than she'd been wearing earlier—this one a full-length, emerald green evening gown, complete with long white gloves, and moved very gracefully for a chicken who'd just put away six martinis in a row.

I was itching to get backstage and question her more. But I've got to admit that I found myself enjoying her act. It was just a standard bump-and-grind, but she did it with real appeal. Every time she shed a new piece of clothing, the drummer did a loud drum roll on his snare, and she was so sexy that I got charged up right along with the rest of the crowd as she slowly unwrapped the package.

Pretty soon, she was down to just her black brassiere and slinky panties. That's when the bubbles started coming up around her. They rose from two little trap doors that had opened in the floor. Big bubbles, small bubbles, and in-between size bubbles—all iridescent and shimmering, they soon enveloped her.

The crowd whooped and hollered. "Yeah, yeah!" they went, like they'd been expecting this part of her act.

Then I got it. Yeah, sure, her flaming red hair all surrounded by bubbles while she stripped, hence her moniker: Bubbles LaFlamme. Pretty simple. Pretty stupid, actually. But pretty damned hot when you saw her in action.

She slipped out of her panties, ever so slowly, revealing the teeniest-tiniest red G-string I ever saw. Then she gyrated back and forth, the bubbles coming up faster and faster.

"Take it off! Take it off!" yelled the crowd.

She obliged. Off came the black brassiere, which she threw to the side of the stage. Her big breasts had little, red, long-tasseled pasties covering her nipples. As the band picked up the tempo, she began to twirl them—faster and faster, around and around. Soon, just as Heine had mentioned, the tasseled pasties did begin to resemble the spinning props on a B-25. She kept at it until the whole joint was ready for take-off.

The band reached a crescendo, and I thought that her act was over. But she gave me and all concerned a major surprise. Bubbles stopped twirling her tassels, stood stock-still and faced the audience for a moment. Then a wicked gleam came into her eyes.

"How about the whole enchilada, boys?" she asked.

The crowd roared. The M.C. got a horrified look on his face.

"Yeah," said Bubbles. "I'm about ready for it, too."

The M.C. ran up and tried to pull the curtains. But Bubbles was too fast for him. She smiled broadly, then reached up with both hands and popped her pasties off, revealing her fully bare nipples to everyone. "How's that, boys?!" she hollered, giving her breasts a vigorous shake. "Fuck the law!"

Near pandemonium broke out at Bubbles's forbidden display. She laughed like crazy, then danced off the stage.

"Boy, oh boy," said an old, bald guy beside me. "I sure never saw nothin' like that before! Woo-eee!"

I hopped to my feet, and made my way through the tables to the exit door by the stage.

The backstage area consisted of a long, dimly-lit hallway that smelled of stale cigarette smoke and sweat. The first door I spotted was up the hall about forty feet. Wide open, it had light and a lot of female titter-tatter spilling out of it. Closing the last few feet to the door, I kept thinking about how the devil Henry Jamison could've ever afforded to abscond to Tahiti with a hot and expensive bauble like Bubbles. Whole lot of moola just to get there, let alone leave his insurance business behind. Maybe he had other sources of income. I'd have to check that angle. Provided, of course, that Bubbles had been on the level about Henry leaving his wife for her and the south Pacific.

I stepped in front of the open door, and found myself staring into a large, communal dressing room. Roughly thirty by thirty feet square, it was ringed by big, lighted makeup mirrors, and contained six or seven different strippers waiting to go on stage, some dressed, others in various stages of undress.

"Well," said a pretty and buxom black-haired broad, sitting topless across the room, as she worked to fix a pair of bright green tassels to her pendulous breasts. "Good for Bubbles. These damned pasties are a pain in the ass."

She abruptly shut up when she saw me in the doorway.

"Hey!" she complained, quickly grabbing her Navy WAVE costume from her dressing chair and holding it up to cover herself, like nobody was supposed to see a stripper without her clothes on. "What d'ya think you're doing, mister? There's no customers allowed back here."

Some of the other girls covered up, too. Some didn't. A couple of them smiled at me.

I smiled back. "Looking for Bubbles," I said. "Got a date with her. Where's her dressing room?"

"Second door down," said a strawberry blonde, putting on her lipstick at a nearby mirror, and paying more attention to its application than she did to me.

"Thanks."

"Lucky Bubbles," the black-haired dame ventured, as I turned to go. "You strike out with her, handsome, come see me sometime. Just ask for Wilma."

Just then a shot rang out—a low, booming blast.

I pulled my .45, and ran toward the shot. Two doors down, I found Bubbles's room locked tight. I turned the door handle for all I was worth, yelling, "Hey, open up in there!" It didn't budge and I got no reply. The other strippers started pouring out from their dressing room, and I stepped back and gave the door a hell of a kick. The top hinge gave way, and it splintered around the lock, but it still took two more foot-killing kicks to finally break it down.

Ordering all the chirping dames to keep back, I stepped through the busted door. The room was empty, except for a very dead Bubbles LaFlamme, still topless, and sprawled forward in the chair at her makeup table, one side of her face blown away, blood and brains splattered all over her lighted mirror. A white bread sandwich beside her had also caught some of the blood, but the glass of milk and plate of cookies and donuts and cinnamon rolls next to it had come out unscathed as far as I could see. The small room's single window to the outside was all broken out, shards of glass littering the hardwood floor. This kind of damage, I thought, she must have been shotgunned through the window.

The strippers saw what was left of her and started screaming from the doorway.

They were soon drowned out by an even louder scream.

"Bubbles! Bubbles!" came the hoarse yells of Tony from behind me. I turned, but all I saw was a fist about the size of Mt. Rushmore speeding straight into my kisser.

When I came to, big Tony was sitting on the edge of the makeup table, cradling Bubbles's ruined head in his arms.

As I sat up, he said, "Sorry, I thought you done it." Then he started blubbering like a baby and rocking Bubbles back and forth. The big lug looked deep into my eyes, his tears running like a river in flood, all his meanness and fight gone somewhere far, far away.

"Look, look," he cried. "Just look at what they done to my pretty Miss Bubbles . . ."

Chapter

13

I DIDN'T WAIT AROUND FOR THE COPS. LAST thing I needed was to give Captain Blevens another excuse to jam me up. I took only enough time to poke my head through the dressing room's blasted window to check for any clues her killer might have left behind. I found two items of interest on the grated metal fire escape that led down to the alley out back: a half-smoked cigarette, still burning, and an empty book of matches laying near it. I climbed quickly through the window, and gingerly picked up the matchbook by its edges. Bright red in color, the black lettering on it bore the name of a chop suey joint in Chinatown called the Ming Palace.

Whoever had used the matchbook had a curious way of striking the matches. All twenty of them were used up, but were still connected to the inside of the matchbook. Instead of pulling each match out to be lit, the person had curled them over, as needed, and struck them against the friction strip. It was the same one-handed method of lighting a match that I'd seen several soldiers use during the war.

I put the matchbook into one of the envelopes I always carried to preserve evidence, and squirreled it away into my vent pocket. Could be prints on it, and I wasn't about to leave it to be overlooked, or maybe even tossed, by whatever boys in blue showed up at the murder scene.

I did the same with the single 12-gauge shotgun shell that I found just below the fire escape in the alley. Then I beat feet for my Buick, up and around the corner. I was just pulling away from the curb when two squad cars peeled to a stop in front of Club Rialto. I'd seen so many hinky things of late that I was hardly surprised when I saw Blevens's lapdog, Lt. Giles, bail out of one of the cruisers and rush into the club with the uniformed cops.

If I could've, I'd have stuck around, been a fly on the wall, maybe gotten an angle on why the good lieutenant showed up, around the dinner hour, at this particular crime scene. That it seemed fishy was obvious. Lt. Giles worked the day shift, not nights, had a reputation for knocking off early rather than late. But I had other fish to fry. Namely, what seafood might be on the menu down in Chinatown at the Ming Palace. I had a real nose for rotten fish. Might be somebody there who could give me a tip on where I could throw out a big old barbed hook or two.

The Ming Palace turned out to be less than palatial. In fact, it was a real dive. Chop suey joints were normally a dime a dozen, but this one looked like a place even a drunken sailor might be wise to avoid. They didn't have any swabbies, but they had an assortment of the skankiest bar girls I'd seen this side of the Philippines. A dark, smoke-filled place with a juke going full blast, a broken ceiling fan, dirty red booths, a littered floor, and only one joe actually eating something over at a side table, it was really more a cheap bar than a restaurant.

"You lookee for good time, joe?" asked a skinny, knock-kneed China girl, who got to me about two steps ahead of a pack of other B-girls without dates. Wearing a Chinese-style red silk dress, slit halfway up her thigh, she had dark circles under her eyes, was probably in her early twenties, but looked like she'd lived hard for a whole lot longer than her years.

"Forget it," I said, pulling my arm away from her bony hand. "I lookee for a man."

She and the other girls tittered. "Oh, you that way, huh?" She smiled wide, revealing red lipstick smudges across her less than white front teeth. "You pretty bold, joe. Maybe we can arrange."

I pulled out the matchbook I'd found outside Bubbles's dressing room, and held it up for her to see. "I'm looking for a man who lights his smokes this way. You know any-body like that, it's worth a sawbuck to you."

"Right there," she said, quickly, pointing at a fellow, his back to me, sitting in a rear booth.

I stuck a sawbuck into the girl's outstretched hand, brushed by her, and strode straight to the guy's booth, my palm resting against the butt of my .45, ready to do a little pistol-whipping and ask questions later if need be.

As I cleared the rear of the booth, I saw a book of the oddly curled matches beside the ashtray on the joe's table. All I could see of him, was the back of his dark-haired head, and one hand holding a lit cigarette.

I got a surprise when I popped around and suddenly

confronted him—recognized the startled joe as none other than Frank Hashimoto, three empty shot glasses in front of him, and a full one that shook in his hand when I suddenly came into view.

"What the hell?" His free hand came up like he was going to put a judo chop on me. "Rossiter," he said, relaxing a bit. "Not wise sneaking up on a man like that."

I slid into the booth opposite him; kept my gun hand ready.

"Did I invite you to sit down?" he said. "What do you want?"

"You've got a mighty queer way of lighting a match, don't you, Frank?"

"What?" he asked, then picked up his matchbook. "You mean this?"

"Yeah."

"So?"

"I just found that matchbook's twin outside a local strip club."

He didn't say anything. Just sipped at his drink.

I leaned across the table, riveted my eyes to his. "Where were you about a half an hour ago, Frank?"

"You got some nerve. You trying to pin something on me, Rossiter?"

"Where were you?"

"I was right here, drinking alone, until you crashed in."

"Prove it."

He threw me a sarcastic smile, then turned and waved at the B-girl who'd tried to pick me up when I first came in. "Hey, Ling-Ling," he called. "Come back here for a minute."

She sallied right over, with a big smile on her puss,

anticipating a little action at last. "What you need, joe?" she said, seductively, ready to pile into the booth at the first invitation.

"Where was I tonight?" Frank asked her.

"What, you crazy or something?" she said, putting both hands on her hips. "You been right here."

"You sure about that?" I asked.

"Sure. Of course, sure."

"Yeah?" I pulled out a double-sawbuck, and slid it up to her end of the table. "How sure?"

She snatched the bill and tucked it away into the slit-pocket of her red dress. "Sure as can be. We don't like him, much," she said, pointing a long-nailed finger at Frank. "This Jap-boy, he always coming in here, but never buying us girls no drinks. Not never. Yeah, we always remember him, sure enough."

"See?" Frank told me. "What'd I tell you?" He toasted me with his glass, then tossed off the shot. "Just what were you trying to stick on me, anyway?"

"You don't want no girlfriend?" the bar girl asked me before I could respond to Frank.

"Not this time, sister," I told her.

"Too bad," she said. "You generous. You remember Ling-Ling you come back around here, huh?" She smiled, then returned to the table up front with the other B-girls who were awaiting dates.

"A stripper got murdered tonight," I told Frank. "Just uptown a ways at Club Rialto."

"And you thought I did it?" He laughed bitterly. "Too rich for my blood, Rossiter. I'm out of work, or haven't you noticed? I don't have the dough for those ritzy joints."

"Sorry, Frank, it seems I may have misjudged you." I took out a Philip Morris, and tamped it down. "We'll see . . . I'm still not totally sure about you, pal."

"Tough," he said. "No skin off my nose." Then he twisted around abruptly and signaled the barkeep for another glass of rotgut. As he turned, though, he grimaced and let out a little gasp of pain.

"Hurt yourself?"

"What do you care?" he said, through clenched teeth, as he faced me again, his jaw closed tighter than a clam shell. "I've still got some shrapnel in me left over from Italy. Nothing that a bunch of whiskey doesn't help, though."

I didn't say anything. Thought about the shrapnel in him. Thought about the steel plate in his head. Thought about how a whole load of Scotch had always helped me with any leftover aches and pains from the war.

I hollered for the barkeep to bring me some Scotch along with Frank's order.

After our drinks arrived, which I popped for, I said, "I noticed you got the Silver Star. Bronze Star, too."

"Don't mean shit," he said, downing half of his hooch.

I remembered how Heine had almost bought the farm saving our squad on Guadal Canal. "They mean quite a bit, actually."

"Maybe for some folks," he said. "Sure didn't mean anything for my uncle."

"What about your uncle?" I asked.

"My Uncle Hideki was a World War I vet. Served with the infantry in France. Had medals up the ying-yang. Bronze and Silver Star, just like me. Well," he said, sipping at his drink, "to make a long story short, my uncle couldn't believe it when we got the news about having to be sent away to the camps right after World War II started. He called the newspapers, wrote his Congressman, you name it. Nobody would talk to him, let alone speak out against that crap. But Uncle Hideki found a way to make his point."

"Which was?" I asked.

Frank frowned. "Day before we were supposed to get bussed down to the main transit point in Pullalyup, some garbage men found my uncle in the alley behind the Federal Building. He'd gotten all dressed up in his old uniform, put all his medals on his chest, hung a sign around his neck, reading, "I am a W.W.I. veteran and an American Citizen," then laid down and blew his brains out. They barely mentioned it in the papers the next day, when we shipped out for the camps. So, that's the story on my uncle, and fucking medals."

We finished our drinks in silence for a time.

"So, I'm curious," Frank said, taking out a Lucky Strike, and lighting it with his peculiar one-handed method. He let the cigarette dangle from his lips as he continued, his eyes dark and brooding. "Except for this business with the matchbooks, what made you think I'd of killed some stripper?"

I answered his question with one of my own. "Did you know she was connected to your late insurance agent, Henry Jamison?"

He got his back up. "How would I know that? I don't even know what her name was," he snapped.

"Bubbles LaFlamme."

"What, you still think I had something to do with it?"

"You've got a sad story. But like I said, alibi or no alibi, I haven't entirely made up my mind about you."

"This is bullshit!" He stood up so quickly that he banged into the table. "You still going on about that shit, huh? Go find some other sap to pin it on, Rossiter. I've had enough of people trying to push me around. I'm going home."

"You've got a hot temper, Frank," I said, also getting to my feet. "You could get these girls to lie about your where-abouts easy enough. And the last time we met, you told me to get out; you were taking care of things yourself. You can't blame me for not closing the book on you quite yet."

"You're way off base, Rossiter. This is just like the war—I gotta prove myself over and over again, huh? Well, screw you!" He wheeled, and strode quickly for the front door.

I followed, double-timing to catch up. "Hold on, you and me still need to talk."

He blew out into the night. I caught him just up the wet sidewalk in front of the seafood market that adjoined the Ming Palace.

He jerked his elbow away from me. "Keep your hands to yourself," he said, ready to rumble.

"Look, pal, I—"

"Rossiter!" somebody shouted from the street.

I turned just in time to see a big, late-model Packard slowly rolling by. Too dark to make out who was driving, there was no mistaking the glint of the silver pistol pointing at me through the rolled-down, rear passenger window.

"Hit the dirt!" yelled Frank, pushing me down as I reached for my shoulder holster. Two rapid shots rang out. I heard Frank grunt as the slugs tore into him, but he held on, still covering me as the Packard sped off.

I hadn't even cleared leather. Frank Hashimoto had saved my life.

"Damn," I said, rolling him over as gently as I could. "What the hell'd you do that for?"

"No time . . . to think . . ." he gasped, his face contorted with pain. "Couldn't let . . . a fellow war vet buy it . . . now, could I . . ." Then he passed out, bleeding badly.

With my left hand, I put pressure on the only wound I could see, a big hole, spouting a torrent, just under his right shoulder blade. I filled my right hand with my cocked .45 in case the Packard circled back around for another go at us.

All alone on the street, I shouted for help. None was coming. Fucking Chinatown, nobody wanted to get involved. I could see the B-girls' faces, all plastered against the Ming Palace's front window, staring just up the way at us, their lips moving a mile a minute, but nobody coming out to help, or offering to call an ambulance. Same story in the other buildings around us: a few lights had come on here and there, but no one was even opening their windows for a better look at what had happened. Frank was a goner if he didn't get a medic but quick.

I ran to the Ming Palace, kicked open the front door and stepped through it. Blood dripping off my left hand, I waved my Colt at all the startled faces. "Somebody call for a fucking ambulance right now or I'm going to shoot the shit out of this joint!"

The barkeep hopped right on the phone. I hurried back out to Frank, stuffed my handkerchief into the hole in his shoulder and pressed against it for all I was worth.

"Hang in there, soldier," I told him.

"Hey, mister," said a small, female voice behind me.

Startled, I jerked around sharply. The voice belonged to one of the Chinese B-girls from the bar. She was very young, had her hair done in a bob, and wore the same style dress as Ling-Ling, only hers was a deep blue, with an even higher slit up the thigh. "I just come to tell something to you."

"What?" I asked, trying to keep as much pressure on Frank's wound as I could.

She knelt down on the other side of his unconscious form, careful to avoid the blood that had puddled up around his shoulder. "Ling-Ling tell me you looking for this joe who light his matches funny."

"I thought I'd found him," I said, nodding toward Frank Hashimoto.

"Not only this Jap-boy." She shivered a bit in the cold. "I know another who do matches that way. See him tonight. I think he is not so nice."

"Why are you telling me this?" I asked, wary of her being so forthcoming in Chinatown.

"I need money."

"Fair enough. I'll give you money. Providing you're on the square."

"Need twenty dollar."

"Start talking."

She stood, wrapped her hands around both elbows, and shivered mightly as she spoke. "This man, he come by maybe hour and a half, two hours ago."

"At the Ming Palace?" I asked, hearing a siren starting to wail somewhere off in the distance.

"Yes, but outside," she told me, biting nervously at her lower lip. "He don't come inside. I see him meet our cop out front after he leave."

"Your cop?"

"Beat cop. Same one always shake us down. He come by regular like every Wednesday night. We pay, we don't get no trouble." She paused, looked up and down the empty street, like the sound of the approaching siren was making her anxious. "Anyway," she continued, speaking more quickly. "I'm up front, waiting for date at our table by the window. This joe, very big, he meets cop right out front on sidewalk. He has hat pulled down low, and coat collar pulled up high. Can't hardly see face, but he is acting nervous, and I'm thinking he is maybe vice cop going to raid us. But no, our cop hands him big, fat envelope. This joe looks in envelope, nods, and puts away in his overcoat; then he takes out smoke but doesn't got no light. Our cop hands him pack of matches. I notice when big joe lights, he keeps one hand in coat pocket, lights matches just with other hand. Has to try twice because it's windy. When match works, I see his face more better. He has small nose, and scars on his face. He sees me looking out window, and makes ugly look at me. Very scary, I jump back. Our cop, he just laughs. Then he goes up street one way, twirling his baton, and this big joe goes real quick up street the other way."

"What's your beat cop's name?" I asked.

"Moody," she said. "Ronald, Donald, something like that, I think. So, I told you what I see about scar-face man with matches. You gimmee my twenty dollar?"

"I'll give you extra if you take care of my friend, here, until the ambulance shows up."

She looked surprised. "This Jap your friend?"

I looked down at Frank Hashimoto's unconscious form.

"He sure acted like a friend," I mumbled, thinking out loud.

"What you say?" asked the B-girl.

"Look, just do it, O.K.?" I said, handing her two twenties. The approaching sirens were making me nervous. I didn't know if they belonged to cops or the ambulance. I couldn't take a chance; had to beat it out of there but fast.

"Okay-dokay," said the B-girl, grabbing the bills and stuffing them into her dress. "But I don't stay here for long."

"You won't have to," I said, the sirens now sounding really close. "Thanks."

I ran for my car, then sped away into the night.

Chapter

14

I WOKE UP FROM A VERY GOOD, BUT VERY BAD dream about me and ZaZu. Good, because she was just as wowzer as ever and desired my physical attentions. Bad, because she was just as naughty as ever and was setting me up for another big fall. I'd just reached that stage of the dream where my brain took over from all the bodily excitement and screamed, *Judas, Jake, not again, get outta here!*

That's the point where I sat bolt upright in bed. Still in that netherworld between sleep and reality, I couldn't believe that I'd almost succumbed to her Mata Hari act again, then mercifully realized that it'd all been a dream, and I was awake. I also had some vague recollection about getting totally snockered the night before, while trying to connect all the unconnected info I'd been gathering on my cases. I remembered one drink leading to another as the connections seemed deliciously close, then alternately as far away as Earth from Pluto. Which was about as far from my office as I found myself after my bender: clear out north on Highway 99, closing the bar at Lefty's Roadhouse, then getting behind the wheel of my Roadmaster and letting it drive me home, where I crawled into the sack still wearing my suit and overcoat.

Yup, that was the straight dope about my night, I thought, as I sat on the edge of my bed and viewed the rumpled condition of the overcoat still wrapped around me. My head hurt from all the hooch, and my lungs felt raw from all the smokes I'd sucked in, even while they yearned for my first morning fag.

Strong java was what I needed. Dark and thick. Best enjoyed with chain-smoked Philip Morrises, a bottle or two of Bayer Aspirin, and a little hair-of-the-dog.

I stood up, felt wobbly, both from my weak knees and pounding noggin, then noticed the music that was playing in the outer office. I swear to God it was the same song that ZaZu had been spinning on her phonograph while she was trying to seduce me in my dream. This caused me a *déjà vu* that turned my mood from foul to positively rank.

"What the hell's going on out here?!" I yelled, throwing open the door to the outer office.

I was answered by the fresh and rested, I-ate-my-Wheaties face of Miss Jenkins, as she pored over files at her desk, Manny Velcker lounging in the armchair next to her, snappy in his two-tone jacket, and happily smoking a cigar and grooving to the tune playing on Miss Jenkins's portable radio.

"Good morning," she said, cheerily, ignoring my condition.

"Jeez, Jake," said Velcker, sitting up in his chair, and doing just the opposite. "What'd ya do, sleep in your threads?"

Not bothering to try and smooth out my overcoat since it was a lost cause, I ignored Velcker and asked Miss Jenkins, "What are you doing here? You're supposed to be at home."

"That was yesterday," she said, looking up at me. "Today's

a new day." Then she burrowed back into the files on her desk, adding, "Some of us have work to do."

"Yeah, she's a real hard worker, Jake," said Velcker, tipping his cigar ash into Miss Jenkins's waste basket. "You sure don't have to worry about anything with her on the job. Shot one day, then nose to the grindstone the next. Even came in an hour early. Don't know how she does it, but she's as dedicated as she is pretty."

Miss Jenkins, who was never early, glanced over at him and smiled at his compliments. Then she dove back into her files—the files from Henry Jamison's office, I noted—telling Velcker, as she flipped the pages, "Dinner and dancing last night certainly helped my constitution. Thank you again, Manny."

"Just what the doctor ordered," he said, with a wave of his stogie.

"Dinner and dancing?" I asked.

"At the Trianon Ballroom," Miss Jenkins said, coyly. "It was swell. Manny can really cut a rug."

"Yeah, you shoulda been with us," Velcker told me. "Course, I'm glad you weren't," he added with a wink.

I took a couple steps toward him, the sudden movement aggravating my aching head. "Hell's bells, man, you were supposed to be guarding her."

"I was."

"He guarded me very well," said Miss Jenkins. "Guarded me very close."

"Yeah, I kept a real close eye on her."

"I bet you did."

"What, are you jealous?" Miss Jenkins asked, grinning up at me.

"Well, what was I to do?" said Velcker, quickly, getting up from his chair, and shrugging his shoulders. "She got to feeling better and wanted some fun."

"Yes," Miss Jenkins told me, a teasing glint in her eye. "And what was I to do? Taken off my very first case, then ordered home and grounded like I was some little bobby-soxer. At least Manny knows how to treat a girl right."

"Oh, I get it," I said. "You're hinting at this romantic baloney just to get my goat."

"Not true!" exclaimed Miss Jenkins, maybe a little too emphatically.

"Whoa-whoa," went Velcker, acting all nervous. "What, are you two are a pair or something? Hell, I wouldn't have even thought about cuttin' in if I'd known you two were makin' time."

"*We're not!*" I told him. "That's not what this is about."

"No, it's not," my junior partner agreed, a wry lilt to her tone. "After all, Jake and I have only ever been out together a couple times."

Velcker took this bit of info like he'd just been shot in the butt with an arrow. "I think I'll make myself scarce, let you two sort this out." He grabbed his fedora off the hat rack, and vacated the office pronto, saying, "I'll be down at the pool hall if you need me, Jake."

"Well, I hope you're happy with yourself," Miss Jenkins told me, after he'd left.

"About what?"

"Chasing poor Manny off like that. He didn't do any-thing wrong."

"Who said he did? I got ticked because he was supposed to be guarding you, that's all."

"Oh," she said. "So, you really didn't mind him taking me out for dinner and dancing."

"It's a free country," I told her. "However, it's damned near impossible to guard somebody right when you're dancing with them."

"Oh, so you *do* mind," she said, her greenish-blue eyes twinkling, obviously expecting me to further address the issue.

I wasn't going anywhere near it.

When she realized I wasn't biting, she shuffled the files on her desk for a moment, then said, very business-like, "Well, whatever. Perhaps you'll finally take a look at what I found in the Jamison files."

"What, you really found something? I thought it was just all part of the game."

"See for yourself," she told me, more than a little insult in her voice. She shoved the three open files across the desk at me.

I sat next to her in the chair that Manny had recently occupied, and gave the files a quick once-over.

"I don't see anything new in here."

"That's because you're really not looking," she said. "Turn to the third page in the *S & T* file."

"O.K., I'll bite," I said, turning to the aforementioned page. On it, I saw only more of the same mind-numbing insurance gobbledygook. "So?"

Miss Jenkins stabbed a finger down onto one of the names listed on the paper. "There!" she said, emphatically. "Yoshiru Suzuki. Owned a Japanese restaurant two blocks away from the Hashimotos' store. Evidently managed to hang onto it after the war, just like the Hashimotos. Place burned down in December of '46. Total loss."

"That's a coincidence, all right," I said. "But so what?"

"It's more than a coincidence. Turn to page six, same file."

I did as instructed. She stabbed a finger onto another name.

"Kenneth Tanaka. Haberdasher in old Japantown. Store was gutted by a fire in early '47. Lost everything."

"I can see that," I said, reviewing the information. "But what—"

"And look here and here and here," she went on, quickly pointing out three more names in the other files, all Japanese businessmen, their places all lost to different fires over the last two years.

"That's a lot of fires," I agreed, thinking that it was, indeed, suspicious that so many Japanese joints had gone up in flames. "But what's your point? What's the connection?"

"Don't you get it?" she asked, making a face. "It's plain as day: *they were all insured by Seattle Life & Property*."

"By, God . . ." I muttered, realizing that I hadn't been able to see the forest for the trees. "You're right. The connection's so simple I didn't see it. Every one of these people had Henry Jamison for their insurance agent."

"Voila!" Miss Jenkins smiled her Cheshire cat grin. "And every one of them got burned out. And every fire was listed as suspicious. There are claims filed in here, but never paid. And every one of them lost their stores and restaurants and such. See? All of them are stamped: POLICY CANCELED— OUT OF BUSINESS."

"Yeah . . ." I flipped through the files fast as I could; saw the same cancelation stamped on each of the policies.

"And there's more," she fairly yelled, flush with her

triumph. "They were all put down as possible arson. See? The same arson investigator handled every fire. A Lieutenant Leonard MacDonald. Look where he signed off on them: *no further action taken/claim dropped*."

"Boy, oh boy. I think you grabbed the brass ring with this one, doll," I told her, with a big smile and a nod of my head. "You know, I'm going to have to take Manny's compliment of you a step further: you're not only as dedicated as you are pretty, but you're also as *talented* as you are good looking! And that's one tall order to fill, because you're the prettiest girl in the whole wide world, and nobody's going to tell me different."

Miss Jenkins grinned ear to ear at my praise. Even blushed quite a bit. I liked it when she blushed. It put even more color than usual into her rosy cheeks and really set off her sparkling green-blue eyes.

"Well, anyway, I'd like to talk to this MacDonald character," I continued. "I wonder if he's Fire Department or Police Department . . . You know which one of them's handling arson these days?"

"Why, no," Miss Jenkins answered. "I'd think you would," she added, as if the boss was supposed to know everything.

I quickly seized on something in the files upon which to salvage my pride. "Well, well . . . There's a lot of arson reports in here, but all the cases were closed with no suspects identified. And what have we here? Look who did the investigating from the insurance company's end: none other than old Henry Jamison, himself."

"Yup." That's all she said, like she'd noted that fact long before.

"According to these files, Henry sold the policies, managed them, collected the premiums, and did the investigations, to boot. He was a regular one-man band, wasn't he?"

"Yup."

"Still," I said, tamping down a smoke and playing devil's advocate. "Henry had at least a cursory involvement with the Hashimotos and all these other Jap businessmen. So what? Hinky as all this seems on the surface, if he'd gotten a reputation as a good insurance agent around the Jap community . . . well, you know how they stick together . . . old Henry might have just naturally built up a good business with them, with one account leading to the next . . . Could be all this just has a mundane explanation."

"Except for one thing," Miss Jenkins piped in.

"What's that?"

"Where there's smoke, there's usually fire," she said, somehow making the cliche seem fresh and ever so wise. "You always say you don't trust coincidences, boss. Well, there's so many coincidences here, you could just about choke from all the smoke they're making."

"Quite well put, my dear."

She smiled.

"And, like I told you, this is a darned good job you've done with these files. You know, we haven't been out together for too long, you and me. When this is all over, I'm going to take you to the ritziest joint in town, really put on the dog, give you an evening fit for a queen—maybe even throw in a nice bonus—maybe like a swank pearl necklace to really set off those gorgeous eyes of yours."

"Really?"

"Yup." I bowed, took hold of her right hand, and planted a European-style kiss on it. "For now, though, I'm going to reward you by having you make a list of all these businesses and take it down to the Hall of Records and go over it with my pal Jimmy Corrigan. I'm going to talk to him about it. I need you try to track down all the present owners of those former Jap businesses. And be sure to get their whereabouts and current addresses. You take care of that, while I go out and track down a certain arson investigator named MacDonald."

She frowned. "Are you sure you're not just trying to get rid of me, again? I'd like to talk to this arson guy, too."

"Tush-tush, darling," I said, making for the door. "It's an exciting job, but only one of us can do it."

"But—"

"You do what I told you." I paused in the doorway. "Please. It's turning into a damned dangerous game out there. Somebody's going to get hurt, and it's not going to be my pretty junior partner. I'll have Manny back up in a jiffy to keep tabs on you."

She looked like she was going to protest further, but thought better of it and said, "Be careful."

"I will." I stepped out, letting the door slowly swing shut behind me.

I skipped the elevator and took the stairs down to the foyer two at a time. I was in a hurry. Would liked to have been in two places at the same time. Had two shady characters to track down: the beat cop who'd given the dough to the scar-face Joe who had shotgunned Bubbles, and the arson investigator who seemed to have been playing ball with Henry Jamison.

I powered through the revolving door and piled into my Roadmaster, in the perfect mood to light a major fire under both the cop and arson joe. First, though, I needed to get Manny back keeping an eye on Miss Jenkins. I gave the Buick its head and made it to Ben Paris in a minute flat.

Velcker was just chalking his cue and waiting for some pigeon to fleece, when I walked into the near-empty pool hall.

"Hey, Jake," he said. "I didn't expect to see you so soon."

"Pack it up. I need you to get back to the office and guard Miss Jenkins."

"You got it."

"But cut the *mash* stuff."

"No problem," he said, unscrewing his custom cue and putting it in its leather case. "Especially now that I know what's up with you two."

"Nothing's up!"

He threw me a wink. "Sure, boss, whatever you say."

Chapter
15

"YOU WANT ME TO DO WHAT?" ASKED MY PAL Jimmy Corrigan at the Hall of Records, his voice raising over the phone to the point that it almost hurt my ear. "For a bunch of Japs? What do I care about a bunch of Japs?!"

It was easy understanding Jimmy being pissed off. He'd been in the same unit with Heine and me during the war. Both of us had managed to come back in one piece, but Jimmy had gotten the shit shot out of him and came back with a withered left shoulder and a metal, claw-style prosthesis that took the place of his right hand.

"I don't give a damn about them, either," I told him, nursing my second Cutty Sark in the pay phone booth at the back of Ben Paris's cocktail lounge. "It's just that I hate crooks even worse."

"Yeah, me too, I guess," he said, slowly.

"Just help Miss Jenkins with it, O.K.? She'll be down to see you, soon. It's worth a steak dinner over at the Cedars Grillhouse, Jimmy."

"And copious amounts of Johnny Walker Black?"

"As much as you can pound down, gyrene."

"O.K.," he said. "But I'm only doing it for you, Jake. Fuck the Japs."

"Yeah, screw 'em. I just want the goods on any hood-lums."

"So, let's see if I've got this straight," Jimmy said. "These former Jap businesses Miss Jenkins will give me—you want me to check the records and see who owns them now, right?"

"Roger that, pal. And while you're at it, maybe you and she could see how many other joints in old Japantown changed hands since the war. I'm a few files short of what I'm looking into. Might be others I don't know about."

"Jeez, you don't ask much for a steak dinner, do you, jar-head?" he laughed.

"The Cedars has the biggest steaks in town," I told him.

"Knock-out waitresses, too, I've heard," said Jimmy. "Know any of 'em?"

"We'll get to know them together."

"Sounds good. O.K., I'll get right on it."

"Thanks. Keep your powder dry, pal."

"And your bayonet fixed, gyrene," he said. "Out."

I hung up, glad to have Jimmy on my side. My only regret might come when I took him out to dinner. It could be embarrassing, him trying to make time with the dames, but them being put off by the extent of his injuries. It wasn't like that right after the war. All the crap we went through was still fresh in people's minds, and Jimmy didn't have too much of a problem getting a date, being a war hero and all. But times change pretty quickly. People forget. It was hard for Jimmy, now, to be looked on as just a cripple. I'd have to see if I could fix him up with one of the girls I knew to come out to the Cedars with us. Maybe I'd even bring Miss Jenkins along for a double date.

Right now, though, I had more pressing things at hand. I plugged another nickel into the phone and spun the dial. Just took a quick call to the downtown Fire Department Headquarters to find out that they, and not the cops, were currently in charge of all arson investigations. Due to politics, arson had flipped back and forth between them over the years, but yes, it had been in the Fire Department's pervue since just before the war, and, yes, Lt. MacDonald was their lead investigator, and, as a matter of fact, he'd just stepped out for coffee at the Manning's Cafeteria across the street and should be back within the half hour, did I want to leave a message?

I said no thanks, I'd catch him later. Later meaning: just as fast as I paid my tab and got my Roadmaster rolling the dozen or so blocks south to the Manning's across from Fire Department Headquarters.

I found Lt. MacDonald, nametag on his crisp fireman's dress uniform, sitting alone and dunking a donut at one of the small, chrome-legged tables that lined Manning's huge plate glass front window. It was a big, noisy, serve yourself place, pretty packed with folks of all stripes, evidently very popular with the coffee break crowd. I didn't bother getting any java, though. What I wanted were answers. So, without further ado, I grabbed a chair at the lieutenant's table and introduced myself.

"Hi. I'm Jake Rossiter."

Startled in mid-dunk, he pulled the dripping donut out of his mug and asked, "Do I know you?"

I flashed him my private detective's license, smiled, and watched closely for any signs of nerves as he took in what I did for a living. His gray-blue eyes went from the photo-portrait on the license to my face without so much as a blink.

"So, you're a private dick," he said, taking a bite of his donut before the soggy end fell off. "What do you want with me?"

"I understand you investigated a string of suspicious fires in old Japantown over the last couple years."

"I handle a lot of fires. What's it to you?"

"Let's just say I'm an interested party."

"You must be working for somebody," he said, calmly dunking his donut. "Who?"

"These businesses were all insured by Seattle Life & Property."

The mention of Henry's company got a slight rise out of him. "You working for them?"

"That bother you if I was?"

"No. Why should it?" He stuffed his face with the last of his donut, then wiped his mouth with his napkin. "What are you getting at, anyway? If there's a point to all this, you better get to it, Mr. Rossiter. I'm due back at the office in a few minutes."

"How many arson dicks work in your department, Lt. MacDonald?"

"I've got four men working under me. Why?"

"That many people in your command, I'm curious why you'd have personally handled all these Japantown cases yourself."

"The answer's very simple." He took a bent, briar pipe out of his jacket pocket and loaded it up from a tin of Velvet tobacco as he spoke. "Six similar fires in such a small area, I wondered if they were connected."

"Were they?"

"You seem to know so much about this," he said, carefully lighting his pipe, "I have a feeling you already know the answer."

"Tell me your version."

"The only real connection I could find was their suspicious nature," MacDonald said, a big cloud of pungent smoke blowing my way as he spoke. "Accelerants were used in each case—gasoline, kerosene, lighter fluid in one instance; they were the last Jap-owned businesses left down there and hadn't been doing that well from what I could tell, so they all had something to gain from these fires. But they dried up and blew away when threatened with court action."

"All except one," I said.

"Yes. The last fire we had. The Hashimotos." He drained the java from his mug. "I'm testifying at Frank Hashimoto's trial next month, as a matter of fact. Don't tell me that's who you're working for."

"What if I am?"

"What, are you some kind of Jap lover?"

I answered by saying nothing and keeping my right hand from socking him in the jaw.

Lt. MacDonald picked up his hat from the table and got to his feet. "Each to his own, I guess," he said, fitting the gold-braided, white saucer-cap snug on his head. "I don't know what your game is, Mr. Rossiter, but you picked yourself a criminal for a client. In my opinion, Frank Hashimoto ought to be facing charges for Henry Jamison's murder, as well. He threatened to kill him, you know."

I stood up. "When was that?"

"When Jamison offered him a small settlement in lieu of litigation."

"The same as all the others, huh?"

"That's right. Although I'm not sure about the exact amount in each case. How do you know about that?"

"I've seen the files."

He laid a nickel on the table for a tip. "Well, I've got to get back to the office. Good luck, Mr. Rossiter."

I followed as he headed for the door. "Why would Henry have offered these folks any money at all?" I asked.

"That's between them and the insurance company," he said, holding the door open for two well-dressed women coming in. We both tipped our hats to them and got a couple nice smiles in return. Stepping out onto the sidewalk, where a chill wind had started blowing, MacDonald continued, "Maybe he felt sorry for them. He insured every Jap establishment down there that I'm aware of. Who knows? Anyway, the insurance boys often offer a token amount to settle disputed claims. Costs everybody money to drag things out. They can go on for years. Once the poor saps realize that they usually take what they can get and drop the claim."

"But not Frank Hashimoto," I said, pulling my coat collar up against the wind.

"Nope. It's his funeral."

"You didn't prosecute the other cases, why this one?"

"Better evidence," MacDonald said, cupping a hand over his pipe.

"What kind of evidence?"

"I'm not at liberty to discuss that," he told me. "You'll have to talk to his mouthpiece in that regard."

"And who might that be?"

"Some schmoe from the Public Defender's Office." He cleared his throat, then smiled. "Look, Rossiter, tell you what . . . I don't really want to beat on a man while he's down . . . Your client's already lost his store. You want to do him a favor, tell him to back off on all this. He does, I'll put in a word with the D.A., see about getting these charges dropped."

"Why would you do that?"

"Maybe I feel sorry for him; who knows?" He took the pipe out of his mouth and tapped it against the heel of his left shoe, knocking the burning embers onto the wet pavement where they sizzled for a second then went out. "At any rate," he continued, returning the empty pipe to his pocket, "the courts are backlogged, and I'm a busy man. It'd be much more expedient just to settle this once and for all. I imagine the insurance company would still be willing to settle. They've never retracted their offer as far as I know."

"You're a real prince, aren't you?"

"Hey," he said with a frown. "Why look a gift horse in the mouth?"

"Why back off on your prosecution? You're holding all the marbles. Unless you're afraid I'll find something."

MacDonald tensed. "I don't like your insinuation."

"And I don't like gift horses that smell like dead flounders."

He looked like he wanted to throw a punch at me, then thought better of it. "That's the offer, Rossiter. Take it or leave it. Goodbye."

He turned and marched down the street.

I called after him. "I'm sticking on the case whether Frank takes your deal or not."

He slowed in mid-step, then picked up his pace and hurried on.

My conversation with the good lieutenant left me primed for my next task. I went back into Manning's and used their pay phone. The desk sergeant at the station house picked up on the second ring.

"This right number for police who work Chinatown, yes?" I asked, in my best sing-song voice and pidgin-English.

"Yeah, that's right," the desk sergeant answered. "What can I do for ya?"

"This the Ming Palace on Occidental Street. We need our cop, officer Moody, come see us right away."

"Moody doesn't come on duty 'til 2:00. He works the swing shift."

"That O.K., yes," I said, really hamming it up. "You tell him come see us chop-chop, first thing. It important."

"You got some kind of problem?" he asked, not really sounding too interested.

"No-no, no problem. Just important. You tell Moody, huh?"

"Yeah, fine, I'll leave him a note."

"Thank you. Goo-bye."

I hung up. Checked my Bulova. It was pushing 11:00. I had a little time to kill before I waylaid Officer Moody outside the Ming Palace. He was going to tell me the who and why about the money he'd slipped to Bubbles LaFlamme's killer, or I was going to teach him the finer points of boxing.

Chapter

16

I WHILED AWAY THE BETTER PART OF AN hour searching the late Bubbles LaFlamme's dressing room. It wasn't hard to get in. I simply took the same route the shooter had used: stood on a garbage can in the back alley, pulled down the fire escape ladder, and climbed up to the landing outside the dressing room window. Somebody on the inside had covered the broken window with a piece of plywood, and some cop on the outside had stretched a piece of CRIME SCENE—DO NOT ENTER tape across the window frame. I didn't let either stop me; pulled off the tape and pushed against the upper right corner of the plywood. It gave easily, held in only with a couple small finishing nails. As the hunk of plywood popped free, I grabbed hold and set it gently and quietly to the floor. Once inside, I didn't worry much about being disturbed. Since they'd sealed off the window with crime scene tape, I was certain they'd done the same with the only door to the dressing room. I didn't have to worry much about making noise either. They must have had a booming lunch trade, because I could hear the band playing and the crowd applauding.

The room was almost exactly as I'd left it, including Bubbles's blood and brain matter splattered all over the mirror. Two things were different: somebody had set a bouquet of red roses on the makeup table, and every drawer in the place had been pulled open and left that way. The drawers I could understand—probably cops looking for clues. But the roses, well, that was a mystery.

I rummaged through everything anyway—the boys in blue were notorious for missing evidence—and, voila, as Miss Jenkins would say, found a couple items they'd overlooked. Train tickets to Frisco, the same train that Bubbles and Henry would've caught the day before, plus a short poem, handwritten in block letters on a small piece of cream-colored stationery:

ROSES ARE RED
VIOLETS ARE BLUE
YOU DON'T KNOW IT
BUT I LOVE YOU!

I didn't know what to make of the poem. Didn't think it was Henry's; not bawdy enough. Secret admirer, I guessed. Maybe even the same person who'd left the roses. Didn't seem to matter much. Strippers undoubtedly had a million secret admirers.

Then I noticed one other thing. Somebody had been snacking on the pastries from Bubbles's makeup table. I was sure there had been more left on the plate last night than there were presently. I had to wonder who'd be stuffing their faces at a murder scene. Probably the flatfeet.

Just then, somebody started jiggling the door handle.

I hopped into the closet. I was taking a chance sticking around, but I was curious about who would be entering a forbidden crime scene. A cop would've just barged in like he owned the joint. This person was taking the time to open the door as slowly and quietly as possible.

Peeking out the crack I left in the closet door, I was surprised to see big Tony, Mr. Fish, edge into the room. I had a good view of him as he moved quickly to the makeup table. He sniffed the roses twice, each time a huge sob escaping from him, then he wiped his eyes, and went to the small dresser just past the table, where he rifled through its top drawer.

When he turned around, he held a bright red G-string in his giant mitts. He rubbed the silky little thing between his hands, then the floodgates opened and he blubbered and bawled, gasped and shuddered, all the while using the G-string to wipe away the river of tears that ran down his ugly mug.

I stepped out of the closet; helped to dry up his tears with a cocked .45 pointed directly at his sternum. "Get hold of yourself," I told him. "You're going on worse than an Italian opera. You want to attract everybody's attention, make them come running in here and find you with your beak buried in that G-string?"

He didn't say anything. Just took the G-string away from his schnoz and stood there sniffling.

"What are you doing here besides getting a snootfull of unmentionables?" I asked, keeping a safe distance from him.

He took to shuddering and crying again, his tears and sniffles soon reaching a crescendo. "I loved her!" he wailed. "I really, really loved her!"

"So I've gathered," I told him. I stepped over and poked

my Colt hard into his chest. "Sit down and shut up. You'll draw us a crowd, and we'll both have some explaining to do."

He did as he was told; collapsed onto the chair in front of the roses and blood and brains at the dressing table, still crying softly, while I ducked over to the door and listened at it, hoping that no one had noticed his outburst. I heard a door close just up the hall. A female voice said something, followed by the click-click-click of her heels coming our way outside the door.

I backed away. "Get a grip, for God's sake," I whispered loudly at Tony. "Somebody's coming. Some dame."

"Nah," he said, keeping a grip on the G-string. "None of those broads will come in here. They couldn't care less. Only one who ever really got along with Bubbles was Bunny. But she ain't around today. She's in the hospital."

"What's Bunny doing in the hospital?"

"Got herself a bad dose of food poisoning, I think," he said, carefully unfolding the G-string and smoothing it out across his lap. "They said she started barfing her guts up not long after Bubbles got . . . got . . . ohhhh . . . shot . . . ohhhh . . ."

He started losing it again. I slapped him three times, hard, across the cheek.

He quieted down, and I went back to the door and listened. Whoever I'd heard out there just kept right on going. As their footsteps receded into the distance, I unglued my ear from the door panel, and turned back to big Tony.

"Poor Bunny," he muttered, gazing down at his lap. "I hope she's all right. She loved Bubbles almost as much as me."

"That so?" I crossed over to him. "Way I heard Bubbles talking, sounded like she didn't think much of Bunny Sunday."

"That was just over who got top billing. They was all palsy-walsy. Real birds of a feather, those two."

"What hospital is she in, do you know?"

"Seattle General, I guess. It's the closest. Why?"

"I might want to talk to her," I said. "See if she knows anything that could help me dope this mess out."

He sat up straight in his chair, his fists balling up like two sledgehammers. "You gonna try and find out who killed Miss Bubbles?" he asked, like a boxer straining for the bell to ring so he could begin his fight.

"Yeah. That's part of it."

"I wanna wring their neck like a chicken!"

I felt at my sore jaw, where he cold-cocked me the night before, grateful that he'd only knocked me out instead of mistaking me for said chicken. "I'm glad you've gotten it through your thick head that I didn't have anything to do with her death," I told him.

"*I wanna wring their neck like a chicken*! I wanna help ya find 'em."

"Look, if you want to be any help to me, you just stick around here and keep your eyes and ears open. You might get something valuable. That'd be a big help."

"Yeah?" he asked.

"Yeah."

He rocked back and forth in his chair, thought about it for a minute. "If I hear something, I call you, right?"

"Roger."

"Well, O.K . . . I can listen real well," he said, at length.

"And sorry for pasting you. I don't think too good when I'm mad."

"I'll try to keep you happy from now on."

He managed a little smile—first smile I'd ever seen cross his face.

I went to the window and prepared to take my leave.

"Say," he said, standing up as I got one leg out the window.

"What?"

"You won't tell nobody, will ya?"

"About what?"

"About this," he said, sheepishly rubbing the G-string between his fingers.

"Oh, that . . ."

He stared lovingly at it. "I just wanted something to remember her by."

"Don't worry, pal," I said, climbing all the way out. "Your secret's safe with me."

Chapter

17

I SWUNG BY SEATTLE GENERAL. THE MORE I thought about Bunny Sunday being gal-pals with Bubbles, the more I thought she might have some skinny that went beyond who shot her fellow stripper. Maybe even something that could shed a little light on who bumped off Henry Jamison. He was like a damned albatross around my neck. Everything swirling around the Hashimoto case had little loose threads that seemed to trail back in his direction. Something told me that if I latched onto the right thread, and tugged on it until it unraveled, it could lead me to Henry's killer and, even more importantly, exactly *why* he'd been bumped off.

I found out that Bunny Sunday had, indeed, been admitted to Seattle General. But, unfortunately, the duty nurse also informed me that afternoon visiting hours were from 3:00 to 5:00—no exceptions. Yes, Miss Sunday was out of danger and resting comfortably, and, yes, I had a nice smile, and, yes, the nurse could use an extra ten-spot, but, no, it wasn't worth losing her job, even with a fancy dinner invite thrown in, and, double-no, that was that, I'd have to come back only during the prescribed hours, but, yes, if I still felt like dinner sometime, her phone number was EA-4107.

I left disappointed, but full of hope. 3:00 would roll around soon enough, and the shapely nurse had bedroom eyes.

Only an hour and a half to kill before my date with Officer Moody, I drove up to Broadway Bob's, got some grub and a few fingers of Scotch, then made a phone call to check up on Mrs. Jamison over at the Olympic.

She picked up on the first ring.

"Oh, Mr. Rossiter, I'm so glad that you called me. I've been trying to reach you since you left."

"What's up, Mrs. Jamison? Everything O.K.?"

"I'm lonely."

"Sorry about that," I said. "But my man Vic Croce's pretty fair company. Isn't he—"

"I sent him away."

"You what?"

"I wish you'd come stay with me."

"Vic's supposed to be guarding you," I told her. "Where is he?"

"Out in the hall. He keeps knocking on my door every hour or so, asking if I'm all right. Well, I'm not all right. It's hard being all alone—especially here in the Honeymoon Suite. Why can't you come watch over me yourself?"

"I'm busy, that's why. I've got a lot of things cooking."

She was quiet a minute, then asked, "Have you found out who killed my Henry?"

"I've barely gotten started, Mrs. Jamison. But I did track down one of the women on that list you gave me."

"Is she pretty?"

"Not anymore. She's dead."

"Oh . . ." She was quiet for a long time. Then she said, "Oh, Mr. Rossiter, I've just remembered something important you need to know about Henry."

"What?"

"Do you have plans for dinner?"

"Not exactly. What's this about Henry?"

"Come to my room, and I'll tell you about it over dinner. We can order from room service. Won't that be grand, just the two of us? Say 4:30?"

I hesitated. She'd been stringing me along, trying anything to get me to come over again. However, Mrs. Jamison just might have been holding something back about Henry. Maybe it was high time for me to string *her* along. Probably only a one-in-a-million shot, but I figured why not play the game just in case. I wasn't all that hungry yet, but I might be after my bout with this cop, Moody.

"O.K., I'll be by," I said. "But only on my terms."

"Whatever you want," she quickly agreed, ever so light and cheery.

"First," I told her, "I'm not having dinner in your room. I'll meet you in the hotel dining room."

"Oh, all right," she said. "At 4:30."

"Second, Mrs. Jamison, you let Vic come back inside to sit with you until I get there, or the deal's off."

"Of course. I can't wait to see you."

"Put Vic on the line, first."

"Don't you trust me?"

"Just get him on the line, Mrs. Jamison."

There was a small clunk as she set down the receiver. Vic picked up a few moments later.

"Jeez, Jake," he said, all exasperated. "What kind of a

cockamamie set up is this? This broad's had me cooling my heels out in the hallway ever since I got here. Won't even let me in to take a whiz—and I been needing one bad."

"Well you're in now," I told him. "And make sure you stay in until I get there. I've got a 4:30 dinner date with Mrs. Jamison."

"Fine, whatever," he said. "O.K., we done? I gotta go now, Jake. I mean *I really, really gotta go.*"

I motored south down First Avenue, hung a left on Yesler, then a right over to South King Street, and parked the Roadmaster half a block up from the Ming Palace. It had stopped raining for a bit, but the sky was still dark—dark as my mood while I lounged against the brick wall at the mouth of the alley that ran between the Palace and the Chinese herbalist joint next door. A little early, I smoked exactly one and a half Philip Morrises before Officer Moody showed up.

Quick-timing it down the sidewalk toward me, he didn't have a clue who suddenly grabbed him by the collar, jerked him into the alley, and slammed him up against the wall so hard that it rattled his teeth and knocked his hat off.

"Jake Rossiter," I introduced myself, keeping him up on his tippy-toes with two handfuls of his wide lapels.

"What the . . . hell?" he stammered. "Who are you?"

I pounded him against the wall for emphasis. "You've got some questions to answer, mister!"

He reached for his nightstick. "You can't—"

I took it away and beat him over the head with it.

He picked himself up off the pavement and went for his revolver.

I took it away and pistol-whipped him with it.

He picked himself up off the pavement again—but much slower this time around—one hand clutching at the huge welt across his right cheekbone. "You can't . . . do this . . . to an officer of the law," he mumbled.

"Seems that's just what I'm doing," I said, then knocked him down again, this time with a short right cross. "Stay put, or I'll keep feeding you to the cement."

He propped himself up on one elbow and tried to shake off the damage I'd caused him.

"What do you want?" he asked.

"I want some answers, like I said." I stood over him. "Listen close. Last night you handed a man an envelope outside the Ming Palace. That same man later rubbed out a stripper at Club Rialto. Who is he?"

"I don't know what you're talking about."

"Look, pal, you're the first person I've been able to lay my hands on who I know for certain has some info. I'm not letting you go until you spill it."

He scowled. "I'm not telling you anything."

"Oh, yeah?" I reached down, and jerked him to his feet. "You cops are good at dishing it out, let's see how good you can take it." I shoved him back against the wall and got ready to belt him some more.

"Wait . . . Wait . . ." he said, waving his palms at me. "I'll talk . . . I'll talk . . ."

"That's more like it," I said, lightening my tone. "Who—"

He suddenly spun away from me, tearing one of his coat's brass buttons off in the process, and ran for the mouth of the alley.

I tackled him just before he reached the sidewalk. He

went down hard, and I fell on him like a ton of bricks. He yelled for help as I picked him back up.

"This is Chinatown, pal," I said, putting a vise-like half-Nelson on him. "Save your breath. Nobody helps anybody down here. Especially a cop."

As if to reinforce my point, the only folks who'd noticed the commotion, an elderly Chinese couple gawking at us from across the street, immediately hurried on their way without so much as a backward glance.

I hustled Officer Moody back into the privacy of the alley and worked him over.

After I'd used his head for a snare drum, and turned his rib cage into a marimba, he became considerably more talkative.

"The dough was in my locker, it was in my locker with my usual cut," he sputtered, wiping at his bloody lip with the back of one hand.

"Who put it there?" I demanded, keeping my right fist primed a foot from his face.

"Sarge always divvies up the money we squeeze out of the Chinks," he blurted. "I guess it was him. Please, don't hit me anymore . . ."

"I don't like hitting you. It hurts my knuckles. How'd you know who to give it to?"

"Note on the envelope. It said to give it to this joe outside the Ming Palace."

"Who was this guy?"

"I don't know. I swear. I'm just a messenger boy."

"Ever see him before?"

He didn't respond. Stayed uncharacteristically quiet for a canary who'd just started singing so well.

I squeezed his Adam's apple into applesauce with my left, and cocked my right. "Ever see him before?"

"Oh, God . . ." he wheezed. "I got a wife and kids . . ."

"They'll be trying to make ends meet without you in a couple seconds. Answer my question."

"I think he might be a cop. He's a cop, I think," he gasped.

"Yeah?" I loosened up on his neck. "Why do you think that?"

He rubbed at his neck, and took a ragged breath. "I've seen him around."

"Where? When?"

"Around the Station House. Just a few times. With Captain Blevens."

"Blevens, huh? Figures." Now that Moody had started to really spill the beans, I decided to play nice guy: let him loose, offer him a smoke. But his hands were shaking so bad, he couldn't take hold of the fag.

I put it between his lips and gave him a light. "So, what were they doing when you saw them those times? Blevens and this joe?"

He sagged back against the wall, and sucked on his smoke. "They went into the captain's office once. In a big hurry. This joe had his coat collar pulled way up, and his hat down low like he didn't want to be seen." Moody coughed on his cigarette, then continued. "The other time was in the captain's cruiser out front. Last week. They were jawing up a storm. I don't know what about. I just hustled out to my beat."

"This guy ever wear a uniform?" I asked.

"No. Always plainclothes. Why?"

"Just because you saw him with Blevens, it doesn't necessarily follow that he's a cop."

"Except for one thing."

"What's that?"

"I asked my Sarge about him once. The last time, after I spotted them in the car together. Sarge got bent out of shape, said to mind my own beeswax. This guy was high up. A real hush-hush type. I knew well enough to drop it and play dumb. There's been rumors for years about guys like him—they operate on the Q.T., do confidential stuff for the big mucky-mucks. Nothing good ever happens if you get mixed up with them."

"But you did, didn't you?"

"Yeah," he said, "and look what it's got me: I'm all beat to hell, and I still got my whole shift to work in this condition. I don't want nothing to do with this. Please, just lemme go."

"This guy ever go by the name of Weasel?"

"I don't know. I never heard his name."

"Would you recognize him if you saw him again?"

"Not on your life," Moody said, a look of utter fear glazing over his eyes. "And not on mine, either."

I thought about beating him into agreement, but he superseded my argument.

"Look, Rossiter," he said, starting to shake. "You can keep giving me the treatment 'til the cows come home, but at least I don't think you'll kill me. This joe? Hell, I get into this, I'm a dead man for sure. So, hit me all you want, it ain't going to change anything."

The way he said it, I tended to believe him. I hadn't seen anybody so scared since we hit the beach on Guadalcanal.

"Fine," I said, almost feeling sorry that I'd worked him

over so bad. "But I want you to tell your story to a cop pal of mine from downtown headquarters, Lt. Baker."

"No." He shook his head. "All I did was give the envelope to that guy. You know it, and I know it. But anybody else asks, it never happened. None of this happened. I got my wife and kids to think about. I never saw that joe; I never saw you tonight; I walked my beat like usual, and tripped on something and fell down a flight of stairs, and that's how I got all banged up, and that's the end of it."

"You can trust Baker."

"Trust nobody," he told me.

Much as I wanted more out of him, it was good advice.

I gave him my handkerchief to clean himself up, then told him to beat it—but not before telling him that I'd haunt him like a bad hangover if anything he'd told me wasn't on the square.

After Officer Moody had gone, my stomach started rumbling. Working him over *had* given me a bit of an appetite, as well as a certain empty queasiness caused from the new dope I'd beat out of him. The little bit of hunger I'd take care of over dinner with Mrs. Jamison. The queasiness, well, I'd try to settle it down by looking in on Bunny Sunday and Frank Hashimoto up at Seattle General. Any luck, maybe they'd have some skinny that could act like a Bromo Seltzer for my upset gut.

Chapter

18

"WHO ARE YOU, HANDSOME?" ASKED BUNNY Sunday, shapely as could be even in her light blue hospital bathrobe. She sat in the small chair beside her bed smoking a cigarette. Tall, lithe, she didn't have any makeup on—didn't need it—made me wish I could have caught her act last night.

"Jake Rossiter," I said, closing the door behind me.

"You always come into a girl's room without knocking?"

"Only when I can get away with it."

She laughed; had a knock-out smile. "That's a good line, mister." She flicked the ash off her smoke and crossed a pair of perfect legs that were longer than the Lake Washington Floating Bridge. She wore open-toed slippers, and I noticed that she had her toenails painted with the same deep red polish she used on her long fingernails.

"So," she said, giving me the once-over and seeming to approve of what she saw. "You're not a doctor, you're not a nurse, what are you?"

"Private detective."

Her eyes narrowed. "Figures. What am I supposed to have done this time?"

"I'm here about Bubbles."

Bunny looked relieved, then sad. "Poor Bubbles . . ." All of a sudden, she looked sick, like she was going to throw up. She dropped her smoke into the ashtray and reached for the bedpan on her nightstand. Holding it just below her chin, she groaned a couple times but didn't upchuck. As the wave of nausea passed, she set the bedpan back, then slowly climbed into the sack.

"Damn," she said, "I gotta lay down for a minute."

I helped her pull up her covers. "You all right?"

"Yeah," she said, snugging the light wool blanket around her neck, then shivering slightly. "I will be, I think . . . Those stinking clams . . . I'm never eating clam linguini again as long as I live . . ."

"That's what got you, huh?"

"Ugh," she muttered, with another shiver, "don't even talk about it."

I stubbed out her half-finished cigarette, then sat in the chair beside her.

"You feel up to a few questions, now?"

"Poor Bubbles," she said, still with the shivers. "She was my best friend in the whole wide world. Why would somebody go and kill her?"

"That's what I'm trying to find out. Anybody come to mind?"

"Who'd want to hurt her, you mean? No. Everybody loved Bubbles."

"Not everybody," I said, lighting a butt of my own. "She ever have any run-ins with the cops, by chance?"

"Sure. We all have."

"Anything bad?"

"Nah. They come around from time to time with some

trumped-up beef or other, but we do 'em a few favors, if you know what I mean, and we're all copacetic again."

"Bubbles too, huh?"

"Her more than most," she said. "She had a temper, you know, always got PO'd about something or other. When she did, well, she did dumb stuff, like pulling off her pasties last night, always brought attention to herself—lots of attention."

"Way you put it, Bubbles must've dated a number of cops."

"If you can call them dates." She gestured at her smokes, a pack of Pall Malls laying beside the ashtray. "I'm feeling better now; you want to light a smoke for me?"

"It's dangerous to smoke in bed," I said.

"And it's dangerous if I don't get my smokes when I want them," she told me.

I smiled, and dutifully fired up a Pall Mall for her, then passed it over.

She pulled herself up, leaned back against the head-board, and took a deep drag. "Poor Bubbles," she said, exhaling. "She was so excited about going off to Tahiti with Henry."

I leaned in toward her. "You knew about that?"

"Who didn't? Poor kid." She sighed. "Boy, what a dope I was. When he didn't come by to take her to the train station, I told her he probably just had car trouble or something."

"You talked to Bubbles after Henry got killed?"

"She called me. She and I had been on the outs a little when were were both dating Henry, but everything was all patched up, and we were best gals again."

"Let me get this straight," I said. "You were *both* running around with Henry Jamison?"

"Sure, I dated him, too, at first. He was a lot of fun." She shrugged. "Ah, but Bubbles, she ended up with him, of course. Just like she almost always got top billing at the club. I was happy for her, though. She really deserved him."

"Henry spend a lot of money on you two?"

"Loads." She smiled, and held up her left hand, showing me a ruby ring, surrounded by little diamonds, on her middle finger. "Henry gave me this ring. Others, too. He was a generous man. Course, Bubbles, she got tons more—necklaces, bracelets, a real swank mink coat, you name it. He spent money like it was water."

"I see," I said, wondering where all the dough came from. "So, what happened when he didn't show up to get Bubbles?"

"She went nuts. And I mean cuckoo, brother. She called over to his office. No answer. Tried there a few more times, then, finally, she called his house."

"You're kidding . . . She talked to his wife?"

"Yeah. Pretty ballsy, huh? Well, that was Bubbles," she chuckled. "She had a lot of gumption, that was for sure. So, Bubbles was surprised that Mrs. J. didn't seem to know they were leaving together. Anyway, Bubbles said he was supposed to pick her up, and Mrs. J. told her that he'd gone into work early, like always."

"I see."

"Bubbles was beside herself. Thought Henry was lying to her," Bunny continued, scooting up a little further in bed, and adjusting her pillow behind her back. "Started drinking. Then Mrs. J. called her back and told her that Henry was dead. Boy, that was tough."

"Mrs. Jamison called Bubbles and told her about it, huh?"

"Yeah."

"So, even after all that, Bubbles just went right back to work at the club?"

"Well, what's a girl to do? Gotta make a living. She was out of cash, as usual. Counted on Henry for some. Can't blame her for that."

"No, I suppose not," I said. "Tell me, did Henry have any enemies that you know of? Anybody he ever mention to you or Bubbles?"

"Henry? Enemies?" She laughed really hard. "That's rich. He was just an old softy. A real good-time guy. I never heard him say a cross word about anybody at all."

"He never talked about any problems, huh?"

"No. He never even talked bad about his wife. He just wanted to party."

"He ever talk about the Jap businesses he insured?"

"No." She gave me an odd look. "Why should he?" She took a small sip of the water beside her bed and said, "I sure hope you find out who killed Bubbles."

"Me too." Figuring I'd gotten all the info I could, I stood and got ready to leave. "Glad you're feeling better, Bunny," I said. "I'd stay and visit longer, but I ought to scoot."

"Yeah," she said, giving me her knock-out grin again. "I liked talking to you, handsome. Maybe you'll come down and see me at the club sometime."

"Maybe I will, at that." I returned her smile, then went to the door. Getting it open, I paused, and turned around.

"Just out of curiosity," I asked, "what, exactly, did old Henry have that put him in so good with all the dames? He sure didn't look like much."

"Plenty of dough," she said. "And he was a real gentleman. Didn't expect too much."

"If you say so," I said. "See you around."

"Hope so," she told me as I went out.

Frank Hashimoto's room was one floor up. I got off the elevator and checked in at the nurse's station to see how he was doing. They said he was a lucky man. The bullet he'd taken for me had broken two ribs, but had been deflected and just missed puncturing his right lung. He was on morphine, but doing well enough for a visit if I kept it short.

Frank was looking straight up at the ceiling when I walked in, his eyes a bit glassy, an I.V. dripping into one arm, and a huge mess of bandages wrapped around his torso.

"I would've brought you a Purple Heart," I told him, "but I know you've already got several of them."

He focused on me, standing by his bed, and managed a small smile. "Yeah," he said, softly, the effort of speaking causing him some obvious pain, "who needs anymore of those damned things?"

I didn't really know what else to say to a joe who'd just saved my life, so I just said, "Thanks for what you did."

"Don't mention it."

I sat in the small chair beside him, took out my Philip Morrises, and offered him one. "Smoke?"

He nodded, and I stuck two in my mouth, lit them up, and passed one over to him. Like so many wounded jarheads I'd seen during the war, he took that first puff off a smoke like it was some kind of life-giving medicine.

"You feeling O.K.?" I asked.

"I've felt worse."

"Sorry about figuring you for maybe killing Bubbles LaFlamme," I told him. "I found out there's another joe who lights his matches the same way you do."

"He the one who took the shots at you?"

"Good possibility."

Frank didn't say anything.

We smoked in silence for a time.

"So," I said. "Before your store got torched, you ever have any cops come by and try to put the squeeze to you?"

"The usual," he said. "Sure. Our beat cop down there, Moody I think his name was, he put the arm on us for a fin a week. Protection money, you know," he laughed, then groaned and put his hand on his ribs. "Wasn't much protection."

"How about any plainclothes types? Any of those joes ever come around?"

"You're talking about plainclothes cops, right?"

"Roger."

He thought a moment. "No. Not that I recall. Why? You think one of those boys had a hand in burning us out?"

"And putting that slug in you last night, as well."

"Sonofabitch . . ."

"Yeah. I'm doing my best to get a line on him."

"You do," Frank said, "I'd sure like to have first crack at him."

"Fine by me."

He grinned, his lips tight and narrow. "Beyond that, fuck 'em," he said. "I just want my store back."

Frank Hashimoto was a straight talker. Almost made me forget he was a Jap.

"So," I said, "you've got your trial coming up soon. You ready for it?"

"Oh, sure," he sneered. "This public defender I've got has talked to me exactly once. Just long enough to tell me how busy he was, and that he'd get back to me. He never has."

"What's his name?"

"Mullins. George Mullins. Why?"

"I'm going to have my attorney look into it."

His eyes went hard. "I'm not taking any charity."

"You've got a public defender, don't you?"

"It's not the same. Those guys get paid out of our tax dollars."

"Fine. I'll have Haggerty, that's my lawyer, see if he can handle your case pro bono—meaning he'll just take your public defender's place. If he can't, I've already got him on retainer. You can pay me back whenever you can. Least I can do for you stopping that bullet for me."

Frank thought for a minute. "If your lawyer can act as my public defender, O.K.," he said. "If he can't, forget it. I'm not taking money from you or anybody."

"Deal," I said, shaking his hand, and making a mental note to have Haggerty tell him whatever was necessary.

"He does come in on my side," Frank said, "he ought to talk to that damned Fire Department arson investigator. He told me the other day he could get us another five hundred on the insurance if we'd just stop making trouble and settle. He's lying through his teeth, the crooked bastard."

"Yeah, I got that impression."

"You talked to him?"

"Yeah."

"What'd you think?"

"He's lying through his teeth."

Frank's eyes twinkled, and he smiled. Then, all of a sudden, his smile vanished, replaced by the jaw-clamping expression of deep pain that I'd seen too many times during the war. He groaned low and soft.

"You need more morphine?" I asked.

He nodded.

"Hang in there, I'll get somebody."

When I found his nurse out in the hall, she said he wasn't due for another shot for at least an hour. I told her he needed one right now in no damned uncertain terms. She came in and gave Frank another shot, and put a new bag in for his I.V.

He and I shared another smoke, and I hung around long enough for the new morphine to do its job on him. Frank was comfortable again, if a little woozy, when I patted him on the shoulder and told him so long. Then I headed down to the main lobby and found a phone booth.

It was pushing 4:00 when I got hold of my attorney's office. His secretary told me that Haggerty was due back from court any minute, so I left a message for him about taking over Frank Hashimoto's defense, and said that I'd be back in touch in the morning to go over the particulars. That taken care of, I left the hospital, and hopped into my Roadmaster for the short ride to the Olympic Hotel to meet Mrs. Jamison for dinner. I looked forward to a little good chow. As to being the object of her romantic inclinations, well, I didn't much look forward to that, at all.

As luck would have it, something happened as I put my key into the ignition that completely took my mind off of Mrs. Jamison: the cold steel of a gun barrel unexpectedly pressed against the back of my head.

"Don't make a move, Jake," said a familiar voice from the back seat. "You and me got to talk."

Chapter

19

EDDIE VALHALLA. I COULD SEE HIM IN THE rear view mirror. I kicked myself for not checking the back seat before getting into the car.

"I hope you didn't scratch up my paint job jimmying the door lock," I told him, watching him closely in the mirror.

He smiled his tight-lipped smile. "Nah," he said. "I was always a lot better at picking locks than you were; you know that."

"Where's ZaZu?" I asked.

"She's taking care of a little business elsewhere. Nice of you to ask."

"What's on your mind, pal? If you want to finish our fight, it'll have to be later—I've got a dinner date."

He laughed his wicked laugh. "By God, I miss talking to you, big guy. We always got this—what do you call it?— *witty repartee*. But enough of that. We can reminisce some other time. Right now, I'm here to do you a favor."

"Funny way of doing it."

"Oh, the *pistole*, you mean. Here, how's this?" he asked, lowering the gun from my noggin. "Now it's pointing at you through the back of the seat. Wouldn't want any passers-by to notice, and see you taken down like some chump. You'd be all embarrassed."

"I don't embarrass easily," I told him.

"O.K., here's the favor: you need to back off this case, Jake."

"Which one?"

"All of them. They'll kill you and your pretty little Miss Jenkins."

"Haven't yet."

"Count on it. I wouldn't be giving you this warning, but I kind of like you, big guy."

"That's very gracious of you."

"For old time's sake," he told me. "Think nothing of it."

"And if I don't?"

He laughed again. "You always were thick-headed. Take my advice; you've become a target for a whole lot of folks. You don't, here's a little taste of things to come."

Can't say I tasted anything, except for some blood, when I bit my tongue, as he made his point by koshing me over the head with his heavy pistol.

When I came around, my noggin felt like ten bowling pins after somebody had just rolled a strike. But it was only 4:05, so I hadn't been out that long. Eddie had flown the coop, of course, after making his little gesture of friendship, and I had the car all to myself to make the amazing variety of noises that can come out of a person after getting a good bash in the head.

My unpleasant recovery progressing, I merged into traffic at 4:10, and pulled into the Olympic Hotel's parking garage at 4:20—plenty of time to get inside to meet Mrs. Jamison for dinner, while my brain slowly stopped crashing into the sides of my brain-pan.

All that was left was a little residual dizziness, when she spotted me in the dining room and called me over to her table.

"Oh, Mr. Rossiter, you're very prompt. It's so good to see you!" Dressed to the nines in a very low-cut, blue satin evening dress, she stayed seated and proffered her hand, knuckles up and limp-wristed, European-style, like she was expecting me to kiss it. I gave it a good old American-style handshake.

"Where's Vic?" I asked, glancing around the ornate dining room.

"I sent him over to my house to get something for us."

"He took off?" I asked, feeling my blood pressure rise. "To get what?"

Just then, a white-shirted busboy showed up to fill our water glasses. Mrs. Jamison waved him off, saying, "There's no need for that. We'll dine in my room and order from room service."

"Wait a minute," I said. "The deal was that we eat down here, not—"

She stood from the table. "I think you'll want to be in my room."

"Why?"

"I've got something to show you."

"No way."

"It's some notes to go along with Henry's diary."

"Oh, yeah? A diary, huh?"

"Yes. I sent Vic to my house to pick up the diary. It's very important."

I got to my feet. "You never told me Henry kept a diary."

She came around the table and took me by the arm. "Well, it's very personal. He put all his inner thoughts into it."

"Why didn't you just bring these notes down here with you?" I asked, resisting her efforts to lead me out of the dining room.

"Oh, I couldn't bear to have you reading all that down here in public. It would be too embarrassing. Besides, they have to go with the diary. He put down everything in it. Everything. Even right up to the day he was murdered."

"He did, did he?"

"Yes," she said. "Now, please," she tugged at my arm, "won't you come up to my room? We can eat there, while you look over his diary in private when your man gets back."

Still a little wary of this big woman, I was intrigued by the possibilities of Henry Jamison's diary. It might help explain a lot. So, I went along with her to the elevator.

"Floor please?" asked the young blonde elevator operator, seated on her brass stool by the bank of numbered floor buttons.

"The Honeymoon Suite," said Mrs. Jamison, one arm tightening around my waist.

The young blonde smiled and punched the appropriate button. In no time at all, we hit the top floor.

As we walked down the spacious hallway to the Honeymoon Suite, Mrs. Jamison still glomming onto me, I kept thinking about why I hadn't returned to the Olympic those times I needed a hotel room over the years. Even though it was the classiest joint in town, it wasn't the dough. Far from it. It was the memory of ZaZu seducing me, then slipping me a Mickey, and telling Eddie about my secret witness at the Olympic.

Some Freudian shrink once said that when it comes to memory, you tend to remember two things the clearest: the best things that ever happened to you, and the worst things that ever happened to you. Like the war. I had plenty of lousy memories about the war but, believe it or not, I often looked back on it with some true fondness. The war was simple and clear cut. We were the good guys and the Japs were the bad guys. We fought the good fight and won. Nice and neat. But it sure wasn't that way anymore. Things were getting all blurred up—you never knew who might stab you in the back—like ZaZu's sweet kisses before she stuck it to me.

When we got to the door to the Honeymoon Suite, I'd done my best to shake those rotten recollections of ZaZu off. Ever the gentleman, I took Mrs. Jamison's key and unlocked the door for us, telling myself that this beefy woman with the wonderous cleavage in the blue satin evening dress didn't even vaguely resemble the svelte and sultry ZaZu Pinske, except for her big bazooms and having the hots for me, and that when we went into the hotel room, nothing bad was going to happen. I wouldn't let it.

"Sit with me," purred Mrs. Jamison, her voice all throaty, suddenly pulling me onto the rose-colored, chintz divan just inside the suite's living room.

She was big enough to pull me down beside her, but not

quite strong enough to keep me there. I was up and over to the window fast as a fox ducking the hounds.

I pulled out my pocket notebook. "I need to take a few notes. Lot easier to write at the table." I didn't give her time to argue. I beat feet into the dining room, and sat at the mahogany table.

She went to the phone, called room service, and ordered for us. Didn't give me any time to say what I wanted. Just placed the order, then joined me at the table. But instead of sitting across from me, she took the chair right beside me.

"What's this I hear about you calling Bubbles LaFlamme?" I asked, scooting my chair away a bit. "If I remember correctly, you told me you'd never heard of her."

"I never called that woman," Mrs. Jamison said sweetly, making moon-eyes at me. "Let's talk about us."

"You never called Bubbles."

"No. Who said I did?"

"Bunny Sunday."

"Who's she?"

I studied her a moment. Normally, I'm a pretty fair judge of character. Got to be, in my racket. But I couldn't get a make on Mrs. Jamison. She seemed as genuine as real dairy butter sitting next to a slab of pasty-white oleomargarine. However, either she, or Bunny, was feeding me a line.

"I don't like people lying to me, Mrs. Jamison."

She looked hurt. Her eyes watered up, and her lips began to quiver and pout.

"Why do we have to argue?" she asked, holding back the tears. "Men always have to argue . . . I've been so looking forward to seeing you. Can't we just have a nice dinner and enjoy our time together?"

"So, you never called Bubbles," I repeated.

"No," she said, sniffling a bit. "I didn't even know who she was until you told me about her."

"Try this name on for size, then: Edna Patrick. That was Bubbles's real name."

"I didn't know her, I tell you."

"She didn't show up in this diary that Henry kept, huh? You said he put all his inner thoughts into it . . . I find it hard to believe that he wouldn't have mentioned the broad he was running off to Tahiti with."

"Henry would never leave me!" she snapped, jumping up from the table. "Never!" She belted the table top with the ball of her fist. "Never!"

"Whoa! Take it easy."

"How could you say such a thing?" The dam broke, and her tears started to flow fast and furious. "How could you? How could you?"

"Just doing my job," I told her.

She stood there and kept crying, her big bosom just heaving from all her sobbing. Made me feel like a heel again. I never liked making women cry. Not unless there was something I could gain from it. In Mrs. Jamison's case, I felt like I'd gone close to the bottom of the well.

"Look, Mrs. Jamison . . ." I stood, crossed to her side, and put an arm around her. "I'm sorry to have upset you. O.K.? When Vic gets back with that diary, we can hash it all out. Until then, hey, it's dinner time, and it's been a tough day. I eat alone more often than not; it'll be nice to have some company for a change."

"Really?" she asked, locking her moist eyes onto mine.

"Yeah, really. They serve some fine grub in this hotel."

She smiled and gave me a big hug, almost squeezed the stuffing out of me.

"Oh, my goodness," she exclaimed, when she finally let me out of her grasp. "I must look a mess."

"No," I said, thinking she was absolutely right, her mascara running down her puffy red eyes, "you don't look—"

"I better go fix myself up." She wiped her eyes with the backs of her hands, more than a little wet mascara coming off on them in the process. "I'll only be a minute. You listen for room service; we wouldn't want to miss them." With that, she headed lickety-split for the bathroom.

I sat back down and lit a smoke. I actually did hope that room service would show up soon with our meal. My banter with Mrs. Jamison had added yet another quandary to go with all the rest that were swimming around in my head. I always tended to think better on a full stomach. Especially if my cranium wasn't working quite up to par—which, right now, it really wasn't—due to the aftershocks of the bash that Eddie had put to it.

I called the office. The rude warning from Eddie had given me new worries about Miss Jenkins, and I also wondered about her progress on the tasks I'd assigned her. But after three rings nobody answered, and I called the answering service, which informed me there were no messages. I didn't let it bother me too much. It was the end of the work day, after all. So, I tried Miss Jenkins's apartment. No answer there, either. That did cause me a little anxiety. She was in good hands with Manny Velcker; he was a tough nut—but so was Eddie.

My smoke tasted off, so I stubbed it out in the small

ashtray beside the phone and returned to the dining room table. I hated mysteries. Well, that wasn't exactly true, I guess. It's just that I liked my mysteries more straightforward. I liked them black and white, not all gray and ambiguous. But that's what I was smack-dab in the middle of: a big, gray, rotten, convoluted, amorphous mess. I could hardly tell my friends from my enemies, let alone who did what to whom. To tell the truth, I was feeling a little powerless. If I was an author, I could just paste it all together, even in a slap-dash fashion like the pulp detective stories that Miss Jenkins was so fond of reading, and be done with it. It wouldn't really matter if all the loose ends were tied up, and everything made perfect sense. The story would be done, and the mystery solved. Nice and neat.

But I wasn't an author. I was a real-life private eye. I dealt with the vagaries and deceits of the real world, and knew that some mysteries never did get solved. Which made me sometimes wish that I'd stuck to the ring. At least with boxing, you get a simple decision: you either win or you lose.

A knock at the door interrupted my reveries: room service, with a cart full of silver-lidded trays, smelling of the juicy steaks I used to train on before a bout, complete with a big ice bucket holding a large bottle of champagne.

We got it all set up on the dining room table, and I was just letting out the young joe who'd brought it, when Mrs. Jamison made her entrance from the bathroom. She wore a sheer pink negligee and robe combo, which exposed a whole lot of pudgy leg, and even more bosom.

"I thought I should be more comfortable," she said, then noticed that the chow had arrived. "Oh, my!" She clapped her hands "What a feast! Henry and I had this very same meal on our wedding night. Isn't it wonderful? Come sit down, Jake, and let's enjoy ourselves."

Shutting the door, I noted that she'd called me Jake for the very first time ever. Normally, I might've gotten my guard up, but I was damned hungry, and the T-bone steaks looked damned good. I needed to eat well to stay in shape until the final bell rang on the big bout I was in.

I poured us some bubbly, and got my fork and steak knife into action.

Mrs. Jamison took a bite big enough to choke a whole herd of horses, chewed mightily, and said, "Very tender, isn't it? You know, steak is the first thing that Henry had when he got back from the Pacific. He said that every time he opened a K-ration, he dreamed of a nice prime steak, and just couldn't believe he was actually having one again."

"Henry was in the war?" I asked. "I thought he sat out the war, 4-F."

"He was 4-F," she said, forking in another massive piece of meat. "Had a ruptured eardrum. But he begged them and begged them—wanted to do his duty. He was very patriotic, you know. Finally, they needed men so bad, they let him in the Army. Put him in supply & logistics because he was so good with numbers." She paused, and washed her steak down with a draught of champagne. "Poor Henry," she continued, "he was only in for five months, and then the war ended. At least he'd had a chance to serve his country. He brought home oodles of souvenirs and went right back into his insurance business a happy man."

"Well, I'll be damned," I commented, enjoying my own

steak immensely, and picturing mousey little Henry in an entirely new light. "Old Henry's just full of surprises. Who'd a thunk it? He never talked about being in the war."

"He was like that. Quiet. Very unassuming about his own accomplishments."

"Well," I said, raising my champagne glass. "Here's to Henry."

She clinked her glass into mine. "Here's to us, Jake," she responded, her eyes aglow.

Brother, we were back to that. I guess I knew that she'd eventually return to the subject, but had hoped that I could at least finish my meal and manage a gracious exit without hurting her feelings anymore. That looking doubtful, I tried to change the course of the conversation.

"Where's Vic with that diary?" I asked. "I've got to be leaving soon."

"Oh, he'll be back sooner or later. You've got to at least stay until then."

"I've got places to be," I told her.

"But Henry's diary is important."

"Yeah."

"Don't worry," she said, with a warm smile. "For now, this is our special time together."

I locked eyes with her. "Look, Mrs. Jamison . . . Don't get all upset and wig out again, huh? But level with me, will you? Does that diary really exist, or was it just a ploy to get me up here?"

She didn't bat an eyelash, just kept smiling, and got up and came around to my side of the table.

"Let me cut your steak for you, Jake," she said, suddenly

sitting in my lap. She tried to take hold of my fork and knife. "I always cut Henry's steak for him," she cooed in my ear.

She weighed a ton. "I can take care of my own steak."

She pressed into me even more. "Let me do it for you, Jake."

By God, she had me squashed and almost completely trapped, her hot breath sizzling my right earlobe like a flapjack on the griddle. Now I knew what a dame must feel like on a bad first date with a masher. "Get off of me, Mrs. Jamison."

"Oh, Jake . . . Jake . . ."

She was all over me. All two hundred pounds of her. I was just thinking that I might have to knock her on her can, when she put me in a head-lock. Then she twisted me around and put me in a lip-lock, too. I tried to pull away, but the way she had hold of me, there wasn't going to be any removal of her flypaper lips without some ungentlemanly fisticuffs.

Lucky for both parties concerned, Manny Velcker started pounding on the door.

"Jake, Jake!" he yelled. "We got problems!"

I got my lips away from Mrs. Jamison long enough to holler, "Manny! Help!"

I heard him struggling to open the door, while I struggled with Mrs. Jamison. He kicked it open just as we fell to the floor, taking the tablecloth and half the dinner plates with us.

"Jeez!" Manny seemed dumbfounded when he saw what was going on.

"Get her off me," I gasped.

"No, no," she grunted, on top of me, slobbering all over my kisser, and squeezing the bejesus out of me.

Manny ran over, managed to put her in a half-Nelson, and dragged her off of me.

I got to my feet, straightened out my sports coat and tie, and tried to shake off my embarrassment. Just as I thanked my operative for saving me, Mrs. Jamison went limp in his arms and started to sob hysterically. "What's going on, Manny? Why aren't you with Miss Jenkins? What's wrong?"

"She's got herself in a jam and doesn't know it," he said, struggling to support Mrs. Jamison. "Damn, this broad's a real load."

"I'm sorry, I'm sorry . . ." blubbered Mrs. Jamison, sagging toward the floor.

"Here," I said, grabbing her under one arm, "let's set her down someplace."

Manny and I got her seated at the dining table, where she continued her hysterics while we spoke.

"What kind of jam? Where the hell's Miss Jenkins?" I asked Manny.

"Chinatown," he said, getting his fedora set back straight on his head. "Down at this joint called the Ming Palace."

"Judas Priest! And you left her there?"

"Didn't have any choice," he explained. "After the Hall of Records, we went all over town trying to dig into the info we got, then she insisted on going to Chinatown and poking around everywhere—ended up outside the store those Japs, the Hashimotos, used to run. We barely got there, when this dish with Betty Grable gams and long platinum-blonde hair walks up to us."

"*ZaZu Pinske*," I said, feeling my blood run cold.

"Yeah," Manny said, lighting up a Lucky Strike. "I hadn't ever met her before, but that's who she said she was, alright. Anyway, she tells Miss Jenkins that she's got some important dope for her—wants her to come along to that Ming Palace joint to discuss it over drinks. I tell Miss Jenkins it's a bad idea. But she tells me she can take care of herself."

Before I knew it, I was poking him in the chest, and yelling, "Sonofabitch, Manny! And you just let her go?!"

"Hey, cut it out!" he squawked, swatting my hand away. "What d'ya think? I'd just let her go off with ZaZu? Hell, no. I know you two are lovebirds. Natch—I was gonna tag along."

"Why didn't you?"

"Well, if you'd let me explain," he said, tapping his smoke into the ashtray beside Mrs. Jamison, who had stopped her crying jag and turned around to listen to us. "This big, black sedan pulls up, and ZaZu and Miss Jenkins get into the back seat. I start to get in, too, but ZaZu slams the door on me, and the driver, this big, greasy mug I never met, he sticks a rod in my face and tells me I'm not invited. Then they speed off."

"So, you came here to find me."

"Not right off the bat. What d'ya think, I'm some rank amateur? Shit, I ran my ass all over Chinatown 'til I found that Ming Palace place. I went inside, but no Miss Jenkins. Hell, I thought she'd been kidnapped for sure . . . But, then I saw these four well-dressed Chinamen come in and make a beeline straight to the back of the joint, then disappear down this hall leading to the johns. Well, I'm thinking it's kind of odd that the four of 'em would head directly to the men's can, you know, so I get on their tails and spot 'em just going through this little, narrow, green door at the end of the hallway. I get a glimpse of this big Chink, about the size of King Kong, standing on the landing just inside the door. He closes it from the inside after they've gone in. So, I try the door, but it's locked. I knock at it, but nobody answers. I press my ear to it, and I can just make out the faint sound of music and laughter. None of the other Chinks working in the place will tell me anything about it, let alone even admit that that door goes anywhere. I figure Miss Jenkins must be in there. It's gotta be like an opium den or one of those illegal gambling joints, you know? I didn't know what to do. Then I called over to the office, and Vic was there. He said this Jamison dame had sent him away from the hotel again on a wild goose chase. So, then I hightail it up here to find you."

"You did the right thing," I told him. "C'mon, Manny, we're hitting the bricks straight to the Ming Palace."

I turned to Mrs. Jamison, about to tell her to keep the door locked while we were gone, but she spoke first.

"Is Miss Jenkins your sweetheart?" she asked me, her face all puffy from crying so much.

My first inclination was to say no—hell no, we'd only dated a few times. But I bit my tongue. Maybe if Mrs. Jamison thought I was totally serious about Miss Jenkins, she'd leave me alone. So, I lied.

"Yeah," I told her. "As a matter of fact, I'm thinking about asking Miss Jenkins to marry me."

"Oh . . ." said Mrs. Jamison, all the wind going out of her

sails. "Ohhhh . . . ." she repeated, the word coming out like all the air from a balloon being deflated.

As Manny and I went out the door, I felt that my ploy had been very successful.

"Jeez, Jake," he said, while we rushed for the elevator. "I knew you and Miss Jenkins were sweet on each other, but I didn't have a clue you were gonna pop the question to her."

"Shut up, Manny," I said, reaching the elevator and stabbing at the down button. "Just shut up and forget it, understand?"

He gave me a queer look as the door opened, and we stepped inside.

Chapter

20

I BURNED HALF THE RUBBER OFF THE Roadmaster's tires getting to the Ming Palace. Velcker told me he hadn't seen anybody matching Eddie Valhalla's description anywhere around when Miss Jenkins had split with ZaZu. I said where ZaZu went, Eddie was sure to follow, and asked if he was carrying more firepower than the snub-nosed .38 he usually had in his shoulder holster. He said, yeah: blackjack, switchblade, and a small .32 caliber automatic in his jacket's inside pocket. Good, I said, that pretty well matched my own backup arsenal, and we might just need every one of our weapons before the night was through. Velcker nodded grimly and checked the ammo in both of his rods, while I screeched to a halt at the pay phone booth outside Warshall's Sporting Goods just north of Pioneer Square and put in a fast call for Lt. Baker.

Like I figured, he'd already gone for the day. I left a message for him with the desk sergeant, anyway. Told him to try to get hold of Baker and have him meet me at the Ming Palace. It was urgent. But no, I wouldn't say what it was about. It was for the lieutenant's ears only. Then I piled back into the Roadmaster, and we blew the last eight blocks to the Ming Palace so fast I barely had time to shift into third gear.

Before we went in, Velcker told me that Miss Jenkins had dug up the name of some holding company based in Hawaii. It was called Kajimura Enterprises, and the Chinamen who'd taken over all the former Jap businesses in Seattle were sending it buckets of dough week after week.

I asked how she'd found that out. Velcker said that they'd gone into most of the old Jap joints, and, at a couple of them, he'd been able to keep the owners occupied while Miss Jenkins slipped back to their offices and sneaked a peek at some of their accounting ledgers.

Well, he'd never been very good with numbers, himself, but even he could see what Miss Jenkins pointed out about their revenues. Both places where she'd been able to peek at the books, a fish market and a small restaurant, listed their weekly revenues at over thirty grand. No way could little joints like that be turning that many dollars. They'd be lucky if they could do five hundred to a grand in weekly volume. What's more, they were sending over twenty-five thousand a week in profits to this Kajimura Enterprises company.

Hell, no question about it, Velcker told me, these places were part of some kind of money laundering scheme. Probably all the former Jap-owned joints were. At the end of the day, he and Miss Jenkins were just about to break into the Hashimotos' old store to verify their theory, when ZaZu showed up.

"I knew there had to be some kind of scheme," I said, checking my own ammo.

"Can't say I did, Jake. Not until Miss Jenkins put it all together. She's a real bulldog, huh?"

"She is at that, *compadre*. Problem with bulldogs, though, is sometime they bite down and don't know when to let go." I slid my .45 back into its holster. "Let's go, Manny. See if we can spring this particular bulldog from the pound."

"Roger," he said, as we got out of the car.

We took a quick gander through the Ming Palace's slightly fogged-up front window; saw that the joint was doing a pretty fair business this evening—almost full-up with sailors and other johns for the B-girls to party with—but saw no sign of Miss Jenkins in the throng. As we opened the front door to go in, the place's raucous revelry and loud swing music spilling out at us, Velcker threw me a wink, and said, "Yeah, Jake, you better watch out. That Miss Jenkins is a pretty sharp operator. Way she cut to the heart of this case, and considering you and her are about to get hitched, she might just end up being top dog around the Rossiter Agency one day."

I responded by giving him no response whatsoever. Just bulled my way through the crowd, Velcker in my slip stream, back to the rear corridor that led to the lavatories. We got to the green door so quick that none of the B-girls had a chance to try and sink their hooks into us.

I rapped at the door—just for the hell of it, tried the secret knock that had been popular at so many speakeasies during my old bootlegging days: "Da, da, da-da!" went my knuckles against the thick and solid wood.

Lo and behold, it was still popular. The door opened and swung outward about a foot. The huge Chinaman Velcker had mentioned gave me a quick eyeball from the other side.

Just as he realized I wasn't on the approved guest list, I threw a straight shot to his larynx with the knuckles of my right hand. He clutched at his throat, gurgled, but didn't cry out. Couldn't. I'd bruised his voice-box so bad, he'd be lucky if he could manage a whisper over the next couple days.

Jerking the door open, I sent the big Chink off to dreamland with a judo chop to the base of his neck. Like Mrs. Jamison, he was a hell of a load, but Velcker and I managed to set him down gently on the landing, so he wouldn't draw any attention by crashing to the floor. Then we headed down the steep stairwell to crash ZaZu's party.

We descended three flights of stairs in all. Must have gone two full stories below the Ming Palace before we reached the entrance to what turned out to be a large, illegal gambling club. All those flights of stairs made sense, I thought, as I took a quick peek into the big room in the joint's sub-basement: if they got raided, it would take the authorities quite awhile to reach the gambling den proper, leaving the proprietors, and guests, plenty of time to get out through a secret exit.

The room was about forty by forty feet square, with bare, red brick walls, deep maroon, Oriental carpeting, and a large, ornately carved teak bar. The bar had brass footrails, complete with an enormous beveled mirror, set between the well-stocked racks of hooch, which reflected the multitude of folks, mostly well-dressed Chinese, who were plying their luck at the various gaming tables—roulette, poker and blackjack, one long craps table, and a couple others set up for mah jong.

At first, I didn't spot Miss Jenkins, and my heart sank. Then I glimpsed Eddie Valhalla, dressed in a black tux, having an animated conversation at a white linen-covered round table set up at the far end of the room. I couldn't see who else he was seated with. Too many people in the way. I changed my viewpoint slightly and caught a glimpse of Eddie's companions: ZaZu, resplendent in a shocking red, Chinese-style silk gown, and none other than Miss Jenkins, in her print dress, sitting smack-dab between the two of them, having herself a glass of bubbly like she was just out on the town for a good time.

"You see them?" I asked Velcker.

"Yeah, I see 'em. That's the broad who grabbed Miss Jenkins, alright. That joe must be Eddie Valhalla, huh?"

"In the flesh," I said, noting that Eddie was drinking straight shots from a bottle he had at the table. Probably his loco cactus juice. Not a good sign. He smiled as he spoke to Miss Jenkins, but I knew he smiled when he shot people, too.

"Miss Jenkins seems to be enjoying herself," said Velcker.

"Appearances can be deceiving."

"How do you want to play this?"

"Let's walk right up and join the party," I told him. "Keep your right hand on that .32 in your pocket, so they know we mean business. Any funny stuff, you take ZaZu, I'll take Eddie."

"Roger."

Velcker's hand went straight to his pocket; then we weaved our way across the crowded gambling floor and up to Eddie's table.

"Hey, big guy," said Eddie, spotting me about twenty feet away. "Fancy meeting you here," he continued, grinning crazily as we approached.

We stopped in front of the table. Neither Eddie nor ZaZu reached for any weapons. Both just smiled at us. Miss Jenkins, however, stopped smiling.

"You all right?" I asked her.

"I was just getting somewhere." She sounded annoyed.

"Yeah," said ZaZu. "We've been having quite a conversation."

"Pull up a chair and join us," said Eddie. "Your Miss Jenkins is a real Crackerjack."

Velcker and I sat down—him, across from ZaZu; me, across from Eddie, who was still grinning, even though his eyes were dead serious, alert and ready for any sudden moves.

"Yeah, a real Crackerjack," Eddie repeated, following it up with a burst of high-pitched, crazy laughter. "She's been sitting here pumping us for info. Doesn't have a clue what kind of pickle she's in."

Miss Jenkins's sulky expression didn't change, but Eddie's last statement did cause her eyes to dart toward him, then over at ZaZu, and finally to me, where they stayed, and rapidly blinked three times, like she was thinking, *Uh-oh* . . .

"She carries an awfully big gun for such a little lady," ZaZu said, her voice smooth as satin. "A .44 caliber Ruger. My goodness," she continued, "it's so heavy, I've got it sitting in my lap as we speak."

Velcker suddenly became even more alert.

Miss Jenkins's head snapped toward ZaZu. "You took my pistol?"

ZaZu grinned, her teeth so white, and her smile so fetching and bright for such a dangerous dame. "You left your purse beside you on the floor, *dah-ling*. I'm just naturally curious."

"Like your little lady, Jake," said Eddie, snapping his fingers at the nearby waiter, telling him to bring over two more glasses. "Too curious, by half." He jerked his head toward ZaZu and spit, "Why'd you have to bring her here? Couldn't you leave well enough alone?!"

"Eddie, Eddie," cooed ZaZu, "I'm just watching out for you, you silly boy."

"This is nothing but a frigging complication! Frigging-fucking-complication!" Eddie yelled, glancing back to me. "Wouldn't be such a dilemma if ZaZu hadn't been so loose-lipped," he mused, communing with two rapid shots of tequila in a row.

ZaZu smoothed her long hair back, and told him, "I was just toying with her, Eddie."

"Yeah, like a cat with a bird," he sniped at her. "Always with the claws out . . ." He tossed down another shot. "Fuck! Who needs this?" He riveted his eyes to mine. "I've got an important man coming any minute. Maybe it won't really matter," he told me, like I knew what he was talking about. "Maybe then you can all go . . . Yeah, that might be O.K. after all . . ."

Just then, the waiter arrived with the glasses for Velcker and me. Eddie tipped him a whole fin from the dough he had sitting in front of him, then sent the joe on his way.

"Who's this person you're expecting?" I asked Eddie.

"Eddie," said ZaZu. "That won't do. Miss Jenkins knows too much."

"Only because you told her!" He slammed a fist into the

table—everything on it bounced, but nothing spilled. "You don't like them being a pair, do ya? You don't like that Miss Jenkins has obviously got the hots for the big guy. You still want Jakey-boy for yourself. You wanted her to know too much so that we'd have to rub her out."

"She was getting onto us anyway," ZaZu said. "Why delay the inevitable?"

Miss Jenkins just sat there looking embarrassed and scared.

Likewise, me.

Velcker, however, had to put in his two cents.

"Well, they *are* getting married," he said, as if that bone-headed statement would've somehow defused the situation.

"We're *what*?!" exclaimed Miss Jenkins.

"It's all a misunderstanding," I told her. "I'll explain later."

"Nah," Eddie told ZaZu. "We might not have to go to extremes." He checked his wristwatch. "Then, again, we might. Hard to say."

I thought about drawing on him right then, but Eddie was as quick with a rod as I was, and I had to consider that ZaZu had Miss Jenkins's .44 in her lap. Instead, I offered a suggestion in order to buy some time for a better opportunity.

"What, exactly, does Miss Jenkins know?" I asked. "Maybe I can help sift through it and see if we can all go home safely tonight."

"Yes," ZaZu told Miss Jenkins. "Tell him." She tossed off a shot of vodka. "I'd like Jake to know."

Miss Jenkins hesitated.

"Yeah, go ahead, sister," Eddie told her. "Tell him. The

big guy's trying to figure some way out of this mess. So am I. For once, we agree on something. Anyhow, ZaZu gets her way all too often."

"Well," said Miss Jenkins, taking a quick sip of her champagne. "To start with, Eddie was brought out here to kill Henry Jamison."

"But I didn't get the chance," said Eddie. "Somebody beat me to it."

"Who?"

"Damned if I know." He swirled his tequila around in the shot glass before drinking it. "Whoever it was sure did have some snappy sense of style, now, didn't they?"

"So, who are you expecting?" I asked him again. "Guy named Weasel I suppose."

"The Weasel?" Eddie laughed. "Nah. As far as I know, he had one job and one job only—which was taking care of Bubbles 'cause maybe she knew too much."

"That so?"

"Yeah. Forget the Weasel. Once he did his work, his services were no longer required. We'll just let the joe I'm waiting for be a surprise to you, Jake."

"Who hired you, Eddie?" I asked.

"Quit pressing me!" he snapped. "Anyway, you're interrupting Miss Jenkins. She's been doing a nice job with the story. Let her tell it."

"I don't know everything that's going on," said Miss Jenkins. "But it has to do with those former Japanese businesses and the money laundering."

"How?" Velcker asked.

"Henry Jamison was blackmailing the big Kahuna in Hawaii."

"Kajimura, huh?" I asked, thinking about what Velcker had told me about Kajimura Enterprises in Hawaii.

"Doesn't matter," said Eddie. "With Jamison and my upcoming visitor out of the picture, there won't be any proof."

"This is a set-up, isn't it, Eddie?" I asked. "You're going to rub this joe out."

He grinned wickedly. "Keep on with your story, Miss Jenkins. It's a good one."

"Was it Kajimura that Jamison was blackmailing?" I asked her.

"Oh, yes," she said, taking another sip of bubbly. "Kajimura runs this big drug and gambling and prostitution empire from Hawaii. Still kept running it during the war because they didn't intern any Japanese Americans in Hawaii. But when he heard about the internment on the West Coast, he saw an opportunity to expand to the states. He scooped up Japanese American stores and such for a song. The people who managed to hold onto their businesses until they got out of the camps, well, he just burned them out and took them over anyway. Like the Hashimotos."

"You mean this Jap, Kajimura, has been taking advantage of his own people?" asked Velcker.

"Keep going, *dah-ling*," said ZaZu. "You're doing wonderfully. She knows ever so much, doesn't she, Eddie?" asked ZaZu, making a slit-your-throat sign as she spoke.

Eddie frowned.

Miss Jenkins swallowed hard.

"Oh, Jake," said ZaZu. "You don't think I want to kill her because of you, do you? It's really only because I'm naturally mean."

"You'll have to go through me first," I told her.

"Yeah, that's the problem, old buddy," said Eddie. "You come butting in like this, it doesn't leave much leeway. Think hard for a solution. We're coming down to the wire. My man's going to be here any minute. No way to change it. I can't see any way out for the three of you, as it stands. That'd be a real shame."

I drank a shot of tequila—didn't like it anymore than our situation.

"Tell me about Jamison," I said. "I know he was connected to those Jap businesses through his insurance company, but how was he working this blackmail and why?"

"That one's easy," said Eddie. "Jamison was hand-in-glove with Lt. MacDonald, the chief arson investigator. MacDonald's the one who set all those fires. You need an expert torch-man, you hire an expert!" he cackled. "After the Jap places burned, Jamison would only offer a tiny little settlement, and most of 'em took it. Those that didn't, like Frank Hashimoto, got threatened with arson charges. Pretty sweet, huh?"

"A package deal," said ZaZu.

"Yeah," Eddie laughed. "Then Kajimura's people offered the joints to Chinamen. They're glad to have their own little businesses, and all they had to do in return was run bunches of the combine's dirty dough through to clean it up. So everybody's happy, see?"

"It's just terrible," said Miss Jenkins.

"A real tragedy," mocked ZaZu.

"And what's more," Miss Jenkins said, leaning toward me across the table, "Henry Jamison never really filed any insurance claims on behalf of those poor Japanese people.

He couldn't have if he wanted to: he'd been pocketing their premiums for years."

"Henry was a sucker for a pretty girl," said ZaZu. "He spent too much on all his dames, then got greedy, saw an opportunity to make a bundle blackmailing Mr. Kajimura through MacDonald, then run off to the South Seas to live the life of Riley."

"He wanted a quarter million," said Eddie, putting away more tequila. "Little bastard. I was supposed to deliver the money to him the morning he got killed. Too bad. It was just a ruse, of course."

"Yes, it's a tragedy," said ZaZu, obviously enjoying herself.

Eddie suddenly smiled and pointed off to my right. "Better watch your back, Jake. Somebody's coming up behind you who wants to have a word with you."

I turned, saw the big Chinese gorilla who manned the door making a beeline toward me. But before I could get up to face him, Eddie put up a hand and stopped him in his tracks.

"Lay off!" he ordered.

The Chinaman halted about ten feet from me, tried to argue about it, but his voice wasn't much more than a whisper.

"I ain't telling you again," Eddie told him. "One word from me, your boss'll have you on a boat back to Shanghai in a heartbeat. Now, get back to the door and do a better job of watching it. *Comprende*?"

The man grumbled, but did as he was told—however, not before giving me a look that said, *I'll get you yet*.

As the big ape lumbered back to his post, Eddie said,

"Boy, Jake, you got a real knack, don't you? Everywhere you go, you got people gunning for you."

"Clean living," I said.

Eddie howled, like he thought that was the funniest line since Rochester and Jack Benny got together. When he stopped laughing, he had tears in his eyes, and said, "Damn, it's too bad you and me parted ways."

"We're going to part ways, again," I told him. "Like right now. Nice of you to give me all the skinny, but the only way I see out of this dilemma is for us to leave. Unless you try to stop us."

"What we got here," Eddie said, his eyes narrowing to the thinnest of slits, "is a Mexican standoff." We all stared at each other for a brief moment, still seated at the table, trying to figure our next moves.

"Only we're holding all the cards," said ZaZu, all of a sudden grabbing a handful of Miss Jenkins's hair, and jerking my startled junior partner close to her.

"Owww!" yelped Miss Jenkins, taking hold of ZaZu's wrist, and pulling herself away. "I'm not afraid of you, you witch!" she yelled in ZaZu's face.

Out of nowhere, ZaZu snapped open a six-inch stiletto and held it up to Miss Jenkins's nose. "Maybe you better be," she hissed.

Miss Jenkins froze.

I tensed.

"Hey," said Velcker.

"Cut it!" Eddie ordered ZaZu.

ZaZu smiled. "That's just what I intend to do, darling," she said, waving the thin, double-edged blade.

Then Miss Jenkins surprised me. Up came her left, and

batted the knife aside, followed by her right fist, with a straight belt smack into ZaZu's kisser—knocking her onto the floor as the stiletto went flying. The .44 from ZaZu's lap went clunk under the table. Miss Jenkins pounced on ZaZu, and they began rolling around on the carpet, screaming and tearing at each other's hair, as the various gamblers around the joint all stopped and watched in stunned silence.

I came out of my own shock and started to stand up, worried that Miss Jenkins was pretty petite compared to the taller, and infinitely meaner, ZaZu Pinske. But Eddie quick-drew his pistol and had the drop on Velcker and me before I could get to my feet.

He laughed his crazy staccato cackle and said, "Let 'em fight. This is rich."

ZaZu quickly got the better of it and yanked Miss Jenkins to her feet by her curly, strawberry blonde locks. Miss Jenkins kicked her in the shin: once, twice, thrice! ZaZu let go of her hair.

"Witch!" screamed Miss Jenkins and tackled her like a midget football linebacker.

Down they went again—arms and legs and feet and fists flying everywhere. They made screeching sounds like two alley cats fighting. ZaZu scratched Miss Jenkins across the cheek. Miss Jenkins came back with claws of her own, routing out four, deep, bloody furrows across her opponent's forehead.

"Damn," said Eddie. "Your little lady's a real bearcat."

"Sure as hell is," hollered Velcker, rooting Miss Jenkins on like he was attending a championship boxing match. "Give it to her! Use your right! Smack her again!"

Miss Jenkins and ZaZu got to their feet once more, bruised, bloodied, and battered. Their hair and clothes a torn mess, they circled each other like a couple bantamweights. ZaZu suddenly lunged for the stiletto laying near our table. But Miss Jenkins stopped her in her tracks with one of the sweetest combinations I'd ever seen: doubled up on the left jab, threw a right cross into ZaZu's chin, then finished her off with a damned decent left hook.

ZaZu was completely flattened. K.O.'d, she sprawled on her back on the floor, her arms and legs all akimbo.

"Judas . . ." mumbled Velcker, as amazed as I was.

"Where'd you ever learn to box?" I asked Miss Jenkins, who stood over her fallen foe, fire still in her eyes.

"Sugar Joe's Gym," she told me, breathing heavily, as the crowd of gamblers whistled and applauded. "I figured I should learn some self-defense after you made me your partner."

"Well, I'll be damned . . ." I said.

"Likewise," Eddie muttered, still keeping Velcker and me covered. "Never seen old ZaZu lose a fight before—fair or otherwise."

"How about you, Eddie?" I asked. "You want to do the same? Just you and me? Settle this man to man?"

"Love to, Jake." He gave me his wicked grin; didn't bother to help ZaZu. "But you know I can't. Got my professional duties to attend to." Something drew his attention at the far end of the room, and he quickly focused on it. "Well, well, speaking of which, here he comes now."

I turned, still half expecting the Weasel no matter what Eddie had said—was pretty surprised to see Lt. MacDonald, the arson investigator, entering the joint. He wore civilian clothes, a light sports coat, dark shirt, and casual slacks. He slowly made his way through the crowd, looking around like he was trying to find somebody.

Eddie slid his pistol under the table. "I still got you covered, Jake. You turn back around and face me and play dumb. You, Miss Jenkins, sit down, and do the same." She took a seat, fairly close, I noted, to where the stiletto lay near ZaZu. "MacDonald hasn't caught sight of me yet," Eddie continued. "When he does, keep your traps shut. He might get edgy seeing you here with me."

"You *are* going to kill him, aren't you?" asked Miss Jenkins, using a napkin to dab at the crimson scratches across her cheek.

Eddie just smiled.

"You can't shoot him in here with all these witnesses," she said.

"This is Chinatown, doll," he said. "Not one of these Chinamen will say a word."

I couldn't let Eddie kill MacDonald without trying to stop him. I put my hands in my lap, and brought them up until they touched the bottom of the table. Even if I took a bullet in the process, I'd toss the table in his face before he could take his shot.

"Hey, Valhalla," said MacDonald, coming up behind me. "I don't know why you're still in town, but what's so important that you got me down here? You and me shouldn't even be seen together."

To hell with Eddie's warning. I turned my head around and faced the good lieutenant. "You better dive for cover," I told him.

"Rossiter!" shouted MacDonald, taking two quick steps

back. "Going to feed me to the wolves, huh, Valhalla?" He produced a small automatic from his front pocket and pointed it at me. I was surprised that Eddie hadn't tried to bring his gun up and take his shot—he easily could have.

The gamblers around us started yelling in Chinese and ran for the far end of the room.

"Fuck you!" yelled MacDonald, thinking he had the drop on us. "I'm not going to be anybody's patsy! You're dead!" he screamed at me, starting to squeeze the trigger. "You meddling private-dick-sonofabitch!"

I ducked and reached for my .45, even though I knew I'd be too late, when, *Bam-Bam*! two quick shots convinced me that I'd gone to meet my maker.

But I was still alive.

The smoking pistol in Eddie's hand gave evidence to that fact.

Lieutenant MacDonald lay in a heap on the floor. There were two, dark holes right between his eyes.

"You saved my life," I told Eddie.

"Yup," he said, blowing the smoke off the barrel of his gun. "Clear cut case of defending you, big guy."

"By God, Eddie . . ." Now I realized why he had held his fire. "You knew MacDonald would wig out, didn't you? Knew he might try to shoot me."

"Figured it was a good possibility, Jake." He started with his crazy cackling laugh, and went over and helped ZaZu to her feet. "See," he told me, as ZaZu leaned on him, "I'm always trying to look out for you. So, I've done my job, MacDonald's out of the way, and there's no solid links left whatsoever to me or my employer. Thanks, Jake, it was almost like the old days. We was always real good together. Like they say: *All's well that ends well.*"

Just then, a shot rang out. Eddie's gun flew out of his hand, and he crumpled to the floor, taking ZaZu down with him, a huge, gaping hole in his shoulder. He moaned, barely able to move.

"Don't even think about reaching for your rods," Captain Blevens ordered Velcker and me. Where he'd come from, I didn't know, what with all the commotion going on. But here he was: greasy Captain Blevens advancing on us with a big revolver in each hand, smiling like the cat that just ate the canary.

"Take 'em out, and drop 'em, boys," he told us.

As Velcker and I laid down our pistols, the last of the gamblers beat feet out of the joint. Blevens stepped up to Eddie's prostrate form, his huge, fat figure towering over Miss Jenkins, who was still in her seat beside him.

"You look like you been through hell, little lady," the captain told her.

"I have," Miss Jenkins said.

Blevens kicked Eddie in the side. While he writhed in pain, Blevens smiled and said, "Rossiter, you look about as surprised to see me as old Valhalla, here."

"It's always a pleasure," I told him.

"Your wit's about to come to an end, wiseacre." He glanced back down at Eddie. "Thanks for doing the jobs for us, Valhalla. But now that MacDonald's out of the way, I've been assigned to put you out of the way. Won't be any connections to anybody left, especially not to Mr. Kajimura. Ain't it sweet?"

Blevens pointed the pistol in his left hand at Eddie's head, while keeping the one in his right trained on us. "Course, I'll have to kill all of you, too. But I can live with that. Now, say your prayers, you'll need—"

Miss Jenkins made a quick movement.

Blevens noticed it and aimed his guns at her. But before he could shoot, she'd already scooped the stiletto off the floor and poised it to throw. With a sudden flick of her wrist, Miss Jenkins sent the wicked blade flying. The stiletto seemed to hang in the air for a moment, then found its mark. Blevens gasped—froze in position. His eyes bulged in disbelief as he looked down at the handle of the stiletto that had just plunged straight into his heart. Then his eyes went blank, and he fell over backwards, the stiletto's black ebony handle wiggling for a moment as he lay still and stared up into nothingness.

"I had to do it. I'm sorry," said Miss Jenkins, her face white as a ghost, her words coming out in a monotone.

I took her in my arms. "I'm not," I said, just before I kissed her.

Chapter

21

THE NEXT MORNING DAWNED EARLY AND bright. Too early and too bright. Even though everybody I cared about was safe, I'd been in a blue funk about the way things had turned out. Lt. Baker and Heine had blown in to the rescue, a day late and a dollar short, just after Miss Jenkins had stuck the pig-sticker to Captain Blevens. Heine had been chasing his tail around after losing Eddie and ZaZu for the umpteenth time, and had finally gone back to the office to wait and see if I called or showed up, when Baker called to see if anybody was there who could shed some light on why I needed him down to the Ming Palace. So, they hooked up together. The rest is history, like they say.

Anyway, when all was said and done, Baker and Henie and me all had a real case of the blues. Sure, we'd cracked the case and gotten some bad apples out of the way, but we had no solid evidence to tie anybody but Blevens and MacDonald and Henry Jamison into the crimes in old Japantown, plus we still didn't have a clue who'd killed Jamison. To boot, Eddie Valhalla was getting off scot free: he was being watched by Baker's own men when Jamison was beheaded, and he had only killed MacDonald while defending me. Couldn't be prosecuted for it in a million years. Even Haggerty confirmed that. I wanted Eddie and ZaZu bad, but, like always, they'd put one over on me, and were free as birds.

Therefore, while Velcker took the ever-surprising Miss Jenkins home to get cleaned up and have some well-deserved rest, Baker let his men clean up at the Ming Palace, and him and Heine and me hit the town to get blind-drunk and commiserate.

Well, we commiserated until the bars closed, then got some more hooch and shared a cheap room at the Vance Hotel, where we drank and blabbed the night and our hard feelings away. Baker kept trying to tell me that it was O.K., and I kept telling him that it wasn't O.K. and he fucking knew it, and Henie just kept going on and on about how he'd never lost a tail like he had on Eddie and ZaZu so many times in his whole life. I kept trying to tell Heine that it was O.K., and he kept telling me that it wasn't O.K., and I fucking knew it.

So, after going around and around like that all night, somewhere in the wee hours we ran out of all our hooch and commiserations and energy, and either passed out, or fell asleep, until the morning dawned too early and too bright.

We all went up to the Doghouse, where nobody cared what anybody looked like that time of the A.M., and choked down enough breakfast so that we didn't feel too hung-over, then went our separate ways: Baker, to Downtown Headquarters to fill out mountains of paperwork on all the events; Heine, down to the pool-hall at Ben Paris to try and shark a few fins out of a few pigeons to make himself feel better; and me, back to the office, to get cleaned up and ready for the new day, which would include copious amounts of the hair-of-the-dog that always resided in my desk's bottom right-hand drawer.

I must say, when I blew into the office, just after 8:00, I wasn't expecting to see Miss Jenkins. Yet, there she was, on time for a change, sitting at her desk in the outer office, perky and chipper as ever, the deep scratches on her face hardly visible under a slightly heavier than normal application of make-up. There was a big plate stacked full of big cinnamon rolls sitting on the edge of her desk.

"Good morning, boss!" she said, brightly.

"Miss Jenkins," I said, taking off my fedora and trying to smooth back my disheveled hair. "Are you all right?"

"Of course," she smiled.

"I mean, after last night, are you sure you don't—"

"Feel as bad as you look?" she asked. "No, no," she went on, before I could complain about her jibe. "I always pride myself on my professionalism. What's done is done. Water under the bridge. I've cleansed my soul. This is a new day, and we've got to get on with it."

"Oh . . . Well, all I can say, Miss Jenkins, is that you're a real pip, no two ways about it." I paused a moment, took off my rumpled overcoat and draped it over my arm. "About that business Velcker mentioned last night regarding you and I getting married, I, uh—"

"Skip it," she interrupted, getting all serious for a second. "I figured it was . . . all just some sort of misunderstanding . . ." We were both silent for a bit, then she turned chipper again. "Cinnamon roll?" she asked, picking up the plate and offering it to me.

I waved it off. "No thanks. I've already eaten. What I really need is to get cleaned up."

"They're fresh and still warm," Miss Jenkins said, putting the plate down in front of her. "I was just going to have one myself."

"Where'd they come from, anyway?" I asked, heading for my office.

"Mrs. Jamison brought them by for me."

I stopped at the door and turned back. "She did?"

"Yes, wasn't that sweet?" Miss Jenkins selected the largest roll on the plate and picked it up. "She's waiting for you in your office right now. She said it was really urgent that she see you."

"She did . . ." I muttered, thinking, *good lord*, all I needed right now was another bout with Mrs. Jamison. "Well, all right . . . I don't have much choice but to go in and see her, I guess."

"Don't worry, I'll hold your calls," Miss Jenkins said, blithely. "She just needs a shoulder to cry on, boss."

"Sure," I said.

"Yum, this looks delicious," she said, biting into the roll.

I opened my inner office door, and there was Mrs. Jamison, sitting in the chair opposite my desk, dressed in a powder blue suit, with a matching pillbox hat. She jumped to her feet when she saw me, threw me a huge smile, then glued her gaze past me to Miss Jenkins, a strange expression coming over her face as Miss Jenkins bit into the cinnamon roll.

I suddenly made the connection. Henry Jamison had been eating cinnamon rolls before he died. Bubbles

LaFlamme had cinnamon rolls in her room when she got shot. Bunny Sunday had "food poisoning," maybe not from clam linguini, but from nibbling on one of Bubbles's cinnamon rolls. And here were cinnamon rolls yet again, with Miss Jenkins biting into one!

"Don't eat that roll!" I ran over, and knocked it out of Miss Jenkins's hand before she could take another bite.

"What'd you do that for?" Miss Jenkins asked, as the roll bounced off one of her filing cabinets, and came to rest near her wastebasket. "Are you nuts?"

I gave the other rolls a sniff, searching for any other discernible odors than cinnamon, such as the smell of burnt almonds. "I think they're poisoned."

"*What*?" She spit out what was left in her mouth.

"I just baked them," said Mrs. Jamison, standing in the doorway to my inner office. She smiled ever so pleasantly. "I went home early and baked them just for you, my dear."

I took Miss Jenkins by the shoulders. "You didn't eat any before I got here, did you?"

"Well, no," she said, looking back and forth between me and Mrs. Jamison, who now took a few steps toward us.

"Not even a nibble?"

"No." Miss Jenkins went a little pale.

"You can't marry her!" Mrs. Jamison suddenly ran at me. "You can't have him, he's mine!" she yelled, wrapping her arms around me and burying her head into into my chest so hard I thought it would leave a bruise.

"*What*?" exclaimed Miss Jenkins, utterly flabbergasted.

"Let go of me, Mrs. Jamison."

She just squeezed me tighter and grew hysterical. "She's

not good enough for you! You mean the world to me, Jake!" she cried in big, wheezing sobs. "The world to me . . . I'll never let you go . . ."

She was all over me. Had me wrapped up like Two-Ton Tony Gallento. So, I decided to take a different tack. I relaxed and gently patted her broad shoulders.

"I know," I said softly. "I know."

"You do?" Mrs. Jamison looked up at me, her chin digging into my sternum.

"Yeah, kiddo, I do."

"Ohhhh . . ." she sighed, tears overflowing her brown eyes. "I'm sooo glad . . ."

Miss Jenkins stared across her desk at us, sadly shaking her head.

I kept patting Mrs. Jamison. "You poisoned Bubbles LaFlamme, didn't you? Don't worry, I understand."

"Yes. It was all her fault . . . all her fault . . ."

Yeah, I thought, Bubbles was probably lucky that somebody else was after her and she got shot before the poison had a chance to work on her. At least she went quick.

"I couldn't let her get away with it," Mrs. Jamison told me with total candor. "You understand. That tramp was the reason my Henry was dead."

I nodded and smiled at her. "You tried to poison Henry, too, didn't you?"

"Oh, no, I didn't poison Henry. Too good for him. He only ate some of my normal cinnamon rolls." She shook her head and hugged me tighter. "No, instead, I dissolved some of my barbiturates into his thermos."

"That's why he looked so calm," said Miss Jenkins.

"Shhhh," I told her.

Mrs. Jamison began rocking back and forth in my arms. "Henry hadn't been home for two days. He did that sometimes. But I was glad he was back. I'd just made him his favorite breakfast, French Toast, with real maple syrup, and scrambled eggs," she said, quietly. "Henry was reading his morning paper and told me he was leaving me. He said it like he was just talking about a stock report, or a good sale at Rhodes. Like it was nothing out of the ordinary . . . I felt numb . . . I didn't know what to say . . ." She began to moan and cry.

I hugged her a little tighter.

"I didn't think I'd heard him right," she continued. "I knew about all his tramps, that stripper, Bubbles, too . . . but I couldn't have heard him right . . . I asked him to repeat it. He did. He said he was going to Tahiti with Bubbles LaFlamme. He had to go into the office to pick up some money, then I'd never see him again . . . All those years . . ."

Miss Jenkins sniffled, looked like she was going to start crying herself.

"He finished breakfast and went upstairs to get his bags," Mrs. Jamison went on. "I was in a daze . . . I packed his cinnamon rolls, like usual, and his egg salad sandwich for lunch . . . then I knew what I had to do when I poured the coffee into his thermos. He came back down and told me he'd always hated my egg salad. Then he took his thermos and his cinnamon rolls and his suitcases and left. He didn't even kiss me goodbye . . . he never really did, anyway, just a quick peck . . . but I didn't even get that . . ."

Mrs. Jaminson began crying harder and harder.

" . . . treated me like a doormat . . . like a doormat . . ." she moaned. "I knew what he deserved. I went downstairs and got one of those old Samurai swords from the collection he brought back from the war. Then I drove after him to the office. He was flat on his back and sleeping like a baby in the middle of the floor when I got there. He looked so peaceful after he'd made me feel so terrible. Then I did it. I raised that sword and *whack*! Off came his rotten, cheating head. Then I wiped my fingerprints off the handle and went home and baked . . . I baked and baked and baked . . . and then I met you, Jake." She started kissing my neck. "I did everything a wife was supposed to do . . . I cleaned and I cooked and did the laundry and made us a nice home . . . and Henry didn't care . . . didn't care . . ."

She gazed deep into my eyes. "You won't ever treat me that way, will you, Jake?" she asked, tenderly. "Will you? You won't ever, will you?"

"No, Mrs. Jamison, I won't," I told her. "I promise."

She smiled and sighed, then put her head back on my chest like it had always belonged there.

I rubbed her back, and quietly told Miss Jenkins, "Call Baker for me, will you, doll? Tell him to go easy when he gets here."

Epilogue

"WHAT THE HELL KIND OF GAME IS THIS, anyway?" I asked, as Miss Jenkins took yet another of my pieces.

"One you're not very good at," quipped Heine.

"It's called Go," said Frank Hashimoto, bringing another small bottle of warm saké to the card table he'd set up in his new store. "Very old Asian game. A lot older than chess. One of the oldest games of strategy in the world, as a matter of fact."

"I know what's it called," I said, trying to figure out my next move, which wasn't easy, considering Miss Jenkins had about four times as many little, white circular pieces left than I did my black ones. "I just don't like it much."

Miss Jenkins grinned, ready to pounce if I screwed up again. "You'd like it well enough if you were winning."

"Bull," I said, making my move, which promptly resulted in another lost black piece. "Haven't you got some Scotch?" I asked Frank, who'd gone back to help his brother, Harry, and his mother set up a bunch of Japanese food on the long counter by the cash register. There was sushi, sashimi, raw octopus, and a whole mess of strange stuff I'd never seen, most all of it looking godawful and ugly, although some of it didn't smell too bad.

His mother looked at me like I was being rude, then smiled politely and returned to arranging the food.

Miss Jenkins reached across the table and gave me a jab. "You stop acting this way, right now," she hissed in a loud whisper. "Maybe they couldn't afford any Scotch. They put all their money into getting this store ready to open. This is a party in our honor. You promised to come and behave yourself, so stop being so rude!"

"I still don't like it," I told her, politely keeping my voice down.

"Me either," said Heine. "All this crap gives me some bad memories."

"I might have just what the doctor ordered," said my lawyer, Haggerty, loud and expansive as ever. He and Manny Velcker strode over to our table, from where they'd been jawing near the GRAND OPENING sign on the front window.

He produced a large, silver hip-flask from his five-hundred dollar suit, and held it out to me. " 'Voila!' as Miss Jenkins might say," he told me.

I quickly unscrewed the cap. "Down the hatch!" I said, in return.

"Hey," said Heine. "Don't hog all the hooch."

I hogged it for a moment, anyway.

"Try some saké," Miss Jenkins told Heine. "It's surprisingly good."

Heine grabbed the flask from me, "Gimme," then took a big slug. "Now this is the good stuff," he said, wiping his lips, then handing the flask to Velcker.

"Only the best," said Haggerty. "Twenty year old single malt."

"Don't know what that is," said Velcker. "But it's damn fine rotgut."

Haggerty moved behind Miss Jenkins and lightly rubbed her shoulders. "I always bring cases of that on safari, my dear."

Miss Jenkins closed her eyes and hummed happily, as Haggerty kept rubbing.

"Hey, watch it!" Velcker told Haggerty. "Jake and her are getting hitched."

"Good God . . ." I said.

"*Good God*," repeated Haggerty, pulling his hands back like he'd just put them on a branding iron.

"You've gotta be kidding," said Heine.

"It's not true," said Miss Jenkins, reaching for more saké. "I'm still free as a bird."

Velcker furrowed his brow. "I don't get it . . ."

"And you never will," I told him. "Shut up."

"In that case . . ." said Haggerty, a gleam in his eye, "I may as well get back to massaging these delectable shoulders of yours, Miss Jenkins."

She pulled away from him this time, and scolded, but not too angrily, "That's enough, you big wolf."

"Excuse me!" said Frank Hashimoto.

We looked over, and there he was, lined up facing us in the middle of the room, with his mom, and his brother Harry. They all bowed low before us, then said, in unison, "*Arigato. Domo arigato.*"

"What's that mean?" Miss Jenkins whispered.

"Means *thanks, many thanks*," Heine whispered back.

Haggerty leaned in and said, "We should all bow back. That's customary."

"Not on your life," I told him.

Miss Jenkins gave me a dirty look, then got up and bowed toward the Hashimoto family along with Haggerty.

The Hashimotos stayed bowed down until Haggerty and Miss Jenkins popped back up, Mrs. Hashimoto giving me a bit of a dirty look, herself, before coming fully erect again.

"Before we eat," said Harry Hashimoto, "we have some gifts for you all, our honored friends."

"Oh, you shouldn't," said Miss Jenkins.

"It's rude not to accept," Haggerty quietly told her.

The mom went behind the counter with Frank, then they came back with their arms full of nice gift-wrapped boxes. Each of us got one, along with yet another bow.

"For Haggerty," said Harry Hashimoto, "for suing to get us enough money to open our new store."

"*Arigato*," said Haggerty.

"For Velc-ker-san and Hei-ne-san," said the mom, having trouble with their names, "for being brave men," she said.

"Yeah, thanks," they told her.

"For Miss Jenkins," said Harry, bowing so low I thought he'd hit his head on the floor, "for believing in us." She got the biggest package, I noticed.

"And, last but not least," said Frank Hashimoto, walking up to me, and handing over a teeny-tiny little package. "For Mr. Jake Rossiter, who, frankly, surprised the hell out of me by helping us. Thanks."

The others all opened up their presents. I held onto my tiny little one and waited until last.

Heine got a small Go game. We'd have to see how good *he* was at it.

Velcker got an origami box, complete with folding-paper and instructions to make small cranes and such.

Haggerty got a bottle of Suntory Whiskey—only useful gift, yet.

Miss Jenkins got a real silk kimono, of all things, bright red with frigging white drawings of Mt. Fuji on it. It was quite lovely, though, I had to admit—very delicate and light. I wondered what Miss Jenkins would look like in that kimono . . . For a minute, I tried to imagine it, but, appealing as that was, I put it out of my mind.

Finally, I opened my present. Have to say, I was damned surprised by what I found inside: a Purple Heart—the real McCoy.

"It's one of mine," Frank told me, with a smile. "I thought it would be appropriate considering how many times you got wounded fighting for my family."

I didn't really know what to say.

I sat there and thought about it for a minute.

Then I stood to attention, and saluted him.

As I held form, I thought about the war. So many losses. So much pain. And for what? Freedom. We all fought for freedom.

Frank Hashimoto returned my salute, crisp and sharp.

Miss Jenkins set down her saké cup and brought a napkin to her face. She must have gotten something in her eye.

ACKNOWLEDGEMENTS

My thanks and affection to Waverly Fitzgerald for her invaluable help with this book.

The author wishes special thanks to Carolyn Marr and the fine staff at Seattle's Museum of History & Industry, as well as all the wonderful folks from the King County Library System. Kudos, also, to HistoryLink.org for all its terrific resources.

More thanks to my many dear friends who supported me while writing this book. You know who you are!

Extra thanks to the dynamic UglyTown team of Tom Fassbender & Jim Pascoe!

And last but not least, my sincere gratitude to all the veterans of W.W.II, who made sure America was still here when I was born.